BLACKSTONE

By the Author

Nightshade

Blackstone

BLACKSTONE

by
Shea Godfrey

2014

ISBN 13: 978-1-62639-080-5

This Trade Paperback Original Is Published By
Bold Strokes Books, Inc.
P.O. Box 249
Valley Falls, NY 12185

First Edition: August 2014

Credits
Editor: Ruth Sternglantz
Production Design: Stacia Seaman
Cover Design by Shea Godfrey (sheagodfreymail@gmail.com)

Acknowledgments

Thank you to the fans of *Nightshade*. Thank you for all of your support and encouragement over the past few years, and thank you most of all, for your patience. To the Facebook fans—you're the best. Every thumbs up and comment of support, each one had a part in fostering the energy needed for the sequel. I hope you like it. I appear to be the DMV of writing, but you have held to your tickets faithfully, and I appreciate all of you. This one's for you.

The toil which stole from thee so many an hour,
is ended,—and the fruit is at thy feet!

—Percy Bysshe Shelley

CHAPTER ONE

The deep colors of the fire moved within the breeze that snaked up the chimney, and the embers beneath the cedar wood spoke softly. There was an odd harmony to their song, the hiss and the crack, and like spirits lost upon a dark Solstice Eve, the reds became entwined with the oranges and the yellows melded with gold as if they sought the company of someone familiar.

The Princess Jessa-Sirrah, only daughter to King Bharjah of Lyoness, was soothed by the interplay, her feet tucked beneath her as she sat upon a deeply cushioned chair she had pulled close to the hearth. The chamber within the royal family's guest wing in Blackstone Keep was quite lovely, and it was well furnished and had welcomed her and her lover as if they had been its expected residents, although nothing could be further from the truth. She missed the intimacy of her own rooms, but it was a small matter when she considered the pivotal events of the past few months.

Jessa's right hand turned as her arm stretched forth along the chair and her finger beckoned a small flame. A spark of bloodred fire floated upward and twisted along the wall of stones in response to her gesture.

The room was filled with a plush warmth that had very little to do with the fire, and the emotions that were stirred within her by its rich presence were new and strangely ancient all at once.

Darrius Durand, the warrior daughter of Arravan's High King, slept in silence upon the bed as the presence of her majik expanded within the confines of the chamber like the heat of a summer's day. Bold and yet ethereal, safe and yet wonderfully dangerous, her lover's life force was a thing to be reckoned with even as Darry lay dreaming.

Before the spring moon, Jessa could not have imagined such a wondrous thing.

She had imagined love, of course, within the sterile heat of her home, the Jade Palace, which had offered little warmth and even less enchantment. Her home had been a prison, and though she had moved freely within the shadows, they were just that, shadows. A darkness cast by immovable stone that, no matter how much force she exerted against their weight, could not be moved or banished in order to gain true freedom.

Neither could her majik dissolve the invisible chains that had bound her, for duty was not a thing one could escape. Unless she was willing to abandon those around her to the consequences of her actions.

Her true family was one of choice and she had chosen the Lady Radha, and Radha had always been her responsibility. Their fates were bound not only by time and love, but by their faith, as well. The Vhaelin gods had long ago chosen them to be teacher and student. Radha had served Jessa's mother before her mother's death, and though Jessa cherished the link to her parent, Radha was more precious to her than any ghost. If Jessa had tried to escape the Jade Palace, there was no telling what her father, Bharjah, would have done to the old woman, despite Radha's more than considerable powers. Her father had many weapons at his disposal, and Radha had forever been old, too old for a prolonged pursuit with no allies who might have helped them.

Jessa knew she had not possessed the courage, anyway, and she felt shame as she looked down at the arm of the chair. She pulled absently at a loose thread. Distance from the Jade Palace had given her an interesting perspective on things, and many of those insights were not what she had expected.

Jessa had not seen their journey east as an opportunity, though Radha had. That they traveled to Arravan so that Jessa might be given in marriage to the Crown Prince, should he find her fit to be his bride, had never been a happy truth for Jessa. Radha had seen something else. *"The world is wide, my child,"* Radha had said. *"When the moon rises and we leave upon the road east, it shall be a road that you know nothing of and the world shall open to you..."*

Radha had been right. Radha usually was.

The logs of the fire shifted smoothly as their essence changed, and a gust of displaced air pushed ash and embers upward into the flue.

Jessa looked to the bed and caught sight of Darry's face, cast in the faint light that had managed to reach across the room. The rich golden curls of her hair seemed alive as they tumbled this way and that upon the pillow.

Thank you, my gods, for showing me joy. Thank you for smiling upon me. Thank you for letting me move upon the Great Loom.

She had spent many weeks within the walls of Blackstone Keep and had come to know the royal family of Arravan quite well. She had watched them all with a keen eye, as Radha had taught her, and what they allowed her to see, she had taken in with skill and care. She had played the part of the shy, foreign princess, and it had not been so much an act as it had been a slow awakening from a very long sleep.

She had been presented before the court, and she had met and dined with Prince Malcolm. They had shared tea, and walks in the gardens. He was handsome and tall and his blue eyes were rich in color, though they were in want of something essential. In want of a spirit that sent fire through her veins. In want of so many things that Darry possessed without even trying. His casual cruelty did not beckon her, nor did a vision that narrowed the farther away he looked.

Jessa had made friendships here that had been completely unexpected, and she had opened her eyes to the truth when it was revealed to her. She remembered the Queen's Garden and how the moonlight had poured down like silver upon Darry's skin, and then standing within the safety of her arms as they waited for their chance to escape detection. That first touch of Darry's lips beneath her fingers, and how the contact had made her ache with the want for more.

That she desired a daughter of the House of Durand and not the son she had been sent to please had been a startling truth. It had also been the most natural of things for her to experience and accept, for it was the truth of her heart.

Each moment she and Darry had spent together had been stolen, as if they were thieves, each shared heartbeat taken from beneath the eyes of those around them. They had lifted their intimacy from the purse of the gods as if each moment was a golden coin. Coins that paid for each glance and every touch, until what grew between them could not be denied, no matter the cost.

Radha had been right about that, as well. There was a price to be paid for such things.

The Durand family relationship was still something new for her, and at first, she had thought that all was idyllic, that their love and their bonds were unshakable and true. For the most part, that first impression remained accurate, though beneath the surface they had their own machinations and their own troubles.

Perhaps the Jade Palace, for all of its blood and darkness, was an easier place to maneuver. At least there, she knew where she stood. At least there, she knew her enemies and what they were willing to do in order to get what they wanted.

Jessa's gaze traveled along the stones beneath the mantelpiece, anchoring herself in the present as she considered the past.

At least there, she recognized her father's webs like those of the Masis spider, its threads invisible until you were caught within them. At least there, one could understand the advantage of retreat, despite the apparent lack of imminent danger.

That she was backwards and wanted only the love of a woman would mean death in Lyoness. Here in Arravan, one who loved the same sex did not walk such a dire path, but it was unknown what would become of them now that their love had been declared to the High King. Acceptance was often a long journey from the heart of intolerance, and not everyone was capable of surviving the distance.

Our love is not without its price in either place, Jessa thought as she looked to the bed once more. *I have been exiled from my people and the land I know, and you have exiled yourself from your beloved family in response to their betrayal. What further price we might pay when the truth is known to all, I have no idea.*

Darry had relinquished her title and her rank, and as soon as it could be managed they would set out on a new journey. Into the world, away from the safety of the capital and the protection of Blackstone Keep, they would make their way into the unknown. She would not marry Prince Malcolm, and their two countries would never find peace through such a union. She knew peace had not been Bharjah's endgame, though her father's plans—as yet unknown—did, in fact, hinge upon her presence in Arravan. To her consternation, she had yet to figure out this crux.

Jessa rose from her chair and moved quietly across the room, unable to stop the rush of love as she slid onto the bed. Darry turned as Jessa lay along the warmth of her body and tucked her face against Darry's neck. Jessa breathed in the scent and closed her eyes as she draped her right leg over her lover's.

The not knowing what would happen was a freedom, as well. Jessa slid her hand beneath the waist of Darry's tunic. Her body lay against Darry's as it was always meant to, and the reassurance and heat of Darry's flesh eased her thoughts. A strange surprise, such knowledge. Radha would laugh at her, no doubt, when she told her.

CHAPTER TWO

The Lady Radha was certain of her way as she moved through the darkness of Lokey, her knowledge of the Arravan city a rare thing for a citizen of Karballa. Her agenda had always been very specific in nature, and despite the demands of others, she had satisfied her own needs first and foremost in order to achieve her goals. She had explored the city at every opportunity, familiar now with its rhythms and respectful of its diverse energies. She knew what to expect when the sun was high, and she understood the dangers that the night would bring. She enjoyed the former, for the city of Lokey was a gracious place for the most part; and she did not fear the latter, for she was a High Priestess of the Vhaelin.

When the crowded markets of Lokey ruled the day, the open bazaar of Bayside Square was a constant hum of activity beneath a pungent deluge of smells. Bayside Avenue, Lokey's most traveled thoroughfare, rolled in a smooth decline from the square to the sea, where it sprawled to an end before the planked boulevard of the wharf district.

The wharf, which serviced Arravan's largest port, moved along the shoreline from one end of Alirra Bay to the other. Warehouses clung to the last of the cobblestones from east to west, long, low storage buildings interspersed among a seemingly infinite number of inns, pubs, and stables.

The east end of the wharf, while questionable in its safety and reputation, underwent a blatant change in attitude as it moved westward. The old brick lodging houses and worn boards of the shops and pubs eventually gave way to the painted planks and smooth sandstone bricks of more established businesses. The seasoned character of the east blossomed as it sidestepped into the west, younger and cleaner as it catered to the Bloods of Arravan society and the more reputable businesses of the Guilds and Master Crafters. The east was brutish and often deadly after the sun went down, while the west was unsullied and quiet, the two wed somewhere in the middle in an oft times precarious union.

This lively center of the city was known as the Circle, crowded with tenement flats, markets, and local shops. Populated by the working-class people of the city, its beat of life was strong and fierce, for the people there took pride in what was theirs no matter how poor they might be. Radha had learned quickly, however, that the temptations of both borders were always present in the Circle. The flip of an Arravan gold might determine whether you would be taken advantage of or find an honest deal.

It was deep within this neighborhood that Radha approached her destination, as she avoided the holes in the cobblestones as if she had walked the same dark streets for many years.

The back door of the planked, two-story house hid within the shadows of the alley with but a single lamp as a guide, the darkness made to tremble and turn beneath its small bit of flame. Radha climbed the weathered stairs and knocked twice upon the door, followed by a pause and then three more raps upon the wood.

The door opened onto an inky blackness that the night air of Lokey could not match, and Radha was quick as she stepped within. The latch clicked hard into place behind her as she threw back the hood of her cloak.

A flint was struck, a lamp was lit, the room revealed. Three men stood about a small, round table as one of them replaced the glass flue of the lamp in order to shield its flame.

They were warriors of the Red-Tail Clan, and they had shadowed Jessa's caravan from the moment the princess had crossed the border into Arravan. They and Radha stood for the blood of Jessa's mother and her people. Their leader was Mesa White, and he had brought with him the most dangerous men of the Ibarris Plains in order to carry out Radha's wishes, no matter what they might be.

"Lady Radha," Mesa said, relief in his expression. He was dressed in the homespun of Lokey, the earthen colors he had chosen plain but clean. There was a sword against his left hip, the weapon held close by a green sash that was doubled about his waist, the tasseled ends left to hang along the outside of his left leg. He was lean and tall, his thick black hair pulled back in a long tail that fell to the small of his back. "We were beginning to wonder, *Hava*."

Radha's chuckle was as soft as it would ever be, which she knew was not soft at all. "Greetings, Mesa. It is good to see you."

He bowed his head to her. "And you, Lady Radha."

"She was followed." A fourth man spoke up as he entered from a darkened hallway on the opposite side of the room. His name was Durasha, and he was known for his deadly bow and the quickness of his many daggers.

"Yes," Radha acknowledged. "Just as I planned. Three men. Three of Serabee's dogs."

Lord Serabee El-Khan was known to them all, and the High Priest of the Fakir was their greatest enemy. He was Radha's opposite on the wheel of power and they had danced about their hatred for many years. The gods of the plains, the Vhaelin, had always been at war with the nameless gods of the Fakir.

"Durasha, take Enders and find the—"

"No," Radha said. "I have other plans for them. I will need one of them alive."

"What are your wishes then, my Lady?" Mesa asked.

"Keep the looking glass close. When I send for you, meet me at the main crossroads just south of the Gonnard Forest. We will make our way home from there. The first battle will be very soon, for Serabee has grown impatient. I could smell the hunt in his blood the last I saw him. We will have but a short time to prepare."

"And the princess?"

"She shall walk her own path from this day forth, though she will find us in the end."

Mesa frowned. "Luka will not like that. Is she in danger?"

"Luka has no say, boy, and Jessa has always been in danger. Luka may be a chieftain, but he holds no authority when it comes to the gods. She is not a helpless woman who needs looking after. When the battle comes at last, Jessa will become the Vhaelin priestess she was destined to be. None shall rule her actions ever again."

Mesa blushed at her tone. "Yes, Lady."

The man named Enders cleared his throat, a tangible anticipation bright in his eyes. His hair was plaited and the long braids, too numerous to count, fell onto his shoulders and down his back. He was young and his build spoke of easy strength and speed, the green sash he wore about his waist tied as Mesa's was. "What of the prophecy, Lady Radha? Has she come back to us?"

Radha considered his question with the scrutiny it deserved. "The sword of our people, or the daughter of the gods?"

"The sword of our people, Lady Radha," Enders answered. "Is not the Princess Jessa the daughter of the gods?"

"She is," Mesa said, and his warm laughter drew Radha's gaze. "Then the sword of the people has returned to us, as well, has she not? And I believe that I have seen her."

"Yes," Radha confirmed. "Jessa has met her match. Tannen Ahru has returned to us."

Enders gave a sharp call and then looked contrite, though his brown eyes were vivid with pleasure. "Forgive me."

"It's all right, boy, I did the same," Radha said, soothing him, warmed by the excitement that filled the room. It was a prelude of hope, and hope was something her people had done without for far too long. "She will be as your dreams have shown you—though she is her own even more, does this make sense?"

His grin was a bit giddy. "Yes. Yes, Lady."

"Purchase the steel you will need," Radha instructed Mesa, "and the gear that Luka wishes for, and whatever else you feel our people will need. It shall be a fair bit of time and then some before we shall find again the likes of what Lokey has to offer. Keep in mind that there will be times of blood between that day and this."

"It is a rich city," Durasha added. His hand rested with ease and experience upon the hilt of his sword. "Their king seems a fair man."

"Who's to say?" Radha answered. "I suppose time will tell, though for now, we must deal with the Fakir. There's a bit of a trick to what I wish for. Who will help me?"

"I will," Enders said, volunteering, the emotion in his smile no longer sweet but decidedly lethal. "Give me the privilege, Lady Radha."

"And I," the fourth man said. His name was Alain, and he was dressed as the others were. His hair was a dusty blond and he let it flow free and straight about his shoulders. "Allow me, my Lady."

Radha was pleased at their confidence as well as their genuine respect. It was an honor she had earned many years past, yet it held the feel of a courtesy that was no longer familiar. "Do not forget to leave one alive, yes?"

Chapter Three

J essa opened her eyes in the darkness and lay quiet beneath the fast beat of her heart. She knew that she had slept, though her sojourn in the land of dreams had been a strange one. She could not remember what she had seen. She remembered a voice that spoke with an urgent, fiery passion, and the warmth of a touch upon her face, but that was all. She remembered a warning, perhaps, for the voice had told her she must wake up.

The shadows that hovered about the bed were thick, and she turned her head upon the pillow, Darry close beside her and fast asleep. *No such dreams for you, my love. You always seem to sleep so sweetly, though perhaps that is Hinsa's doing. The blood of a golden mountain panther would seem a wonderful gift to have when one wishes for sleep. Only a cat in the sun appears so satisfied.*

And then it hit her. The smell.

She set her hand upon the mattress and sat up.

It was dark beyond the closed shutters, for she could feel the night and she could taste the difference in the air. It was not yet too late, but the moon was high and the world had changed with it. She moved beyond her lover's touch, and Darry's bandaged hand slid to the quilted spread, as if content with the warmth that Jessa left behind.

She could smell it. Jessa could smell it with her very blood.

A narrow column of moonlight fell between the the outer balustrade door and its frame, the pale light upon the floorboards barren and without warmth as she swung her legs over the edge of the bed and stepped to the floor. Someone had opened the chamber door, though it had been locked when she had finally taken her rest.

"Darry, wake up," Jessa whispered as she moved to the end of the bed.

It was a cold and bitter smell, like the scent of blood upon a blade.

The words of a verse moved suddenly through her mind, cloaked in the cadence of Radha's long-ago voice, the child's poem all but forgotten until her senses remembered its song. *Like winter's icy chill, their blood flows thick for naught but ill. Upon the blade their hate runs hard, they smell of death and bitter char—*

A surge of panic burst within her chest and she let out a shout. *"Ahla fahleece!"*

The spell pulled hard at the faint light in the room, the energy around her compelled from its natural state and bound beneath her immediate control. The witchlight formed upon the palm of her right hand and curled into a ball of blazing white fire. She cast, and it sped across the length of the chamber.

"Darry!" Jessa shouted as the darkness came to life beneath a shower of white and blue streamers. *"Zaneesha Fakir!"*

Darry leaped from the end of the bed as Jessa stumbled back beneath the reach of dark arms and the flash of a knife. She slapped aside the blade and slammed into the man's chest, both of them taken to the floor. Darry grabbed his head with both hands and cracked his skull against the floor as the curved knife sliced through the waist of her shirt. She fought for the weapon with one hand and threw a punch with the other, his jawbone rock hard against her knuckles.

A colossal figure rose up behind Darry as she struggled and Jessa answered the threat. *"Bella Vhaelin,"* she summoned, and the man spun about. Jessa's open hand landed firmly against his chest.

The fingers within the grip of Darry's left hand caved beneath the pressure she exerted, and her opponent cried out as bones were snapped. She snatched the dagger from his hand and, without hesitation, pushed the blade through the skin beneath his chin.

Jessa stood as still as stone but a few feet away, her right hand upon the chest of a man nearly twice her size. The air around them swirled and her black hair moved within it, lifted from her shoulders like heavy tendrils of dark smoke.

Darry rushed forward, and Jessa tried to keep the spell within her thoughts as her lover slid upon a knee. Darry spun sideways beneath Jessa's outstretched arm and her blade sliced with precision through the tendons at the back of the giant man's knee, Darry on her feet within the next moment as the balustrade door was kicked open.

Jessa felt the light of the Vhaelin churn low in her belly and rise up as her eyes locked upon the hooded face before her. She felt the influence of her blood as the words danced through her mind as never before, words that she knew but had never used in earnest. Power sang through her body as the spell came to life, and she wanted to laugh aloud at the endless depths, at the heat that raced like a downpour of sunlight through her veins. There was no substance that it could not pass through and she knew it.

Jessa recognized at once that the words were right. She understood their true purpose as her hand pushed through the muscles of his chest as if they were made of thin parchment.

Across the room, Darry turned the oncoming sword with her dagger and pushed, afraid that if they did not clear the room Jessa would fall victim to their brawl. She took a blow to the shoulder, but her left hand closed upon the guard of the attacker's sword even as her right struck fast and true, her stolen weapon finding a new home deep in his belly. She grabbed his tunic and shoved until they stumbled through the door and toppled to the stones of the balustrade.

Darry rolled to the side, pushed to her feet, and took a breath in order to cry out for the guard, but instead she was yanked backward, her left hand caught beneath a wire garrote. She planted her boots and shoved as the cord burned along the underside of her jaw. The cord sliced through her sleeve and into the skin beneath, but it gave her the leverage she needed to turn her head and drop clear.

The back of a hand slapped her and she spun farther onto the balcony as yet another enemy appeared. She used her momentum and tumbled smoothly over her left shoulder, landed on a knee, and seized the hilt of a fallen sword. The oncoming blade missed her by inches as she twisted at the waist, dropped her shoulder, and struck.

The weight of his body pushed back against her blade, and she stood up beneath it, his tunic ripping as her sword pushed through and through. She took possession of his sword before he dropped it and shoved him aside.

The whistle she gave pierced the night as she tossed her new weapon into her right hand and attacked.

She feinted to the left before her two remaining opponents and then spun to the right, her weapon held high and close. The sword sliced through one throat and stopped at the second as her steel slid along a thicker blade. Both swords were pushed to the floor and then back around as she was forced to defend.

The sound of their battle rang out against the stones of the terrace and Darry accepted the final swordsman's advance. She marked how he played to her left, allowed him the move, and then let his sword through. She leaned close as he was pulled off balance and struck him with her fist, whipping his head to the side. Darry hooked the pommel of her sword over the tang of his own, pushed their weapons downward, slammed her boot upon the steel, and pulled the unguarded dagger from his belt. She sliced his throat.

She stepped over his body, picked up his sword, and shouted at the top of her lungs. Her voice echoed along the terrace and into the night as she called for the Palace Guard.

❖

Emmalyn Durand, the eldest royal daughter, pushed to her feet and the chair scraped against the floor with a lonely sound.

She stared at the papers strewn across the surface of the desk, deeds of land and titles of ownership that she had not looked at since the anniversary of Evan's death. Once every few months she would attend to the business of her first husband's inheritance, but the deeds she would only look at once a year. She would lay the papers out and run her hands upon the parchment; and she would gaze upon Evan's signature and that of his father and his older brother, Cieran. She would drink cool spring wine from the pewter chalice that had been Evan's upon their wedding day, and she would drift within the memories of a love that had been taken from her much too quickly.

His death had been meaningless, and though she could still see her brothers carrying his lifeless body into the Great Hall, it was not a memory she chose to dwell on. That such a great horseman had fallen to his death during an afternoon ride through the Gonnard Forest was not a legacy that her heart chose to honor.

She would remember his long hands and the fall of his unruly blond hair and his deep blue eyes. She would remember his mouth and his kiss, and how he would sit at the end of their bed, his lean body naked upon the sheets, as hers was. She would listen to him tell of how he would build a new manor upon their land, and a stable that would rival even the king's. He'd wanted to breed horses, and he would laugh when she teased him and demanded to know when, always when. *Not long now, my peach,* he would say, and she would run her hand along the skin of his thigh.

She would remember making love to him, and the feel of his flesh inside her body. He had been as tender a lover as he was a man, and Emmalyn remembered how she had prayed even that first night that she would have a child as soon as possible. She had wanted Evan's children. She had wanted his seed to take hold inside her body and grow. She had wanted to watch him with their sons, blond-haired boys set loose in the long grass and sunshine.

Her touch moved with care upon the parchment as she thought of her new lover. "So different than Royce…"

Perhaps it was time to let go just a bit more, and Darry was an heir that would be worthy of Evan's dream. When she had come of age and had her choice of lands, Darry had claimed but a few titles, none of which held any great value. A stretch of land beyond the cliffs of Antioch where the beaches were as soft as silk, and a massive swath of territory through the heart of the Green Hills. It was wild and completely unlivable and their father had fought with her that it could not be used for anything, except for getting lost in and eventually mauled by something that was faster than she was. Darry had only smiled and signed the papers.

But Evan's lands would give Darry power should she need it, and the people who lived there would take to her, Emmalyn was certain of it. Eventually her sister and her lover would find their way to the haven it would represent. She smiled to think of Darry and Jessa together. She could see even now how Jessa had sat beside her sister as Darry had lain with fever, Jessa's touch so very tender when she thought no one would see.

She took a drink from Evan's chalice as she turned back into the room and wondered if their father truly understood all they would lose if Darry disappeared from their lives.

Emmalyn swallowed hard upon the tart spring vintage and slowly lowered her goblet.

The man beside her bed pulled the black hood from his head. He did so with his left hand, for in his right he held a sword. He spoke in a rough but quiet voice, and Emmalyn recognized the Lyonese words at once, though she did not understand their meaning.

"Blessed Gamar," she whispered and the blood roared in her ears. Her hand trembled as she raised her cup and gauged the distance to the door. "I believe you are lost, yes?"

The man considered her with a curious expression and then smiled as she took another sip from her drink. "*Pittan cunta,* pretty whore."

Emmalyn raised an eyebrow as she noticed his damp hair, his weight, and the curved daggers at his belt. "No," she responded, and though her voice trembled her hand no longer did. "Not a whore, just a bit of royal blood."

His brow came down and he took a step forward.

Emmalyn backed into her chair with a clumsy step.

He stopped his advance. "Pontius. Bartik."

Emmalyn's attention was drawn to the balcony that overlooked the palace gardens, whereupon one man, and then another, stepped from the dark of the terrace and into the light.

Emmalyn heard a high-pitched whistle moving through the night.

"*Cunta,* yes?" One of the late arrivals laughed at his own question, and Emmalyn's blood turned to ice as he reached down and began to unbuckle his sword belt.

She eyed the man beside her bed and thought of the thin rapier that Darry had given her for Solstice, and that it now hung useless in her dressing room in its polished leather sheath. She raised Evan's chalice. "Wine?"

Her shoulders gave a small flinch as he approached, every ounce of control she possessed rooting her boots to the floor. His fingers brushed against hers as he took possession of the cup.

Emmalyn seized the pewter decanter from the desk and swung it as he drank. When it struck the side of his head, she grabbed for the closest knife on his belt.

❖

The High King Owen Durand pushed forward in his chair and cocked his head as the hairs lifted upon the back of his neck. He shifted upon the cushions and looked back across the chamber, the lamp upon the table warm in its glow. He had been deep in thought and on the verge of dozing off, despite that every fiber of his being was in some way restless. Exhaustion had its uses, he knew, and he wondered if he would ever again experience a night of untroubled sleep. The distant call that had roused him had most likely been a trick of the mind. Or perhaps a nighthawk.

He rose from his seat and moved across the room in order to satisfy the tick of nervousness that fluttered through his chest. With a quick glance toward the archway that led to the bedroom, he noted that Cecelia, his queen, had finally put out the lamp. He did not think she slept, though she might pretend for his sake.

He opened the chamber door and took a step within the shadows of their private corridor, in search of the familiar tabards of the Palace Guard. He found no one at the end of the hallway and his instincts warned him back at once. He grabbed the door, recognizing the distant cry that called forth the guard. Darry.

The bolt from a crossbow took him high in the right thigh, and he let out a howl of anguish as he stumbled and tripped into the room. He hit the floor with a grunt and the pain exploded throughout his hip.

"Cece!" he yelled and grabbed the edge of the door. A second bolt buried itself in the heavy oak but an inch above his hand. He surged to his feet and used all his weight, a rattle in his bones as the door slammed shut beneath his momentum and he threw the lock.

He grasped the quarrel where it jutted from the flesh along the outside of his thigh, and with both hands he snapped the shaft. His head went back and he let out an angry snarl.

"Owen?"

His eyes snapped open at his wife's voice, and he yanked his sword belt from where it hung upon the peg. "To me, Cece!" he shouted in a booming voice as he pulled the blade free.

She screamed.

Chapter Four

*A*s *still as death* were the words that came into Darry's mind as she knelt before the foot trunk at the end of the bed. *Or close enough to it,* she amended beneath a swell of panic. Her hand trembled as she reached for Jessa's leg and wondered if she would encounter stone or the warmth of her lover's flesh.

"Jess?"

Jessa seemed caught somewhere else entirely and perhaps beyond her reach, though the heat of Jessa's body burned against Darry's hand. The entire world seemed to move in Jessa's eyes, though not a breath was taken, nor the blink of an eyelid given. Darry could see nothing in her expression, and yet there was everything. The moon and the stars raced behind her lover's dark eyes, and a depth of such strange wonder that Darry could actually see it. Darry could feel the pulse of Jessa's majik flow beneath the glow of witchlight.

Jessa's right sleeve was soaked with blood and the tunic clung to her arm, though the blood was not hers and Darry knew it. "Jess, it's me."

When she received no response, she pushed forward and kissed Jessa, her lips soft at first and then more forceful, her hand at the back of Jessa's neck as she forced Jessa's lips open.

Jessa's shoulders gave a hard jerk, and her thoughts tried to reject the foreign energy that filled her mouth. The power radiated inward and though she tried to throw it back, it swept down her throat and filled her chest with familiar ease. This new fire was different than the one she already sought to control, and her concentration broke beneath its heady flavor.

Jessa struck out in a burst of fear, and Darry turned her face beneath the unkind blow, forced to protect herself.

Jessa saw the blood first, and then Darry's face beneath it.

Darry accepted the arms about her neck, took Jessa about the waist, and lifted her until they both found their feet. When Darry moved back, Jessa followed with an awkward step. "It's all right," Darry said. "Let go, my love. We have to leave this place." Jessa released her and Darry smiled. "You see? It's all right."

Jessa touched Darry's face. "It was all…it's all very big."

Darry's eyes were uncertain but she kept her smile. "It must've been."

"I cannot see the bottom of it," Jessa whispered. "Are you all right?"

"Yes," Darry answered and leaned down to pick up her sword. "But we have to—"

The narrow blade sliced along Darry's left shoulder as she stood up, the knife finding but a piece of its target. Darry squared her shoulders and threw her sword in response. The weapon flipped twice before it found its mark and the assassin stumbled and fell straight back, the sword deep within his chest as he hit the floor.

The watch bells from the barracks rang out, and their call was deep and strong as Darry stepped over their would-be assailant and pulled her blade free. "Jessa, we have to go."

Jessa obeyed and Darry took her arm in a firm grip when she neared. They sidestepped the bodies that blocked their way. An arrow buried its head in the door frame, and Jessa felt its heat as it sliced the air before her face.

Darry hissed in anger. "The other way, go!"

Jessa raced back through the chamber, and though her boots slipped in the blood beside the bed, she kept her feet. The handle turned and she threw the door open, only to have a man rise up before her. The sword came down but Darry was there, her left hand upon Jessa's chest as she pushed Jessa clear and met the weapon with her own.

The blade slid along Darry's and she grabbed a wrist as his knee hit her thigh and she buckled into the corridor. Darry pushed at his face and growled not unlike Hinsa as they fell to the floor. She dragged the edge of her sword beneath his chin and she brought her strength to bear, lifted his head by the hair, and straddled him. His upper body was pulled from the stones as she turned her grip and brought the sword back around.

Jessa recognized Hinsa's presence, and as she scrambled across the threshold to her lover, the man's head came free from his body. Darry cursed as Jessa grabbed her by the shoulders, and they fell back, Darry between Jessa's legs as they sat down hard.

"Darry," Jessa said, and she could smell the panther within her lover's blood. She pressed her face close. Akasha, *come back.*

Darry shouted, and Jessa knew the voice moved in her head, but Jessa held strong. "*Akasha!*"

Darry coughed roughly as she wiped a torn sleeve across her eyes and blinked into the moment. "Up," she ordered in ragged voice. "Up, Jess, let me up."

Jessa obeyed and Darry got to her feet.

"Emmalyn." Darry held out her hand and Jessa took it, pulled up beside her.

"They are Serabee's men, they are Fakir." Jessa kept pace as Darry ran. "We must find Radha, Darry, we must find her now."

"They are Sahwello Clan."

Jessa's eyes went wide as her lover gave name to the most brutal class of warriors within the Fakir tribe.

"We bloody well need the guard." Darry looked into the shadowed distance before them and then glanced back. "I need light, Jess, can you give me light?"

Darry slowed as Jessa pulled up short and slid to the balcony rail. She spoke fast in a language that Darry found unfamiliar, and then it mattered not, for Darry was spun to the right as her sword met another. A scream sounded in the distance, and Darry shouted Emmalyn's name as she parried, thrust, and moved faster than she ever had before. Hinsa's blood fought through her veins for dominance as Jessa called out the last of her spell.

Every torch along the corridor popped and gushed forth with flames along the inner balcony from east to west, the upper tier flooded with sudden light. Jessa turned as another scream pierced the air, pulled into action by the sound.

Darry shouted in disbelief and pressed forward as Jessa left her behind, her opponent pushed to the wall as her sword came down and forced his to the floor. Darry reached across her body, ripped the torch from its sconce, and swung it back in a fierce arc. The assassin lifted his sword to block it and Darry stepped into the opening, her sword buried in his shoulder but an instant later. He stumbled awkwardly to the side and Darry followed him with a long stride, the torch set against his tunic. She kicked out as his clothes caught fire, pulling her sword free as he flipped over the balcony rail and fell to the stones below.

"Darry!" Jessa shouted and set her hands upon Emmalyn's door.

She closed her eyes against the breaking of glass behind the door and tried to summon the words for even a simple spell that would throw the latch. Not a single command moved within her mind, and she took a breath. *Concentrate, Jessa...*

The wood about the lock casing cracked.

"Move!"

Jessa leaped to the side as Darry threw her right shoulder against the heavy door from a dead run, the wood splintering even further from the blow. Jessa caught her breath as the scent of the panther was released, her eyes wide as Darry's majik was unbound in all its fury. Her own blood stuttered, and Jessa stumbled back as the power of the Vhaelin surged in response. She could almost see Darry's strength erupt and swell; she could see Hinsa's essence within her hair, within her eyes, within Darry's very body.

Darry smashed through the door, and the frame about the latch broke free upon the other side. Darry shoved through without pause as witchlight exploded from Jessa's hand and blazed into Emmalyn's chamber.

Darry's eyes were wild as she reached for the man who

struggled with Emmalyn upon the bed, Emmalyn caught beneath him. His hair was in Darry's fist, and Jessa saw Emmalyn's bloodied face and exposed breasts through a flash of hard light.

When a second man rushed into the fray and struck Darry upon the back of the head with his sword hilt, Jessa shouted, her cry filled with rage. Darry stumbled to the side but did not lose hold of her sister's attacker, her hands about his throat as she dragged him from the bed.

The second man swung a killing blow.

Jessa's hand intervened and caught the sword as she wove her spell. The steel rose back and bent within her grip, the man's dark eyes going wide beneath the blood that covered his face from a cruel wound upon his forehead.

She took from the life energy around her, though most especially she drew upon Darry's strength, the panther's power overwhelming all others.

A strange sound blossomed beneath her touch as the steel began to change, and its high-pitched transformation filled the chamber as Darry took her enemy to the floor. She landed on his back with his head in her hands, and she slammed his face against the floorboards.

As if it were made of molten steel, Jessa folded the blade over double as the runes danced along the metal. She turned her wrist and the tip of the sword melted neatly against the weapon's tang. Jessa removed the useless blade from his hand and touched his cheek, her fingers open upon his skin. She felt his breath against her wrist, though only for an instant before the runes she spoke burst into flames within her head. They demanded payment, and his body jerked and spun harshly in answer. The bones of his neck snapped, and as he fell away, Jessa accepted his life energy into the runes, her chest filled with a now familiar dark rush of power.

An unexpected wave of nausea swelled upward, and Jessa stumbled beneath its influence as Emmalyn crawled to the opposite side of the bed. "Emmalyn," she said and dropped to a knee. "*Sheeva.*"

Emmalyn pushed onto her right arm and though it shook, it held as she dropped her legs over the edge of the bed. "I'm all right," she said in a strained voice.

Jessa tried to find her own strength as Emmalyn swayed toward the end of the bed and pulled at her torn shirt. Her hands trembled as she found one button, then another, and Jessa followed Emmalyn's gaze along the dark trail of blood that Darry left in her wake, only to find a man beyond the overturned desk chair. A dagger stood low in his abdomen near the undone buttons of his trousers.

Jessa's attention shifted yet again as Darry let out a savage yell as she heaved and lifted the body over the rail of the terrace.

Jessa struggled to her feet and tried to focus, each movement terribly specific. *Use your hand...yes...your feet now, one foot... watch your skirt. Stand up.* Her mind began to swim forward through the fog and see clearly once more. *Radha, you should have told me...*

A sharp crack of sound. Emmalyn wrenched up straight, and Jessa's focus was drawn to the balcony arch where a fresh quarrel had buried itself in the oak.

Jessa rose, clean in her strength, the spell furious upon her tongue.

The man within the doorway smiled at Emmalyn as he slid his boot into the bow stirrup, pulled back the cord, and set a fresh quarrel. When he looked up, Darry's right shoulder hit him square in the chest.

Jessa's spell was on its way, and she cast her eyes from her beloved, staggering as she tried to turn her power.

She lost control instead.

The floor at Jessa's feet split with a terrible scream, the wood blackened as the spell raced beyond her command. It blazed a path until it hit the stones of the wall and leaped upward. The mortar cracked and the entire room shook as Emmalyn grabbed for the bedpost, fear on her face as the stones of her wall split open and debris exploded outward. She turned and fell to the floor amidst the blast.

Jessa pushed along the bed toward the door through the violent cloud of fragmented stone and dust.

Darry and her opponent grappled and slid across the floor until they slammed into the balcony rail, whereupon the wood split with a screech. Jessa stumbled beyond the brawl and found the railing as Grissom Longshanks, commander of the High King's elite guard, shouted out his presence. He slid to a halt in the east wing foyer of the residence, his gaze lifted upward.

"To the king!" Jessa shouted in command. "The king is here!"

Grissom reacted to the tone out of habit and bellowed the order as Captain Kingston Sol passed him at a dead run with a dozen men behind him.

Jessa saw Darry's oldest and dearest friend. "Bentley! Bentley, to Nina!" Her breath caught and she spun to her left as thoughts of Darry's cousin were replaced by something more immediate. "Fakir bastard…"

Witchlight exploded along the upper balcony amidst a heavy cloud of dust, and blue lightning crackled along the beams of the high ceiling, the smell of a summer storm pungent in the air. Bentley had never stopped, Etienne Blue and Arkady Winnows beside him as he raced up the sweep of stairs.

Darry's opponent broke through the rail and fell over the edge as Darry twisted onto her stomach and grabbed for what remained of the balusters, his hands violent upon her left leg as she followed him over.

Emmalyn grabbed Darry's hand, dug her boots in, and sat down hard. "No you don't."

What was left of the nearest spindle broke in Darry's other hand and her upper body went over. Unable to stop the momentum or the weight of two people, Emmalyn was pulled forward onto her stomach and dragged to the edge. She cried out from the force of it as her arms snapped out straight and her body began to follow.

Jessa watched as Etienne Blue dove onto Emmalyn's legs as they rose from the stones and wrapped his arms about them. He rolled his weight onto the back of her thighs and held tight as a brilliant light exploded near the stairs. Bentley leaped over them both and sprinted beyond.

Grissom Longshanks seized the crossbow from the man beside him, aimed, and released. His shot was true, and Darry's adversary fell away and dropped with a thud to the stones, even as Arkady scrambled to the edge and grabbed hold of Darry's shoulders.

Grissom tossed the crossbow, the soldier beside him having the good sense to catch it. "Secure the residence and the Keep, clear the Great Hall," he ordered in a hard voice. "All of it. Only the main arch and the gardens are to be left open, with access to the kitchens. I want everyone in there." He looked to a second man. "Call up the City Guard and find as many healers as you can."

CHAPTER FIVE

Nina Lewellyn took the blow across the cheek and spun into the bedside table. Light exploded behind her left eye, and the pitcher on the table fell to the floor and shattered. Her hands closed hard upon the basin and she gave a fierce growl as she turned. The porcelain bowl broke against her assailant's face and he fell back, pushed into the man behind him as Nina pulled up her skirt and leaped onto the bed. She stumbled across the covers and jumped to the floor on the opposite side, desperate to reach the door before they could recover.

She cried out as the bolt pierced through the flesh of her upper right arm, spun about until she met the floor. She kicked at the hands that grabbed her legs. Her head banged against the floor and, dazed, she reached out blindly as her skirt was ripped.

She gave a sob at the heavy weight that slammed between her thighs, and she felt a surge of strength within her fright. Her left hand took hold of the bolt still in her arm and yanked it through. Her new weapon struck true as the steel tip met flesh with a vengeance.

Fingers closed hard about her throat and she gasped for breath.

Blood sprayed across her skin and she jerked her face away, the choking hand suddenly gone. The weight disappeared from between her legs, and she coughed as she rolled onto her side and began to crawl even as her gaze was drawn to her rescuer.

Bentley Greeves, Darry's second in command, tossed the dead

man aside even as he ducked with speed and grace beneath a new attack. The sword strike came from his right in a wild lunge, and Bentley knocked the man's weapon aside as his own sword sliced across the man's exposed belly.

Nina's fierce heartbeat filled her head with noise as her eyes focused upon the mud-stained boots just inches from her face. Her last attacker towered above her as she tried to look up without drawing his attention. His mask was torn off and he stared down a loaded crossbow.

"I will still kill you," Bentley promised. "For touching such a woman? I'm going to cut your head off."

Silence followed Bentley's declaration, and Nina felt the utter stillness within the chamber as if it were a living thing. There was pain and there was shock and confusion, but most of all, there was outrage within her thoughts and it blossomed like dry tinder beneath a hungry flame.

Nina grabbed the nearest boot and Bentley moved faster than Nina had ever seen him, the Fakir pulled off balance as he pulled the trigger. Bentley twisted to his right as the quarrel's tip cut a shallow channel across his chest before it passed beyond. He stumbled to the side and fell to a knee.

The assassin rushed him and Bentley rose up, the dagger drawn from his belt as they collided. Bentley brought his head forward as their arms tangled, and the man's nose broke beneath the blow. Bentley sank his blade to the hilt beneath the Fakir's ribs. "Did you touch her?" His voice was intimate as their struggle began to fade. Nina could hear the question despite the quiet tone, and it filled her with fear and satisfaction both. It was a strange combination. "Did you?"

Bentley let him drop to his knee and stepped to the side. He picked up his sword, moved in a tight circle, and swung smoothly as he came back around.

Nina let out a jagged breath as the man's head rolled to the bricks of the hearth and his body flopped to the floor. The front of Bentley's shirt had darkened with blood from his wound, and it clung to his stomach as he sheathed his sword.

Nina cradled her wounded arm and met his eyes as the blood seeped through the fingers of her left hand. "Lord Greeves," she greeted in a wavering voice as he came for her.

Bentley knelt and slipped his arms beneath her knees and back. He gritted his teeth as he lifted her, but that was all the discomfort he showed.

Nina grabbed at his collar, his face close as he looked in her eyes. "Thank you," she whispered and her eyes filled with sudden tears.

Bentley pulled her close and she pushed her face against his neck. "Don't cry, my pretty." He lowered his face to hers. "Please don't cry."

Nina swallowed and cleared her throat. "Fucking bastards."

Nina remembered when she had last seen him, standing tall among his comrades, shirtless, his skin glowing with sweat from the practice yards. Practice that had just come in rather handy, now that she thought about it. She remembered the sharpness of her tongue as she had commented on his lack of clothes. "I like your shirt," she whispered.

Bentley smiled. "I put it on just for you, my Lady."

Nina let out a startled laugh and closed her eyes as her good arm went about his neck and held tight.

❖

Jessa waited within the doorway of Emmalyn's washroom as Darry stood behind her sister, her bloodied hands fisted at her sides. Emmalyn stared in the basin of water on the table beside the tub, and her hands trembled upon its edge.

Jessa noted the blood that stained Darry's tunic at the small of her back and followed its sticky path to the back of her head, Darry's hair soiled as it clung to her shoulders. Jessa knew of several blows that might have caused the wound, and none of them had been any less than wicked.

"Emma," Darry said in a quiet voice.

Emmalyn let out a stifled sob and then sucked it back down.

"I'm sorry I wasn't fast enough."

"They didn't..." Emmalyn turned and looked at her sister, her face pale as tears hovered for a moment and then slipped free. "He didn't rape me."

Darry held out her hand. "It's all right to cry, Em. Perhaps I'll even join you."

Emmalyn gave a startled smile and took her sister's hand. "No, you won't."

"I might...I've caught a splinter from that damn railing."

Emmalyn took a step and Darry gathered her close in response.

Jessa turned away and searched the wreck of Emmalyn's chamber, Arkady Winnows and Etienne Blue ready to command amidst the destruction their battle had wrought. Her mind worked at a furious pace and after a moment she stepped forward. "Where are the rest of us?"

"They breached the walls, my Lady," Darry's third in command, Arkady, answered. "It is the wall that took our numbers from the residence, for we thought the Palace Guard was here."

"Most of them are dead though, Lady Jessa," Etienne added.

"I want"—Jessa shook her head—"I *need* more men, please. Find as many of our number as can be spared. I want a guard upon this room, on the balcony, and at the door, until we ready another chamber for the princess to stay in. I want someone to get these bodies out of here, I want them out of here now."

Etienne glanced at the nearest body. "Yes, my Lady."

"On your oaths, not a word to anyone," Jessa ordered in a strained voice. She felt a bit overwhelmed as she looked to Arkady and he took her elbow, not waiting for her permission. "There is a corpse below the balcony, on the stones. I want these bodies placed with his, or what's left of him, for Emmalyn to burn if she so desires. No one touches them until she is given the choice, understood?"

"Aye," Arkady replied in a dark voice.

"Find Bentley," she ordered. "Find out what has happened to Darry's cousin, Lady Nina Lewellyn."

"Bentley will find her," Etienne assured her.

Jessa's expression was fierce. "That is all well and good, Etienne, but find them anyway. These men were Fakir. Do you know what that means?"

"No, my Lady."

Jessa thought hard and quick about her brother, Prince Joaquin, and doubted very much if Joaquin understood his true place within the hierarchy of power that was suddenly playing itself out.

"They are Fakir, they are of Lyoness. The Lord Serabee El-Khan is a priest of the Fakir and councillor to Bharjah. He is here, do you see? He *has* to be here. He is not in the Green Hills with Joaquin, he cannot be, not when his servants are here and dying. He must be found. My Lady Radha must be found." She knew her mind as she met Arkady's eyes. "No one is safe here until they are found. This is not over. It has only begun."

"And your brother? What of him?"

Jessa considered the question. "Where is the king?" she demanded. "You must get me to the king. You must get me to him *now*, Arkady."

❖

Nina studied Bentley's strong hands as he tied the torn strip of bedding about her wound. It hurt terribly, but he had stopped the flow of blood with a keen knowledge of such things, and he had gone about it in silence and deference to her comfort. He had spoken only to ask if he caused her more pain. She had lied and said no. She studied his damp blond hair as it fell across his forehead, his brown eyes intense as he concentrated upon his task. She had not known that hands so strong could be so gentle as well. Her gaze fell to his chest and the wound that cut across his skin, though it skipped over the valley between the defined muscles.

"You're hurt," she whispered.

"Just a scratch." He glanced up with a smile beneath his mustache. "Did you cut your hair?" His voice was filled with sweetness as he changed the subject. "I remember it being very long when I saw you last."

"Yes." Nina wanted to laugh. It was an odd feeling, amusement in the midst of what had just happened.

"I like it very much, Lady Lewellyn."

Nina hated being called that. She had always hated it. It made her feel very unlike herself and caught within something not of her own choosing. Her heart beat fast at it now, however, and she felt the words deep inside. "Thank you, Lord Greeves."

"Was your mother angry?"

Nina couldn't help but laugh at that. "I thought she'd give birth to Amar his bloody self on the floor of my father's study."

Bentley laughed his boyish giggle and sat back. "I was thinking of a change, as well. I've been thinking of shaving my mustache."

"No, don't," Nina said at once. "It looks quite fine."

"I'm thinking it makes me look like my brother Sebastian."

"Is he handsome?"

"Yes, but he's a dimwit. If he looks up when it rains he would stay so until he drowns, a bit like a cow."

Nina smiled, and though she was still afraid, it seemed entirely acceptable that she was.

Bentley stood up and drew his sword. "We're going to run now, like all seven hells, for the Great Hall and the warm bosom of Granny Longshanks." He held out his free hand to her and met her eyes with a charming smile. "How does that sound to you, Lady Lewellyn?"

Nina took his hand and got to her feet. "That sounds bloody splendid, Lord Greeves."

"Off we go then."

CHAPTER SIX

Owen Durand paced before the dais as Grissom Longshanks entered the Great Hall beneath the main arch. "Where are my children, Gris?"

"Still within the east wing, my Lord, and well guarded," Grissom responded as the queen pushed through the kitchen doors with her lady Margery a quick step behind. Cecelia's dress was hastily worn and there was a long bandage near her collarbone that carried the stain of herbs. He gestured to the bloodstains upon Owen's leg. "Crossbow?"

"Aye. My guard?"

"Dead. Every man so far, though we've yet to find them all."

Owen turned slowly and surveyed the massive chamber, the doors to the minor halls barred shut. "The kitchens?"

"Access for us and no one else."

"The staff quarters?"

"Secure. The residence was their target."

"How in the bloody hell did they get in? And don't tell me that my walls were breached."

"They breached the wall at the southern gate." Grissom ignored him. "Twelve men dead, and two at the armory. The portcullis is up but a foot or two. I have no idea as to their numbers. We must search everything. Everything."

"My children, Owen!" Cecelia called out, and it was not a request. "And where is Nina? Where are my girls?"

Owen looked to his wife. She had not stopped in her duties and as she and Margery began to push one of the heavy tables along the floor, Owen wondered what he would have done if she had fallen prey to a quicker blade.

He had practically carried her to the Great Hall, and quite against her will. She had wanted only to find her daughters, despite the danger of such an endeavor. Such a blatant assassination attempt had spoken of a larger attack, and he had no intention of stepping into an even worse situation with his beloved in tow. He had told her that she must trust in Grissom, and that his men would see to her daughters. It was no matter that he, too, had felt a dark panic that reached into his very bones. Emmalyn was no match for a sword, and even Darrius could eventually be outnumbered by a greater force, no matter her skill.

He would not have his love in the midst of battle yet again, however, and so he had forced her through the residence to the Great Hall. "My sons, Grissom?"

"I've sent the Thirteenth. They ride with all speed to the Green Hills, prepared for battle if need be."

Owen wiped at his face with both hands and pushed his hair back. "I want a tally of their dead. Poll the men and find out."

"From what I can tell, so far it's mostly Darry's doing."

Owen's temper flared but he bit back his words. That Darry had stood alone against an unknown force of intruders tipped his anger with a sickness he had a hard time trying to conceal. She was not untested in battle, but as far as he knew, she had never before encountered such as this. It did not surprise him that she had prevailed, but such violence had never been what he wished for her.

He stared past Grissom and into the distance. He had expected it though, from that first terrifying moment he had seen her wield a sword. And when it became apparent that she was a singular talent, he had started to count the days. In that secret place within his heart, where not even Cecelia was allowed, he had marked the passage of time until Darry's dance with death would begin.

He could not have been more proud of the warrior she had

become, and that she had used her deadly skills to protect their home and their family; he could not even decipher the many levels of pride and anger, both, that swarmed through his heart. But her dance had begun, and Lord Death, be he a servant of the god Gamar, or a deity all his own, he knew her name now. And no doubt he would hear it again and again until he felt compelled to come for her.

Owen refocused his gaze on Grissom.

"Owen, the guards who were on duty are dead. They didn't move on the family until there was no one here to protect them. Darrius was the only one here, aside from you, whose blade would truly count in the thick of it." Grissom made a face that Owen had seen but a few times before. The commander of his guard was uncertain. "And the Lyonese princess," he added. "She's got majik in her, Owen, the likes of which I haven't seen since I was a boy."

"She's of the Vhaelin."

"Well, whatever she is, I'm thinking she took out her fair share as well, for all that she's a slip of a girl. How many did you count?"

"Four," Owen responded. "Two in my own chambers and one of those with his hands about my wife's throat." He stalked away in a few long strides as he tried to shake the image from his mind. "One in the corridor and two more after we met up with Captain Sol and his men."

"They wear a brand upon the chest," Grissom informed him. "A circle with a spar through it, broken in the middle. I've never seen it before."

"Hired swords?"

"I don't know."

"I want one of them alive, do you hear me?"

"I'm working on it."

"Why aren't there more men here?"

"The Thirteenth rode north and the rest walk the wall and comb the grounds. We've been breached, there's no choice, my Lord. We must search everything and guard the staff on top of that. We were unprepared for this."

"Call up the City Guard." Owen was angered at Grissom's

comment, though he knew it for the truth. He should have seen this, or at least had some vague suspicion of it. It pricked him hard and he let it. "I want Joaquin's men at Los Capos taken prisoner and secured. He brought nearly a hundred men with him. I want them all accounted for."

"It appears we were right to house them away from Blackstone," Grissom said in a grudging tone. "All the men we could spare have been sent. Belkip rouses the City Guard and they'll be on the way quick enough. These weren't the men Joaquin brought with him... these men were something else entirely."

"It doesn't matter now." Owen acknowledged Grissom's opinion. "I want word sent to Colonel Winnows at Falkus and Wyatt in the east, and every outpost along the way, Tomms Town, Baylon and Lockley, Avin-Dell and Genoa. I don't want just the Kingsmen, I want you to give the call, Grissom. Raise my army."

"Many are here on leave for Solstice."

"I don't care if they're hiding beneath your mother's skirts, Grissom, find them. I want the warning bells of Gamar's Temple ringing by the end of the hour." Owen turned to his left and stared long and hard beyond the garden doors. There was torchlight and the grounds were lit as they had not been in many years. It was close to three hours until the dawn. "This is Bharjah."

"Perhaps," Grissom replied. "But with his own daughter here?"

Owen frowned, for it was a good point. "I don't know. But it was convenient, yes, that the women of my family were here alone?"

"Darry was here. I am thinking that it was her call that roused the guard."

Owen's lips curled in a smile and he could feel the danger of it in his very bones. "Aye, it was her, Gris. I heard the call, even as I stuck my fool head out the door like a fucking green recruit."

"If it *is* Bharjah?" Grissom asked with a lift of a white-haired eyebrow.

"My Lord!"

Both men turned to the archway as one as the Princess Jessa-Sirrah of Lyoness moved with confidence into the Great Hall, flanked by Arkady Winnows and Tobe Giovanni.

Jessa's neck and right arm were stained with blood, and Owen let out a hard breath at the sight of it. "Are you wounded?"

"No," she replied, "the blood is not mine."

"Darry?"

"First things first," Jessa said evenly, and Owen lifted his brow in surprise. Cecelia approached, her eyes filled with fear. "Will you try and take her from me?" Jessa's voice was clear, and in want of an immediate answer. "For I warn you now that if you ever try such a thing, I will pull the stones of your palace down about your ears."

Owen let out a huff of surprise. "No, I'll not take her from you," he answered truthfully and wondered where she led.

"The word of a king means very little to me," Jessa continued, and though her hands trembled where she held them to her skirt, her spine was straight and her shoulders back. "My own father is a murderous bastard and would not know honor if it woke up beside him. I am thinking, my Lord, that you are very different than him, though you've made your share of mistakes.

"If you give me your word that we are safe to live as we choose, without interference or plotting against us within your lands," Jessa said, "then I am yours. And I will keep your daughter yours as well, no matter what it may cost me, short of her love, of course. There is the condition to my allegiance and those are my terms. My oath will not go beyond that provision."

Owen realized at once that he bargained with a queen. No matter her lack of the title, at the moment she was exactly that, and she was using her power to protect his daughter, while giving him another chance in the bargain. "You have my word, whether you choose to stay or not. Though it is my hope that you will stay."

"Then I am yours, my king." Jessa bowed her head, Tobe and Arkady pulling their shoulders back as she did so. If they were surprised, they did not show it. "You have my oath of fealty to the land of Arravan and the crown of Durand. Upon my mother's name,

Jhannina de Cassey LaMarc, who was once of the Red-Tail Clan and Queen of Lyoness, I swear it."

"Do not bow, Princess. Please."

Jessa straightened and held out her hand to the queen. "My Lady, you are needed upstairs. Tobe will take you where you need to go."

"What, what is it?" Cecelia's fingers tightened upon Jessa's. "Where is Nina?"

"Lord Greeves sees to her safety."

"The blood you wear?"

"It is not Arravan blood, my Queen. Darry is with Emmalyn. She was…Emmalyn was assaulted, my Lady," Jessa explained with great care. "Though violence was done to her, she was not taken against her will. Tobe will take you to them."

Tobe Giovanni stepped forward and extended his hand.

"I know the way," Cecelia said in a terrible breath of a voice.

"Yes, but Tobe will take you nonetheless," Jessa repeated and glanced to the High King. There was disbelief in his eyes, and confusion, perhaps. "We are not safe yet."

Cecelia lifted her hand and Tobe took it in a gentle manner. The High Queen allowed herself to be led, the color gone from her face and her bold strength of but a few minutes before vanished from her demeanor. Jessa noted Owen's struggle, his rage at war with his shock as both emotions fought for control of his expression.

"She was…" Owen began and then cleared his throat.

"There were three men in total." Jessa's voice was calm, though she had no idea if that would help lessen his distress. "She was fighting them off when Darry and I arrived. They are dead now."

His eyes darkened and his chin quivered, though only for an instant. Grissom reached his hand out but stopped short of the king's arm.

"Might we sit down, please?" Jessa noted the blood upon his trousers and the way he favored his right leg. She took hold of his hand and wondered how severe the wound might be. "I'm very tired, my Lord, and I feel somewhat weak." It was but a small lie and Jessa felt justified in its use. She had used powers she had not known she had and woven spells that had always been a mystery to her, though Radha had made her learn them regardless. She had no idea how—or when—she would pay the price.

Owen's eyes cleared somewhat at her words.

"Please, might we sit down?"

"Yes," he answered, and his fingers closed gently about hers.

She walked beside him to the nearest table, her gait equal to his own. She let him sit first before she let go of his hand and took the chair next to his. Grissom had followed, with Arkady but a few steps behind.

"What did you mean, that we're not yet safe?" Owen asked, and Jessa could see his eyes were clear as he asked the question.

"These men were of Lyoness." Her stomach filled with nervousness as she spoke the words. "They were of the Fakir, the Sahwello Clan, I believe. It is the warrior caste of their faith."

"Bloody hell." Grissom growled.

She looked to him. "Do you know of this Clan?"

"Only by legend."

Jessa returned her attention to Owen. "Serabee is a Lord of the Fakir. These men are his. They bear a brand upon the chest? A sort of wheel, with a cross spoke?"

"A spar?" Grissom asked. "Broken through the middle?"

"Yes."

Owen's eyes flared with rage. "You know these men?"

"No," Jessa responded at once. "But I know Serabee and I know the Fakir. I am a Vhaelin witch, and the Fakir have been the enemy of my people for a thousand years, even longer. There was not a time, ever, that the people of the plains did not fight the Fakir. This feud is as deep as blood. More importantly, however, is the fact that Serabee is First Councillor to my father."

"This I know." The king closed his eyes.

You should never have opened your gates, my Lord. "Whether or not this was planned by Bharjah, I don't know. I have only ever been a trinket." She shook her head. "I have no power and no certain knowledge of such things."

"Joaquin has hinted that your father has not aged well, which I took for the complaints of youth. There's nothing as tiresome as an old man, especially when he's standing in your way. But I have spies that tell me he is actually ill. Is this true?"

Jessa was startled by the thought, though in the back of her mind several troubling ideas began to slide into place. A picture was formed, and his unexpected words allowed the colors of her keen logic to flow and paint upon the aging parchment of her frustration. "I don't know," she answered and arranged her thoughts as quickly as they arrived. "The last I saw him, he sat upon his throne and told me that I was…" Her eyes focused upon the past as she remembered her father's throne room. She remembered his veiled amusement, and the darkness that lay hidden just beneath. "I was…"

"What?"

"You may be right." She took the leap and followed where it led. "He said I would be the last piece of jade in his tower." She shook her head. "I thought he meant that I would marry your son, and that one day his blood would sit upon the throne of Arravan."

"And you do not think that now?"

"Well, aside from the fact that I am backwards and in love with your daughter"—Owen surprised her with a smile—"your son is not interested in a marriage to me. He is more concerned with—"

"Joaquin," he finished for her.

"A child would take much too long and my father is old. The fact that he may be ill is irrelevant to that point, for he would not live to see an heir of his blood take to the throne of Arravan even if he was healthy. And besides, my brothers would never allow it. To see a child lay claim to what they feel is theirs to take?" She leaned forward, her eyes intense. "I have twelve brothers, my Lord, and none of them are certain of the throne. They each have claim, and so they will all seek what is yours. To claim Arravan may seem easier to some than to lay hands upon the Jade Throne."

"Sylban-Tenna?" Grissom asked.

"Sylban is first, this is true, but that carries very little weight in my land." She met the commander's steely blue eyes. "They fight like dogs for my father's attention and favor and Bharjah pricks them on, like a stick in their bellies to watch them scrap and fight.

There is no clear succession, for my father's favor changes with the wind. When Bharjah dies…" Her voice faded with the words. "When he dies…"

Jessa sat back slowly as she felt more than just a portion of the world's weight settle onto her shoulders.

"When Bharjah dies, if he has not chosen his successor publicly before his Court of Lords"—she felt somewhat ill as she looked long and hard down such a road—"my country will be thrown into a civil war, my Lord, and it will be a war that will rage until only one of my brothers is left standing."

Jessa met Owen's eyes as Bharjah's puzzle, and her place in it, took on a definite shape. "My Lord?"

"Yes?"

Jessa took a breath to speak and felt fear. *How well do you truly know your son?*

Owen's gaze sparked with something close to suspicion and she knew she had shown him too much. "This is a conversation for another time, I think." She straightened in her chair and focused on their most immediate concern. "Right now? The Lord Serabee El-Khan is here."

"He is in the Green Hills."

"He is not," she contradicted. "If the Sahwello are here then Serabee is here. We are still in grave danger until he is found. Have you sent word to your sons?"

"My best company of men," Grissom said, "aside from Darry's Boys."

"If they attacked us here, then my sons could be in danger as well," Owen informed her. "My help to them will only be as fast as the Thirteenth can ride. If they are in the thick of it, well, I will know soon enough."

"Is there a place where we may wait?" Jessa asked. "We must stay together."

"Right here, the Great Hall. Wait for what?" Owen demanded.

"Wait for Serabee and his majik to come. If your men search the grounds, they are in more danger than ever. You must pull them back at once."

"But Serabee's men are found out. Their best chance is to run—no matter that we have been caught lacking, they're greatly outnumbered."

"No, my King, you are most certainly wrong." Jessa moved to the edge of her chair. "These men are Fakir, they are Sahwello." How to make him understand? "Once blood has been spilled, they will not be able to stop until there is no one left. Whether they are five men or five thousand, any Fakir that came to kill this night has the sole intention of laying waste to everything you love."

She saw it then, that he heard her words. "This dark passion, it is why my people hate them so, and most likely why my father enjoys them and seeks to curry their favor by placing Serabee so high in his confidence. They have no restraint and they kill for the sheer joy of it. Their rites are of blood and they consume it in worship to their gods. The Sahwello are the hardest of these men and not quite right in their minds. There is no land that may be shared with the Fakir, and so since the birth of my people and theirs we have tried to destroy them."

"I thought the Fakir had grown weak."

"Once, long ago, the Fakir were extremely powerful and might have even encroached upon Arravan, had my people not stopped them and dealt them a terrible blow that lingers still. If you search back through your scrolls, no doubt you would find some mention of the Sahwello and their stature among the Fakir. And the Fakir have never been weak—they merely hide with great skill. Darry knows of the Sahwello, and Jacob, no doubt."

"Darry has always known a great many things that no one else seems to know," Owen replied, and Jessa could hear the affectionate frustration in his voice. His brown eyes had changed in a wonderful manner when he spoke his daughter's name, though the pride came and went quickly.

"The Fakir have hidden within the Kistanbal Mountains, in the north country of my land, for hundreds of years. Radha says they have been waiting and sending men like Serabee into the world for whatever purpose they deem worthy of meddling in. And the Sahwello leave only to kill, or to steal women."

Owen lifted a hand and covered his eyes. "And I let them in. I opened the bloody door myself."

"But this is not your fault, my Lord. Access to such knowledge is, well, let us say my father's borders can be unkind to the curious traveler."

Owen let out a soft bark of laughter and met her eyes.

"The Fakir were a legend in Lyoness, spoken of in hushed tones of fear and stories told about the fire to frighten children into behaving. Radha says that when Lord Serabee arrived in Karballa and word spread that a Lord of the Fakir had come, villages at the foot of the Kistanbal Range became deserted overnight, the people leaving for fear that the Fakir would ride again."

Owen stared past her, lost in thought.

"Owen," Jessa's firm voice brought his gaze back into focus. "Serabee will come. There is something here he wants."

Owen's eyes flared in a silent demand for more.

"I know not what it is, my Lord, but he has exposed himself and the Sahwello in a most brazen manner. He has a need, and he'll not leave until he satisfies it. Whether he does so at Bharjah's bidding or his own, I do not know. Perhaps it is both."

"Would Joaquin be involved?" His tone was lethal at the suggestion.

"Joaquin is cruel and clever," she admitted, and her tone was not dissimilar from his, "but he is a *fikloche piton*." She nearly spat as she revealed her hatred. "If he is involved, he is merely a puppet and does not know it."

"Where is your Lady Radha? I would speak with her."

Jessa's frown was instant. "That, my Lord, is a very good question. I've not seen her since midmorning."

Owen looked to Grissom. "I don't care if you have to carry them kicking and bloody well screaming, I want everyone in this hall. I want them here *now*."

Grissom slapped his boot heels together and turned. "Quick now, Winnows," he ordered and walked several feet before he turned back with a snarl.

Arkady waited for Jessa, the question in his eyes.

"Go now, Arkady. Bring my love to me, if you would please, before she does something foolish. Like nearly falling from a balcony again."

Arkady smiled and clicked his heels as Grissom had done. He walked past the older man. "Are you coming?" he called over his shoulder and Grissom followed with a muttered curse.

When Jessa turned back she knew she was blushing. "Darry's Boys have sworn an oath to me," she explained, somewhat embarrassed. "I don't understand why, really, except that they would not let Darry leave them behind."

Owen let out an odd snort of amusement and used the table to help himself rise. "Do not be so modest, my young Queen."

CHAPTER SEVEN

Darry watched as the Great Hall was transformed beneath Grissom's command, the heavy tables moved and chairs stacked out of the way or used to build fortifications around the wounded. The doors to the kitchens swung open at regular intervals, and barrels of water had been set against the far wall beneath the tapestries, blackwood for washing and oak for drinking. The doors to every entrance and minor hall were barred against attack, with only the main arch and gardens left open. Every lamp was lit and torches burned hot in their sconces as they filled the room with light.

Jessa wrapped Nina's arm with herbs and fresh bandages, and though Nina looked tired and frightened, she seemed ready for a fight just the same.

Emmalyn sat upon the dais floor with her back against the wall, her knees close beneath her skirt and her arms wrapped tightly around them. Etienne Blue was a small distance away from her, cross-legged upon the floor with his sword in reach.

At the moment, her father stood within the center of the Great Hall with his hand on his sword. He stared beyond the garden doors, and though she tried to give a name to it, Darry found his expression completely unfamiliar.

Conflicted though she was about her relationship with her father, she was fairly certain that she understood at least a bit of what he felt in this moment.

The Fakir had invaded her home, and though but a few hours before she had planned to leave Blackstone Keep forever, it was still the place she loved most in the entire world. Her memories were here, both good and bad, and it was the place that had always centered her world.

But to the High King, it was the seat of his power. And so how did the attack look to his enemies, both here and beyond the waters of the Taljah? He'd opened his gates in good faith, like a fool, perhaps, and men of Arravan died because of it. Did he have the will to go to war again? Perhaps he no longer had a care for the honor of his own name, just as he had none for hers.

The temper that still simmered in the pit of Darry's stomach began to boil once more and she turned away, only to fall straight into the eyes of her lover.

Jessa took Darry's hand. "Come with me."

She led Darry easily about the tables, past her own men and those that remained of the Palace Guard. Arkady and Tobe stepped aside so they might pass. The talk in the hall was quiet, but as their numbers grew with each passing moment, the air had taken on a quality of dark anticipation. They were under siege, and though there was now a brief respite, they all understood what might come. There were men that lay dying all around as a grim reminder, nothing the Healer could do for them beyond giving them passionflower syrup mixed with valerian root so they might be made as comfortable as possible. Some of those men would die alone, Jessa knew, without their families or their loved ones to comfort them.

Her own love was not among them, and at this she felt a relief and a joy so fierce she found it hard to contain her emotions. She had stood by for as long as she could and let Darry clean up and change her clothes, her wounds dressed quickly and without fuss. She had let her speak with her men and Commander Grissom Longshanks, and she had played her part and helped those she could. The Healer was an able man and he had respected her rank as a peer in the healing arts. He had let her practice without interference, and he had even deferred to her knowledge once or twice.

Yet through it all she had kept an eye upon her lover, and she could see the panther lying in wait. She was proud of Darry's confidence and the love the Arravan soldiers laid at her feet, like the dearest of tributes given to a great lord. She was a natural leader and a warrior that commanded respect, no matter what her rank was. Jessa had known all this, but she had not understood what it truly meant until she had seen with her own eyes.

When Darry had watched her father with a reluctant look of understanding and hatred both, Jessa could bear no more. Darry's anguish tore at her heart, and though she felt some shame at the thought, she cared at that moment for no one but Darry.

They passed through the kitchen doors and were greeted with activity, the fires lit and tended as the cook yelled for more wood and clean linens. There was a guard set upon the doors which led to the courtyard and the kennels beyond, despite that they were barred against attack.

Jessa spied the empty shadows of a far corner near the laundry and moved accordingly. Her heart hammered in her throat and her flesh felt overheated at Darry's presence. When Darry stepped around her and spun them deeper into the shadows, Jessa grabbed her shoulders with anticipation.

Their mouths met and Darry's hands were forceful at Jessa's waist, her arms like steel as she held Jessa tight. Jessa opened her mouth to her and moved as close as she could, Darry's tongue against her own in a kiss so deep that Jessa felt it in her very blood. Her desire for discretion waged a war against her body, a moan held prisoner within her throat until she could hold it no longer.

Jessa felt Darry's hair and bent back at the waist beneath the force of their kiss. Her passion demanded the sort of satisfaction she knew must wait, and yet Darry's hands slipped lower and cupped her buttocks, an openly defiant gesture amidst the labor that was happening but a few dozen feet beyond their secluded corner.

Darry thrust against her and Jessa gasped, suddenly trapped against the wall as her sex throbbed with want and need alike.

She tasted blood in their kiss. "No"—she pulled back, startled—"wait."

She held Darry's face, the panther abruptly docile before her, an exquisite tenderness about her lover that had arrived without warning and replaced her aggression within the span of a heartbeat.

She moved her thumb across Darry's lower lip, the deep cut upon the tender flesh just inside, ardent in its want of her attention. There was a burn beneath her jaw, as well, the mark red and raw from something that had scraped the delicate skin.

She pushed back the damp curls of Darry's hair and saw the bruise already forming against her right temple. "You're hurt, my love," Jessa whispered as a shiver danced about her spine. She felt no fear, but the tingling sense did hold a delightful expectation of what the look in Darry's eyes might mean for her. She let her fingers slide along Darry's neck, and her touch eased behind Darry's head, in search of the wound she knew would be there.

"I'm all right, Jess."

"Are you the Healer now, *Akasha*?" Jessa asked, not without kindness.

"No."

Jessa felt the knot at the back of Darry's head, her touch careful. Darry moved her head to the side and shook her off. "I'm fine, Jess."

Jessa's hand dropped away. "Let me see it."

"Jess."

"Do not be stubborn, Darrius, or I shall—"

"You shall what?"

Jessa covered Darry's dimple with her hand. "I love you." She stepped close and wrapped her arms about Darry's neck. "Do not be falling off any more balconies."

"I love you, Jessa." Darry's lips moved against her ear. "If anything had happened to you…If they had…"

"Hush," Jessa's hand moved at the back of Darry's head.

Darry growled within her throat at the touch upon the tender skin, and she pulled her head away for a second time.

Jessa leaned back against the wall and set her hand at the center of Darry's chest. "You cannot hide that from me, Darry. And do you think you can just be hanging off balconies and smashing through doors? You have a serious wound." Her throat was tight with fear. It was not a pleasant thought. "It might cause you great harm."

Darry did not ignore her words, but neither did she react to them. "Serabee is coming for us, yes?"

"You might go to sleep and never wake up," Jessa whispered. *And then what would I do?*

"That won't happen."

"Why? Because you have Hinsa's blood within you?" She knew that she had spied the truth of it. "Being *Cha-Diah* does not make you invincible, *Akasha*. And so you would leave me when I have only just found you?"

Darry frowned. "And what of you?"

"What about me?"

"How am I supposed to protect you when you go running off without me?" Darry's eyes filled with sudden anger, and a touch of fear if Jessa guessed correctly. "Off you go," she said and took a step back. "Off you go into blessed Gamar knows what while I nearly get my head cut off staring after you!"

"Do not be foolish, Darrius," Jessa argued, her own temper reacting smoothly. It rose to the occasion and she did nothing to stop it. "All you had to do was stab him."

Darry blinked at her. "Excuse me?"

"I do not need you to protect me."

"That, Princess, was made perfectly clear to me when you—"

"Stop being so stubborn!"

"You cracked a bloody wall open, Jessa!"

They stared at one another, both startled from their anger by the reality of the statement.

"Well…only sort of," Jessa responded. "I'm sure it can be fixed."

Darry tried not to smile as she tucked in her tunic. She was pleased that she had found something to do with her hands, rather than breach all good etiquette in the company of others and joyfully molest her lover. Although she was not entirely certain there was a specific rule for their current situation, she assumed it was completely acceptable to apply what little she did know. "If anyone is going to go to sleep and never wake up, most likely it will be you, for you are a crazy woman. Breaking stones and burning floors, making a storm beneath my father's roof as if you were making a bloody cup of tea."

"I was trying not to kill you," Jessa replied evenly. "You move too fast, *Akasha*."

Darry absorbed all that stood before her, and in an instant she saw the grand scope of absolutely everything. Jessa's intelligence and her passion, and those eyes filled with a dark fire she had been blessed to touch firsthand. Flames that could warm and fill her in places she had thought would forever be cold and empty. *And you have the rest of your lifetime to entice those flames into a glorious wildfire of crazy dreams and sweet passion...if you don't thrust when you should parry.* "I really want to kiss you right now."

"I would like that, please."

She took Jessa in her arms and obliged her until she felt dizzy with it and her lip began to bleed once more. "I will let you stuff me with herbs like a Solstice pheasant and drown me in teas and bitter soups and carry me around on your back if you would like," she promised in a whisper against Jessa's mouth. "But after I have killed Serabee."

Jessa swallowed. She looked from Darry's blue eye to her green, her gaze bright and rich with life. "May I keep you in my bed?"

Darry's grin was slow with any number of wicked thoughts. "If that is what you would like to do with me, then I suppose I will have to let you."

Jessa raised an eyebrow. "You do not sound pleased at the prospect."

"If I become any more pleased at the prospect, my head will burst like a ripe melon in the hot summer sun," Darry replied happily. "Please do not be frightened, Jess. I love you, and I'm not going anywhere."

"Do you promise?"

"Do you?"

"Yes."

"Then all is well, my love," Darry said. "Do not distract me, please," she added and kissed her again before she walked away.

Jessa smiled in appreciation as Darry moved, her back strong and her stride determined. Darry pushed through the doors to the Great Hall, and Jessa turned at the sound of a quiet cough.

The queen stepped from the laundry beyond the cellar door, her arms full of linens that were no doubt needed for the wounded. They stared at each other for several seconds, and Jessa let out a troubled sigh, uncertain of how much the queen had witnessed. "Your daughter is very stubborn."

Cecelia smiled, the gesture filled with agreement. "Yes. But she is worth the trouble, I think, don't you?"

Jessa covered her face with both hands and rubbed at her eyes before she pushed her hair back over her shoulders. "I have never been in love before," she countered and felt more than a bit puzzled. "Is it supposed to make your stomach so upset?"

Cecelia gave a quiet laugh. "Sometimes."

Jessa stepped away from the wall and took the sheets from her. The queen's eyes held an expression that Jessa did not entirely understand, though she thought it might be sadness. She frowned and felt her skin darken with heat. "I should not have been kissing her." She felt selfish in more ways than one as she looked down. "It is not the time for that, I suppose. I'm very sorry, my Lady."

Cecelia touched Jessa's chin and lifted her face. "Now is *exactly* the time to be kissing her. It will give her strength, do you see?"

"I don't know what I'm doing," Jessa admitted. "She is very... she's so very strong. Like the desert Washeeki that blows through the southern plains of Lyoness, stripping the rocks of their time and leaving them new. I do not want to be scared."

Cecelia stepped forward and kissed her upon the cheek, startling Jessa with the tenderness. "I am very much afraid as well, dear girl," the queen confessed. "So we shall make a pact to be strong together, yes?"

Jessa liked the sparkle in the older woman's eyes. "Yes, my Lady."

The queen took her by the arm and guided her through the kitchens. "And my Owen is just as stubborn as your *salla de Akasha*," she said in an almost playful tone. "They are more alike than either of them would care to admit."

Jessa was shocked to hear the queen speak those words, and she suspected her reaction showed on her face.

"Yes, I know what *Akasha* means, my sweet, and the book it comes from, as well." Cecelia looked sly as she spoke and much like her old self. "Does *she*?"

Jessa could feel herself blushing yet again. "Please do not tell her."

"She'll not hear it from me," Cecelia promised.

CHAPTER EIGHT

Jessa felt the queen's eyes upon her as she moved about a cluster of chairs and made her way into the Great Hall. Much like her Radha, Cecelia knew things she shouldn't know. Jessa should not have been surprised, and she would remember from now on that her new queen could speak Lyonese, and that she had read obscure Vhaelin scrolls. Jessa had no clue why Cecelia had chosen to do so, but she would damn well remember that she had. She whispered a curse and felt better for it.

Nina slid from the tabletop as Jessa neared. "Nina, sit back down."

"From the look on your face, I'm betting my Aunt Cece just threw a bit of harsh language at you," Nina said with a smile, though her voice lacked its usual vigor.

Jessa could not help but laugh as she set the linens on the table and reached for the shears. "She did no such thing."

"Pity," Nina sighed. "She's quite good at it."

Jessa's attention was captured by the table's surface, her focus pulled from her control as Nina's voice echoed back through her mind. The grain was deep and old, the wood like a map of years as Jessa's eyes slid along the soft grooves and curious patterns. Her touch hovered above the sewing shears, the metal dark and stained with the use of many hands through the decades. The edges were sharp, though, and they flared oddly as a bubble of light slid along the blades as if it were an insect. Jessa straightened as a low hum of power vibrated along her bones. A pale white light spread across her vision, and she became blind to the faces around her as she set her hands upon the table for balance.

"*Radha...*" Her heart swelled in response to the call, more than ample to the task as it encompassed all the love she felt for the old woman. She turned about and her vision cleared with the movement, a sharp stab of pain passing behind her eyes. Her backside faltered against the table and Nina grabbed her arm.

Jessa had refused to acknowledge her fear at Radha's absence, though she was steadfast in her belief that the old woman had her reasons. Jessa had been certain that Radha would appear out of nowhere and scold her for being careless with her majik, or for staring down a king. She had been desperate to hear Radha's scrape of a laugh and her ancient voice. She wanted to pledge herself to her lover before the only witness that mattered, certain that Radha would bless them both.

Jessa wanted to take her hand, which was old and thin, Radha's bones pronounced beneath the skin, her veins purple and blue as they pressed upward as if to win their freedom, her blood still so strong though her body was frail. She wanted to look into those pale blue eyes and ask why she had never been told. Why had she not been told there would be so much power? There had been no warning. There had been no declaration that her strength was even greater than Radha's, High Priestess of the Vhaelin.

For Jessa knew that was the truth.

"Jessa?" Nina's voice seemed very far away.

Jessa wanted to stand before the old woman and thank her.

She wanted to thank her for all those years. All the days and nights they had sat upon the terrace as the old woman taught her the ways of the Vhaelin. She had taught her the path of majik and sworn with confidence by the blood that pulsed through Jessa's veins. Jessa wanted to thank her for letting her argue and cry and dream upon the stars, praying that somewhere there would be a life for her and that one day she might taste of its sweetness.

She wanted to see her *Akasha* and her Radha sit before the hearth upon a chilly night and talk, the two people she loved most in all the world lost in conversation, for no doubt the two of them would find many things to discuss. She wanted to be there when Darry made Radha laugh, so she might bless her gods that such an unexpected reward had been given to the frightened girl who was now a woman.

"Radha, no"—Jessa pushed away from the table—"let me, old woman, don't be a fool."

Darry and Bentley stood at the center of the hall and Jessa was caught the moment Darry turned her head. They were caught for now and for always. She knew it without a doubt as she felt the same depth of connection that Darry had felt within Tristan's Grove, old and bottomless and meant to be. The Great Loom was spinning and *Senesh Akoata,* the threads of all life, had claimed them both in a warm embrace.

"Jess, are—"

Jessa blinked into the distance where the long grass swayed in a sea of movement. It was early summer grass beneath the brilliant sun, not yet at its full height, though how she knew that, she had no idea. The sky rolled into the end of the world in a blanket of lush blue that took her breath away, not a cloud to be seen between where she stood and the end of forever.

She turned in a slow circle and lifted her arms as the air rushed into her lungs. She saw smoke to the south and knew it was the cooking fires of her people, the smell of spiced meats on the breeze.

The ground trembled beneath her bare feet.

Jessa looked to the north once more, and a giant piebald horse broke the calm of the horizon, the stallion's gait beyond what Jessa knew to be wise, though Vhaelin Star could no doubt keep up. The rider rode low, and as they neared, Jessa felt an unbidden wave of happiness flood through her body.

The horse was magnificent, sixteen hands at least, his white coat dense with dark gray spots. His mane was as dark as pitch with a tail to match, silken and rich. His rider sat back and the stallion thundered to a halt, threw his head back, and pawed the ground.

The rider laughed, and Jessa caught her breath at the sound.

It was Darry's laugh, or very nearly, though it was so close that only Jessa might tell the difference. The rider's hair was a dusty, dark blond and her curls were dense with braids that fell about her strong shoulders. She was beautiful in a unique manner, her features chiseled and fiercely tanned from the sun. She wore soft, battered leathers, and as she looked beyond Jessa into the distance, Jessa noted the long scar upon the left side of her face. The wound must have been cruel to leave such a profound reminder, from her forehead to her jaw; the tissue was thick and white within the darkness of her face.

"I did those braids this morning."

Jessa looked to her left and met black eyes very much like her own. "Who is she?"

"She is Tannen Ahru," the woman answered with a loving smile, "and she is the War Chief of the Red-Tail Clan."

Jessa looked back to the warrior. "Is she yours?"

She felt a pang of desire low within her body, and it startled her. Her chest flushed with heat as thoughts of Darry's touch sent an unforeseen wave of desire washing through her. Her body moved with Darry's as their passion rose, slick and filled with heat, as Darry's mouth upon her neck sent a shiver straight through the heart of her.

Jessa took a small step back and let out a startled laugh, embarrassed as she tried to rein in her unexpected thoughts. "Is she yours?" she asked again.

"She is wild," the woman answered and smiled, much like Radha often did, "so I may not claim such as my own, though if she belongs to anyone, she belongs to me."

"And who are you?" Jessa noted the skin so like her own and the black hair, scented ever so slightly with an essence of jasmine she recognized.

"I am Neela."

Jessa's eyes widened slowly, for she knew full well what that meant. "Why am I here?"

"You have always been here, my daughter. We live upon the same thread in the Great Loom of the world."

Jessa felt her heart skip. "Tannen Ahru." She took a step toward the stallion. "But...but Radha told me Tannen Ahru was a man."

Neela laughed. "Then she lied to you."

Jessa's knees felt weak. "We walk the same thread."

"Yes. As do they. Greetings, lover!" Neela called out and then laughed as Tannen Ahru and her piebald stallion danced sideways in the grass. The warrior lifted a hand into the air.

Jessa blinked as the sun caught upon the silver vambrace Tannen wore upon her left wrist. The flash of reflected light upon the wide cuff was more than she could bear, and Jessa was forced to turn her eyes.

"Remember..." Neela whispered.

"Darry," Jessa whispered, back within the Great Hall. Her gait faltered and then evened out with her next step.

"Are you all right?" Darry asked.

The air beyond the patio doors wavered as if caught within a blast of heat that surged up from the ground. "Get out of the way, love."

Language swamped through Jessa's head like a raging river that had overflowed its banks, Jessa determined to stay afloat through the sudden storm. The lexicon of words that Radha had taught her, all of the charms and runes and endless lessons, all of the ceaseless hours spent upon the written spells until she thought her fingers would bleed and she begged Radha to let her stop, begged until the old woman would relent and give her fresh berries dipped in sugar and braid Jessa's hair while she whispered tales of home. They all spilled forth in a tumble and terrible flood of knowledge.

Jessa stepped close and her fingers trailed along Darry's jaw. She met her eyes, blue and green. "Move everyone back, *Akasha,* or they will all die."

Bentley shouted and the room erupted with movement. The High King drew his sword as Grissom bellowed orders, his own blade suddenly free of its sheath. The men behind her scrambled for their weapons as they sought to obey, and though everything was suddenly in flux, Darry was as solid and calm beside her as the earth itself.

She saw it all as if she were somehow above the Great Hall, her senses attuned to a new and unique scale of vision that was vastly different than what she was used to.

There was a high-pitched scream of metal followed by a deep shudder as the colossal pins that held the Grand Foyer doors broke free from their rust. A hush fell across the hall as the massive gates trembled where they hung and the mortar about the frame began to crumble as the doors swung outward from the walls.

Owen shouted in disbelief as the gates swept shut with an explosion of sound that shook the floor. The Durand banner was thrown loose and fluttered free as the Kingsmen stationed in the Foyer upon the opposite side hollered and beat upon the doors.

"Back!" Bentley shouted and ran into the king. He grabbed Owen's arm with a firm hand. "The Lady said to get *back,* my Lord."

"Boy, do not test me this—"

Owen! The king jerked about at Jessa's unspoken command. The nearness of Darry's strength spread in a glorious manner throughout Jessa's body and it filled her with warmth and confidence. *Not yet, Owen,* her voice echoed within his thoughts and his shoulders flinched. *Wait for it. Your time will come.*

The king grabbed Bentley by the collar and turned away. "The tables!" his voice roared out, Grissom at his heels, as he hauled Bentley behind him. Tobe, Etienne, and Emmalyn helped the wounded onto the dais as the tables were tipped and slammed onto their sides in order to provide protection.

"You could have at least brought me a sword," Darry said in a dry tone as they faced the garden doors.

Jessa heard the clash of swords in the foyer beyond the doors. "*Akasha,* please go away."

Darry took Jessa's hand in her own. "At least allow me the illusion of being necessary."

Jessa touched Darry's face as she whispered the spell. "No."

Darry looked at her with a curious expression and then her eyes narrowed in an odd mixture of amusement and suspicion. "And what, may I ask, are you doing?"

The spell faded upon Jessa's tongue, completely inadequate for what she wanted. She tried not to smile as she turned back to the gardens and tightened her grip upon her lover's hand. "Accursed *Cha-Diah*."

"You weren't complaining the other night."

Jessa caught the laughter within her throat before it could escape. "*Sheeva,* Darry, this is not the—"

The Lord Serabee El-Khan appeared amidst a thick shimmer of air, stepped through the patio doors, and walked uninvited into the Great Hall. His clothes were as black as always and he wore two swords, one upon each hip. His bald head caught the lamps and torchlight and his teeth flared as he smiled. From the balcony above, Kingston Sol took aim and fired.

The arrow bounced upon the floor at Serabee's feet and skipped deeper into the room with a clatter. Kingston cursed in surprise.

Lady Radha, High Priestess of the Vhaelin shimmered to life out of thin air, halfway between her children and the Fakir Lord, draped within her many black shawls and fringe. Jessa stepped forward at the sight of her but Darry grabbed her and held her back.

"Lady Radha, how good of you to come," Serabee said and smiled. "I had thought you dead in an alley, along the wharf, I believe. Though when my man returned with word of your demise, I will admit that it seemed somewhat doubtful. But one always hopes for the best."

A loosed arrow bent around Serabee's shoulder and ricocheted through the air. It missed Radha by a few scant inches. "Wait until you have something you can *hit*, boy!" she yelled out, and Kingston stood down.

Serabee laughed and looked beyond the old woman, his gaze intense as he studied Darry across the distance. "We have been waiting for you, Yellow Hair."

Jessa felt her rage rise up, and this too was as deep and old as her love for Darry. *We live upon the same thread in the Great Loom of the world...as do they.* Neela's voice echoed through her thoughts, and once again Jessa saw Tannen Ahru upon her splendid piebald stallion.

Darry let go of Jessa's hand and stepped forward.

"And we have been waiting for a very long time," Serabee said, watching her move. "If only Joaquin had realized what he's truly been poking at. Thank you for not killing him." Serabee laughed. "I would say that you are late, Yellow Hair, but that would be rude."

Jessa heard Darry's name spoken and knew it was the queen. She knew where Cecelia stood within the hall, just as she knew where the king was. It was the Hawk's Eye spell and it was not a comfortable awareness, to see the world from so many perspectives. She had never before had cause to use it, and the spell had come unbidden into her thoughts. This, too, was not a comfortable sensation—that some part of her mind wove together the string of runes without her conscious knowledge.

"My name is Darrius," her lover said clearly for all to hear.

"Your name is of no consequence," Serabee responded. "It is the thread upon the Loom that matters. And your thread will finally be at an end."

"It will be my sword in your throat that matters, Fakir dog," Darry threatened, and there was a low chuff of sound within her voice, almost a purr.

Jessa felt a hitch in her breath at the pulse of majik that poured from Darry, an open flow of power that held absolutely nothing back. It spilled onto the floor at her lover's feet like a glorious wave and rushed forth.

Hinsa, Jessa realized, truly startled. Darry had called her forth. She was calling the great cat from the maze at last and claiming her blood in full.

Serabee smiled. "But you are not wearing a sword."

"And you have one too many," Darry answered with a grin of her own. "I shall just use one of yours."

Jessa stepped forward and set a careful hand at the small of Darry's back.

"Talk, talk, talk, you are unwelcome in my daughter's house," Radha said and reached out. "Let us get on with the killing."

"Radha, no!" Jessa screamed.

Light bowed outward and Jessa was shoved to the floor, Darry's hands hard upon her shoulders as she was taken down amidst the explosion. A discordant wail of strings filled the hall with a horrible surge of noise, and Darry gave a shout as a blast of heat washed over them.

Jessa spoke the counter spell and it surrounded them both as she held fast to the pocket of air that defended them. In her mind the spell was like a bird in her hand, held firmly and yet with great care, each feather an instrument of power that she smoothed with a whispered thought. The torches guttered and spat flames that rose up as the wave of light raced across the Great Hall, only to escape through any opening available. Flames caught one of the tapestries and the ancient fabric was lit afire.

Radha stepped close within the center of the storm as the glass upon the garden doors shattered outward, as did the balcony windows, the archers thrown back from the railing as the unleashed power surged upward.

Radha touched her left hand to Serabee's forehead and met his eyes, her laughter pleased at the fear and shock she encountered. *Not just a witch, you arrogant dog, but a High Priestess of my gods. Not just a nursemaid but your equal, yes?*

The heat that wrapped around the Fakir intensified as she called forth all her power and forced the white flames past the influence of Serabee's icy cold shadow. She could smell his blood, and she closed in for the kill, giddy at the prospect of so quick a victory. But she could also smell the demons of the Northern Wastes swell upward to meet her, and the fingers of her hand became stiff beneath the rival power. *Even so, Serabee, you are no longer hidden within your cold stone...*

Radha reached out with her other hand, and his body trembled beneath her touch, helpless as she drew forth one of his two swords. "My daughter has need of this," she said within the storm of the Vhaelin blood fires called to life. "Thank you for remembering."

She knew the heat pushed within Serabee's veins, and she felt his power arch against it in a frantic manner. His gods required ice and blood, and no doubt he had drunk his fill in the dark, frozen towers of the Kistanbal.

One thing she had not expected, however, was the messenger of her own gods. She had not expected to feel the pounding of its hooves, nor to smell the musky scent of its soft coat beneath the stench of his power.

Radha leaned closer as she sought the stag, her eyes wide as she tried to tame its might and turn it to her advantage. The messenger was truly unexpected and she let the flames grow stronger as she sought its protection against them. She opened herself to the stag's influence, some deep part of her filled with pride that the Vhaelin would come to her in the midst of her greatest battle. She had encountered the animal's genuine essence only once before, those many years ago when Jessa had taken up the bone dagger. And though the stag had thundered past her in search of the girl, it had been enough, enough to keep her prayers faithful and strong.

Serabee smiled in the heat and struck Radha along the throat. His hand passed through the flesh as if he were a ghost, and then he tried to grab hold, at once solid and filled with rage.

The stag's energy shifted, and Radha realized—to her horror— that Serabee had been drinking of the stag's blood and hoarding its power. Her eyes went wide in distress and she stumbled back, spitting blood within the runes of her spell as she seized the totem of her gods from his control. The pure distillation of power splattered across his face and blistered his skin as Serabee fell away with a scream, seared to the bone.

❖

Darry looked up as a gust of wind surged through the hall and replaced the heat with a bitter cold that burned in its own right. Her hair slashed and clung to her face as the perverted frost blanketed the room. She fell onto her backside, and Jessa grabbed her tunic in the crush of silence.

The sudden sounds of battle rang out from the balcony above and beyond the archway doors as Darry took her first clean breath in what seemed like forever.

Radha stood in the center of the room, and though Serabee El-Khan was nowhere to be seen, the High Priestess did not stand alone.

Darry guessed that close to one hundred Sahwello warriors stood in wait behind the old woman, their numbers fanning back through the shattered doors and into the gardens. They were unmasked and exposed, weapons at the ready. Their skin fairly glowed in the light of the few torches that remained, their illumination meager when compared to the power that had filled the vast chamber but moments before.

"*Sheeva…*" Jessa spoke in a shocked breath, and her arm jerked as Darry pushed to her feet and ran.

"Darrius!" Owen bellowed and his voice echoed through the hall.

Darry could feel the grass beneath her feet and the air against her face. She could feel her muscles pump and her feet pound the earth. She could smell the lilacs within the courtyard as the hunt swelled upward and the maze was left behind. She could smell the blood of her enemy, and her tongue was eager for a taste.

Radha turned her back on the Fakir warriors and walked toward Darry with a dark smile as the enemy surged forward. The old woman tossed Serabee's captured sword high into the air, and its twisted silver guard flashed with brilliance as it spun.

"Thank you, my Lady," Darry said as she snagged it smoothly from its downward arc and was past her. She whirled with grace into the steps of the Dance and the wicked blade of the Fakir Lord sliced upward, straight through the first Sahwello that crossed her path.

Chapter Nine

Jessa watched in horror as Darry disappeared into a sea of black, even as her perception was spun high up within the Great Hall as the Hawk's Eye spell graced her with its gift. Thrown off balance by the sudden shift in viewpoint, she stumbled to the side, only to be caught by Arkady's strong hand upon her arm.

Bentley slammed into the Sahwello near the edge of the dance floor, struck the man's sword aside, and let momentum do the rest. They both crashed into the men behind, tumbling to the floor as weapons struck out and steel flashed, Bentley on his right knee as his shin crushed the throat beneath him and his blade slashed upward with the strength of both arms.

Tobe Giovanni slid into the fray beside him and pushed forward as his blade caught the sword at the back of Bentley's neck and shoved it away. The dagger within his left hand stabbed out and found the willingness of flesh.

Grissom Longshanks waded in with both sword and dagger drawn. He chose his first kill, and then made it so as he ignored the blade tip that sliced open the tunic along his sword arm. He flipped the dagger around and threw it as his sword slid in a circle and swung his opponent's blade around and out. He drew a second dagger from the belt at the small of his back and struck, the blade lost to him as the Sahwello fell away.

An arrow pierced the back of the man beside the commander, and Jessa's vision swung smoothly to its source. Kingston Sol nocked another arrow as he slid along the balcony rail, no doubt his second shot as deadly as the first.

The High King of Arravan fought with a mighty sword, the movements familiar to his body and delivered with an unexpected grace. He took a wound upon his left forearm as his sword pulled back and sliced a throat, blood arcing into the air. He bellowed his rage, his eyes wide as his voice rose through the Great Hall above the fray, and he laid both hands upon his sword.

Upon the dais Emmalyn grabbed Etienne's arm. "Etienne, go!"

"No," he replied. "I won't leave you."

Jessa's gaze hovered overhead. Five Sahwello warriors broke free from the center and rushed the overturned tables as Etienne stepped forward with a smile. He moved to the gap and spun, his sword behind his back as he came up. His blade slid through flesh but he never stopped, the second Sahwello unable to defend the unexpected strike. When Etienne came around, the third man fell past him, two arrows in his back. Etienne's sword clashed with the man upon his right, and he pushed him back as the remaining Sahwello charged the gap.

Nina Lewellyn pulled a dagger from her boot, shoved the queen aside, and faced their enemy with a furious expression. An arrow exploded through the front of the attacker's throat, and he crashed to the floor. His body slid to an unruly halt at Nina's feet, and she looked up into the distance. Two more Kingsmen had joined Kingston Sol upon the balcony, both bloodied but capable as they picked their targets.

"The banners!" the queen cried out and ran.

The slow embers had caught fire, and the flames had begun to spread from one tapestry to the next. Emmalyn reacted and shouted for the water barrels to be overturned, Nina close behind her as she ran. Emmalyn grabbed her mother as Cecelia struggled with the Lewellyn family tapestry, lumps and streamers of flaming fabric raining down from above. She spun her to the side and out of harm's way with a shout for help.

Jessa refocused and looked to Arkady, his sword slick with blood. "Arkady!"

He turned toward her voice amidst the sounds of the battle around them and stepped forward with a downward swing of his sword, at her service.

"To the king, Arkady," she ordered and sent the Hawk's Eye in search, leading him through the carnage.

"Hell and hounds, woman!"

Jessa reached out as they went, the words upon her lips a deadly breath as she moved through the battle. She touched a shoulder, whereupon the bones broke and a scream rang out. Her fingers slid through a wave of hair as Arkady turned a sword away, and a spine turned to dust even before Arkady could strike. His sword was cool and precise, a keen partner to the majik that Jessa let loose in order to destroy their enemies.

The Hawk's Eye saw Radha close to Darry as the old woman plucked from her shoulders one of her many black shawls. Jessa stumbled at the sight of them both and Arkady cursed as he steadied her and thrust his sword at the same time.

The Sahwello who swung a killing blow toward Darry's spine turned as the black shawl became smoke along his sword, his eyes shocked as the dense cloud spun thick and heavy about his blade and raced up his arms like a snake. It filled his mouth as he screamed, slithered down his throat, and took him to the floor. Radha plucked another shawl and tossed it, the garment flying past Darry's head before coiling around a throat, slicing along the jaw, and finding the lips of her next victim. It flooded his mouth, poured down his throat, and filled his lungs.

Darry moved like water, the Dance—the discipline of Honshi— guiding her stolen sword. The weight of the weapon appeared perfectly balanced in her hand, as if it were made only for her. She seemed to recognize nothing but the sleekness of the steel as it clashed with the weapons in front of her, first upon her left and then her right, her movements so clean and swift that the Sahwello began to part before her despite their numbers. The force of her blows and the conflict her sword provided were a graceful thing, and within the steps of Honshi, each strike was a deadly blow against one of her opponents. Her sword was alive, and Jessa thought at that moment that her lover had become one with the blade, her will given up to the secrets of the steel.

Jessa turned to her left and reached out, grabbed the throat of an enemy, and then watched as the runes burned a path of fire down her arm. His body jerked and spun as flames burst out in a glorious flash of white brilliance, and then he fell, turned to ash before he could hit the floor. Through the Hawk's Eye spell she caught sight of the king and they waded deeper into the fight.

❖

Darry was at one with the steps until she heard the screams. Her mind filled with a face and she felt the heat of blood upon her tongue, the rush of its flavor hard within her next step. Her sword faltered and she tried to adjust, her concentration splintered by the instincts that could not be tamed: Hinsa.

The blow took her upon the right side, and she crumpled beneath it as pain exploded along her shoulder and into her neck. Her head seemed to split beneath the force of it, and she let out a startled breath as her eyes shut and light burst within her skull. The sword slid into the flesh along her ribs and she cried out. She tried to spin away from it even as she fell, her sword striking as she went down.

Darry saw what appeared to be a black snake wrap thick about her opponent's neck, and he stumbled to the side, taken from the battle as he struggled against a new attack. She lifted her blade in confusion as another Fakir filled her vision.

Hinsa leaped within the fray and landed upon the man's back, taking him to the floor. The golden panther took his neck within her mighty jaws and, with a smooth twist of movement, swung his body to the side as if it were a child's doll. The fur upon her back was bloodstained, and her powerful tail lashed out behind her.

Darry blinked and felt Hinsa lift her head, the Lady Radha standing before the cat, though the old woman was much too tall. Radha was surrounded by brilliant light as the old woman bowed her head in deference, and Darry realized that she was looking through Hinsa's eyes.

Then Radha reacted smoothly to a new threat, and her hand pushed through a chest.The fringe at the waist of her skirt unraveled and thick pieces of twisted yarn pulled free of the material, swirled into the air, and then straightened into deadly quills. The air rippled with a heavy pulse of energy, and the long needles scattered as Darry tipped over. Her vision shifted yet again as she looked up, her senses returned to her own body as the enemy fell before them like stalks of wheat at harvest.

She saw Bentley in the distance with Tobe Giovanni at his back, Tobe bleeding heavily from his left leg though he fought on. Darry pushed to her feet and moved, even as Hinsa leaped into the Sahwello warriors as Tobe went down, his legs kicked from beneath him. Bentley was crowded but he would not leave his companion, as Tobe lay crumpled against the back of his left leg. Darry sliced at a shoulder and switched her blade over in the same move, the weapon brought back around in order to dispatch a second line of attack.

Bentley called out and Darry fought harder at the sound of his voice. They had been pushed deep into the Great Hall and fought just beneath the balcony, a position that had no line of retreat or defensible advantage, and Darry knew this would be their final stand. Hinsa yowled and Darry spun to the side with a furious shout. She knocked an enemy's blade aside with her wounded left hand and stabbed as Hinsa slithered to the right, a gash along her hind leg. A second Sahwello swung his dagger toward her in a vicious arc as Radha stepped into the melee. The fringe of her skirt unraveled and, like a rope, spun in each direction to entangle both Sahwello opponents. Necks snapped to Darry's left and to her right.

❖

The High King looked up from the bodies at his feet when the doors to the Great Hall shook as if some monstrous creature battered them from the other side.

Owen stumbled back a step as Jessa appeared before him, the bolt of a crossbow caught smoothly within her left hand, a foot or two before his very face. The shaft flared in a burst of white flame and she shook the ash free with an almost casual shake of her hand. He met her eyes for an instant, startled to see her smile.

The heavy, ancient wood of the Great Hall doors splintered inward and began to swing as Owen tightened the grip on his sword, and his heart let out a cruel thud. It did not take a master strategist to know they could not withstand another frontal assault.

The City Guard poured into the hall, their gray uniforms disheveled and their weapons sullied, the Grand Foyer a battlefield behind them. The captain held up his left fist and his men came to a halt behind him. Lucien Martins, one of Darry's Boys, walked forward and stood beside the captain, his neck and tunic plastered with blood.

The High King surveyed the carnage that was the Great Hall of Blackstone Keep, and then he looked for the Lyonese princess.

Jessa moved with a purpose through the wounded and the dead alike, and he wondered how many times she might have saved his life in a battle where he had no doubt been the main target of every Sahwello warrior. Arkady Winnows followed her close, and Owen saw then what she sought with such fierce intent.

Darry stood up slowly and Jessa stepped into her arms without hesitation. His daughter embraced her lover, her newly won sword bouncing against Jessa's hip as Darry refused to let it go.

Arkady Winnows lifted his blade into the air with a ragged shout, whereupon the call went up and the name of Durand echoed through the vast chamber.

CHAPTER TEN

Jessa pushed the hair back from Darry's face as she sat beside her on the bed. "They are calling it the Siege of the Great Hall."

"It was more of a mess, actually," Darry whispered as a sleepy smile turned her lips.

They had chanted Darry's name and Jessa would never forget the sound of it, for they had all been witness to her fearless charge. The wound upon Darry's left side was deep, but nothing vital had been pierced. Jessa had only observed the Healer's work, his careful stitches, for her hands had been too unsteady to do it herself. The bruises had turned dark already, Jessa uncertain as to what their final shade would eventually be. "I think you had best not do that again, *Akasha*."

"Do what?"

"Start a fight."

"I won't make a promise that I probably can't keep."

Jessa smiled. "Well then, you had better think of something."

"Or what?"

Jessa leaned forward until their faces were close. She saw in Darry's eyes that the Healer's tonic had taken hold, and it would not let go until it had its way. Darry would be asleep in moments, if her guess was true. Jessa kissed her, Darry's lips soft and filled with heat, her lower lip slightly swollen. Jessa could taste the passionflower herbs that lingered, and the flavor was not unpleasant. "Or I shall not be kissing you again."

Darry's left hand slipped from her stomach and fell onto the soft fur of Hinsa's neck, the panther fast asleep beside her *Cha-Diah* child as the cat took up more than her fair share of the bed. Her wounds had been seen to, though she had let no one but Jessa touch her.

Hinsa had at last made her presence known to all, and within the Great Hall, everyone had stood still and silent as the great cat had moved through the dead to stand at Jessa's side. At the time, Jessa had gauged the wound to be the least of the panther's worries, for several warriors had drawn their bows and taken aim, uncertain as to how they should respond.

It had been the queen who had shouted for them to lower their weapons, and Grissom's men had done so, though reluctantly. They had left the hall in peace with Jemin McNeely—a dark-skinned warrior from Artanis and one of Darry's Boys—in the lead. He carried Darry in his arms as they went, the rest of their small band close behind.

The panther's purr moved through the covers and the feather mattress and Jessa had no doubt there would be explaining to do, though she was still wondering about Cecelia's initial reaction. She had ordered everyone out of the great cat's way, including her shocked husband. Her tone had brooked absolutely no argument from anyone, and even the king had obeyed.

"I think the queen recognized you, Biscuit," Jessa whispered, and perhaps Cecelia had. No doubt that night so long ago, trapped within the maze as her daughter slept beneath the jaws of a wild panther, had left a permanent impression. Such a thing as that, a mother would most likely never forget.

"What if I tell you first?" Darry's voice was a mere ghost of sound as her eyes closed and she began to drift in earnest.

"Before you start a fight?"

"Yes."

Jessa considered the offer and then sat back. "Fair enough." A moment later, Darry's soft, deep breathing signaled to Jessa that her lover slept.

There was a raspy cough from across the room and Jessa turned, tired herself but knowing that it would have to wait. Her eyes searched beside the hearth. "Are you well, old woman?"

Radha dropped the shawl from about her head and her spell fell away as if it were water. For a moment, the chair beside her faded from the light as if made of air. "I am well," Radha answered, though her voice was rougher than usual, and more quiet than Jessa had ever heard it.

Jessa rose from the bed and moved across the room with a purpose. "Radha."

Radha stepped into the embrace. "You did well, child."

Jessa leaned back. "What in the name of the Vhaelin did you think you were doing?" she demanded, a slight edge to her voice. She thought her tone was appropriate, however, so she did not temper it as she might have. "Where is Serabee? Is he dead?"

Radha adjusted the heavy scarf about her neck and shoulders and stepped to the chair, which was now as solid as ever. Jessa reached out quickly and helped her to sit, unaccustomed to the exposed fragility in the old woman's step. It worried her a great deal, but she was uncertain about what she might do to change things.

"I know not where he went, child"—Radha covered her mouth as she cleared her throat again—"though go he did."

"Where?" Jessa knelt beside the chair and gazed up, her hands upon Radha's knees. The thought that Serabee was out there was not a comforting one, though she could not deny that she was glad he was gone, if only temporarily.

Radha gave a raspy chuckle. "I told you, I do not know."

"Where, Radha?" Jessa insisted. "If you don't know, then tell me where you think."

"Most likely, he has run for the skirts of the Butcher."

"After failing to win his purpose? Bharjah might very well kill him, if he can."

"Did he fail in everything?"

Jessa frowned as they fell into their familiar game, the pieces moved about the board without any pretense or preamble. "I do not wish to play, old woman."

"And was it Bharjah's ambition he served?"

"King Owen lives, Radha, and the Sahwello dead are being stacked in the field beyond the north wall, even as I speak. And if it was not Bharjah, then who ordered such an assault?"

"The game is in play, girl, follow the pieces."

Jessa knew very well there was a game in motion, but at the moment she was much too exhausted to even look at the board. Was it Bharjah's will, or that of Serabee El-Khan? Or perhaps Joaquin had finally made his move, though she thought of Serabee standing in the Great Hall as he called out his challenge. He had confronted Darry, though, not the king and not the Durand name. He had called out to the Yellow Hair. *It is your thread upon the wheel that matters…*

"*Sheeva,*" Jessa mumbled. "Let me see your neck," she added, and her left hand pulled with care at Radha's scarf. "You cannot hide your wounds from me."

Radha slapped her hand away. "You can teach me nothing about the healing arts, child, that I do not already know. It is a hard wound, but I will be fine with time. Are the pieces in your mind? Do you see the board?"

"I see them"—Jessa sighed—"even as I see a glass of cool spring wine and fresh fruit to soothe the ache in my belly. I see a bath, with water so hot that I can barely stand it. And I see my lover naked beneath me, causing me to speak in ancient tongues, for she is beyond my best dreams, and I have no words for what she does to me."

Radha's chuckle was quiet but filled with delight.

"I'm very tired, Radha, I need no lectures. The king has summoned us in but a few hours, and I need to sleep."

"Your mind shall ponder things while you rest, you needn't fear."

"Come to the divan and lie down."

"We have no time for that."

"Do not tax me, old woman, or I will carry you there myself."

"Jessa-Sirrah."

Jessa reacted to the use of her full name and sat back upon her heels, her hands folded upon her lap. It was a familiar moment and Jessa found comfort in it, despite her unease at their conversation.

Radha smiled, and her soft, old hand peeked out from her sleeve, her fingers gentle as they tapped Jessa's cheek. "Where did you go in the Great Hall?"

Jessa gave a rueful smile. "You miss nothing, old woman."

"Where?"

"It was not so much *where*…" Jessa began, her thoughts fast and clean despite the aches of exhaustion. "As *when*."

"Ah." Radha gave a nod. "I felt you go and stay at the same time."

"I did not weave the spell," Jessa admitted. "I'm not even sure what it was, or if there were runes to hold it fast. It was…it was a shift, as if a door had opened and I stepped through it. But it was smooth, no more than taking a breath."

"To when did you go?"

Jessa wondered what Radha's reaction would be. "I stood within a sea of grass and spoke with Neela."

Radha hissed in her breath and leaned against the back of the chair. She batted an angry hand at the air and let out a disgruntled sound. "I have sought that for many years!"

"Radha?"

The old woman's eyes were fierce. "Yes?"

"Did you not tell me once that Tannen Ahru was a man?"

Radha let out a gruff sound. "Not exactly."

Jessa felt her eyes flare, fairly certain of the comment that was to follow.

"But I did not dissuade you when you made the assumption, this I admit."

"Damn you, Radha."

"And what should I have done?" Radha countered. "It is not wise for anyone to know their fate completely. With such knowledge, one tends to step to the left, when before, one might have moved to the right." Radha gave a dismissive wave of her hand. "Everyone thinks they are in control, and if they are not, they are determined that it should be so, no matter what the gods may say. You most of all, child. Being a prisoner has done you no favors in this regard."

"I have always done as you have asked."

"You have *listened*, at the least, and this is the most anyone may hope for from their child. What did Neela have to say?"

"We walk the same thread."

Radha remained silent.

"What, you have nothing to say to that?"

"I have known this since you were born. What else?"

"I think…I think Darry and Tannen Ahru walk the same thread, as well."

Radha laughed and her pale blue eyes lit up like the noonday sun. "You think, or you know?"

"All right, I know it," Jessa admitted. It was a thrilling revelation, but she was uncertain of what it would mean for them. Neela and Tannen were the greatest legends her people had ever known. "*Senesh Akoata* is at play."

"Did you ever think it was otherwise, child?" Radha's tone was that of a tired teacher, one who had waited many years for her pupil to understand.

"I have not taxed you so darkly, have I?"

Radha took a careful breath and settled more comfortably in her chair. "No, child, though I have waited some time for you to see the threads that reach back. Back through the ages and into the heart of your own blood."

"But you never told me the stories as you should have, as I asked you. Tell me more of Neela, I would say, and you would not. Tell me more of Tannen Ahru, I would say, and again you would not. So many secrets on your part, that I thought Tannen was a man, Radha."

"And yet you stole through my scrolls for the stories you wanted, yes?"

"Of course I did."

"And what did you find?"

"Only what you wanted me to, apparently," Jessa accused in a dry tone.

Radha laughed, the sound careful as she protected her throat. "Do not be sore, Princess. Your love for Darrius is true and unfettered by old expectations. You have no ancient dreams to live up to, or prophecies to argue with in the dead of night. You have only your lover, for whom you have killed and would crumble mountains to the ground. You hold the heart of a panther in your hand, and it is good and right, and it makes your knees weak. Her passion rattles your bones, and you love it, every moment of it, and it came to both of you as it should, pure and untouched by anyone's need but your own. What more must you know?"

Jessa considered the old woman's words, though it did not take her long. She looked to the bed once more. "What rules did you break by not telling me?"

"The Vhaelin love free will above all other things, child. What would I be, if I had stolen such from you?"

"I do not care who she is," Jessa whispered. "She is mine now."

"I'm not blind, girl," Radha replied. "I don't care either if you must know. Now tell me of your majik."

Jessa's eyes locked on to Radha's and held tight. "The spells I wove, they came to me with very little thought behind them. The Hawk's Eye and the Ashes of Blood. The Song of Steel."

"That is a hard one to hold," Radha said with respect, "the Song of Steel."

"Yes, and I have never spoken the runes before, as well you know." Jessa's voice held an edge once more. "If I am not in control of my own majik, then we are all in a very lot of—"

"You were quite in control and you know it, or you would not be here." Radha's tone was sharp. "You drew upon the panther's strength, yes?"

Jessa rubbed the back of her hand against her forehead. "It was everywhere, Radha." She glanced toward the bed. "I could actually *breathe* it in…It was magnificent."

"You make a good pair, Jessa. Even as you once did, long ago."

Jessa gave her a tired smile. "There's something to think about, yes?"

"You are ready now."

Jessa let the moment hang in the quiet between them, though not for long. "Ready for what?"

"The spells you wove upon this day, my child, are not the spells of a Vhaelin witch, nor are they the spells of a Shaman. They are the runes of a Vhaelin priestess. And do not think I make this decision lightly, for I do not, I assure you. I will bestow upon you the mantle you have earned, and I will tell you the truth of it at last. But first and foremost, I shall gift you with my scrolls."

Jessa let out a breath of surprise.

"And so in this matter, it is the custom that you must make your own way, child, without my help and without my guidance. For if you wish to take my rank from me, that is exactly what you must do."

"I do not wish your title, Radha. You are the High Priestess of the Vhaelin, and that is as it should be. I want no such responsibility."

"No?" Radha demanded, her tone stinging just a bit. "You took your place on that road when your true thoughts called me a fool in the Great Hall and told me that the battle was not mine to fight. Now, when we sit safe in the warmth of a fire, with our bellies full of karrem and the blood washed away, you may not play the apprentice simply because you wish for the familiar comfort of my presence."

Jessa's face was hot with shame. "I'm sorry, Radha. I did not want you hurt, that is all. I love you, old woman, and you know it."

"I know this, just as I know that love was your motivation. But you chose the road of your power regardless, no matter how flattering the reasons may be to me. I'm not saying you were wrong," Radha explained. "Serabee is stronger than I gave him credit for, and perhaps I was too arrogant, as you have chided me, more than once. But I have been fighting this battle for three generations of our people, and I have sacrificed *every*thing I have ever loved—save for you, my child. I have more than earned my place in this struggle."

Jessa took Radha's hands within her own. "Yes, this I know. I'm sorry."

"So my scrolls are yours, Jessa-Sirrah, and there you shall find all the knowledge you will need, though perhaps, not all the wisdom."

Jessa smiled. "This is why I have you, my sweet."

"This is your path, child, not mine. I have my own to seek, and it is high time I was on my way. If you wish my rank and the spells of the Vhaelin Blood Fires, you must earn them. By our custom you must make your own way now, as a Vhaelin priestess of our Clan. And when you are ready to claim the mantle of High Priestess? You, my child, will have to come to *me*."

Jessa stared at her. "What does that mean?"

"Do not look so stricken, Jessa-Sirrah, or play the innocent. You know what it means. You have come into your power. You are a woman full grown, with the might of the Vhaelin at your fingertips and the passion and strength of a lover by your side. And she is no ordinary lover, to be sure. Not a woman to be carrying your trunks of dresses and scrolls. She is Darrius Lauranna Durand, and she walks the thread of Tannen Ahru. And I tell you now, I'll not soon forget how the Golden Panther danced the steps of Honshi within a sea of Fakir," Radha said with a smile. "You have little to fear from the world from this point on, unless you find such darkness in your own heart."

"She is better than I am," Jessa whispered, "and I know it."

"You are different than she, that is all," Radha said, a gentle correction. "The blood of Bharjah was not always black. At one time, your father's people worked the land and held true to their gods, and men flocked to their banner. They were given protection for their loyalty and they thrived. Do not ever forget that, Jessa-Sirrah. You are the rightful Princess of Lyoness. You are the Nightshade Lark and the Woman Within the Shadows."

Jessa accepted all her titles, and they sat less heavy within her chest than they once had. Perhaps being loved and loving someone else in return had proven a balm against the burden of such responsibilities. She could do nothing about her royal blood and the shame it caused her, and she could do nothing to help her people, either. She had always known it. "Yes."

"Just so."

"Yes, Radha."

"Shall I tell you a secret now?"

"Where are you going?" Jessa demanded, her mouth dry and her hands unsteady.

"I am going home, child. I wish to visit the burial ground where my mother lies, and my husband as well."

Jessa listened to the simple words, though she understood that they were far from simple.

"And in the dark of a terrible, black night, a lifetime ago and a thousand leagues away, my daughter's bones were smuggled from Karballa, in a basket stained with the blood of the sacred stag. A basket that was carried home at a great cost, so that she might rest beside them both, my mother, Aba, and my husband, Tinsella."

Jessa blinked and pulled her hands from Radha's.

She had always known that Radha had been married once, long ago before she had traveled with Jhannina, before she had refused to let the beautiful young woman be taken alone to face the Butcher of the Plains. *Tinsella...Tinsella was the name of Jhannina's father, my grandfather. And Aba...Aba was my mother's grandmother.*

Radha leaned forward in her soft chair and held Jessa's face between gentle hands. "And you, my daughter's daughter, had best come and claim what is rightfully yours."

Radha's face blurred in Jessa's vision as a sudden ocean of tears overwhelmed her eyes, though only for a moment before they spilled over. She felt Radha's soft lips beside her mouth, and then the old woman's voice within her head.

My blood, only now do I know that you are safe and free to meet the world with strength and cunning. To meet your fate with a power that no one may ever take from you. Free to make your decisions in life with your chosen lover beside you. A lover whose thread is furious and strong upon the Great Loom...a thread that has been entangled with your own since the birth of us all.

Jessa rose upon her knees and wrapped her arms about Radha's shoulders and held tight. "Blood..." She wept as her grandmother held her with equal strength. "I am your blood."

Radha's quiet laughter was filled with love. "It shall be interesting to see what happens."

CHAPTER ELEVEN

O wen Durand studied both Jessa and Darry, and Jessa could only guess at what he might be thinking—a Lyonese princess with her tanned skin and dark hair beside his very own daughter, who stood pale and straight. Darry's curls were tied behind her neck and she did not wear a uniform, dressed instead in brown homespun and brown boots. Her white tunic was tucked in with the sleeves rolled to her elbows, though more importantly her bandaged left hand sat upon the hilt of her sword in the presence of the king.

It was the sword that Radha had won for Darry, and Jessa remembered the sight of it as it had flared in the torchlight before her lover had seized it with a strong hand. It was a beautiful, fierce weapon, and it sat naturally upon Darry's hip. Jessa's own dress was simple, a black skirt and pale blue tunic, both crisp and clean. She wore one of Radha's fringed black shawls tied about her waist, an unexpected gift from her grandmother, who had given it over with a satisfied smile.

And so what is there here that would announce our royal blood?

"If those from the Green Hills will return," Owen began, "they will be here before the moon is high."

"You are thinking of Joaquin," Jessa replied.

"Yes."

"Was your brother involved in this?" the queen asked simply as she sat to the left of her husband.

"Why do you think I would know?" Jessa countered, curious as to where the answer might lead.

"If you wish to accuse my lover of something, do not play with your words," Darry said in a rather harsh tone.

"Because we do not know him as you do, Jessa," Cecelia answered smoothly. "I am only looking for insight, that is all."

"I know my brother only in the sense that he has been an unwanted presence in my life since I was a young girl," Jessa explained, her tone clear and unencumbered by emotion. "As I told you before, he has been my keeper." She looked to the king. "And as I have told you, my Lord, I know him to be cruel and clever."

"But do you think he knew of Serabee's intentions?"

"That El-Khan would bring the might of the Sahwello to invade your home?"

"Yes."

"No, I do not."

"Why?" Cecelia asked.

Jessa looked at her hands upon the table's surface and studied the bangles she wore as she moved the pieces in her mind. "Serabee is of the Fakir, and my father's dog," she said in a quiet voice, each move on the board leading to another, and another. She looked up. *Why am I here?* was a familiar question to her, and it entered easily into her thoughts, just as it had for months. What was the endgame to be, and who was to benefit by sending her into the very heart of Arravan? Why was she here?

"*Is* your father's dog?" Owen's voice was dark.

Darry straightened her shoulders back at his tone.

"My Lady Radha has told me that he is still alive," Jessa answered as her hand brushed against Darry's for a brief moment. "Which means Serabee is still a threat."

Owen's temple gave a hard twitch.

"He is most likely riding for Lyoness as we speak. Such a defeat as was dealt him will send him into retreat."

"You are certain of this?" Owen demanded.

Darry took a step closer to Jessa's chair. "It's all right, love,"

Jessa whispered. There was no need for her to look. "I am certain of nothing, my Lord. But if I were he, and I attacked the High King of Arravan within his very own palace and failed despite the strength of my dogs behind me? I would be running for the skirts of my master."

"Bharjah." Owen sighed as Grissom Longshanks entered the solar.

"A rider from the Thirteenth has returned. Those from the Green Hills will return several hours before dawn. There was no attack upon the lodges or the lands there," Grissom informed them.

"Then they came for you," Darry said to her father. "Or they came for Jessa."

Owen returned his eyes to Jessa. "I wish to know your opinion, Lady Jessa."

"Serabee and Joaquin are thick," she said at once. "This would not happen unless by my father's bidding. Serabee is a great high-up man among his people. His power is severe, not just political but in majik as well, as you saw last night. To answer to a *fikloche* such as Joaquin? It is only by my father's wish then or Serabee's own design. Perhaps in this attack upon you, Joaquin makes his bid for the throne and works in partnership with Serabee. By striking at the heart of Arravan and succeeding? This would place Joaquin at the foot of our father's throne before all others."

"Even Sylban-Tenna?" Grissom asked.

"Yes," she answered. "I told you before that my father's throne is not like Arravan's. It is a prize to be taken." Jessa turned from Grissom to the king. "Not to be given to the eldest merely because they came first and they cried the loudest. Lyoness must be earned."

Darry chuckled in surprise and then cleared her throat as Owen's brown eyes flared in her direction.

"But if Serabee and Joaquin worked together in this, what is in it for Serabee? Perhaps he looks to the long view, yes? He is on my father's leash because Bharjah is Bharjah and *no* man is greater within Lyoness, not even a Lord of the Fakir. But to be the First Councillor to King Trey-Jak Joaquin? Joaquin will not *ever* be a great man. Serabee perhaps saw his future in controlling a puppet king. This would not be unwise on his part."

There was a long moment of silence, and then Owen huffed. He scratched at a day's growth of beard, his eyes thoughtful.

"Or perhaps I am wrong," Jessa said, reconsidering.

"How so?" Owen asked at once.

"To be within the Green Hills and far away when the Fakir strike? How could it be me, Joaquin will say, and this is all very tragic, for my sister was slain as well. He has become a fast confidant of your son's, and so surely this will help him, should he come under your suspicion. But in the end, when these men are found out to be of Lyoness? Joaquin would be caught within his own trap. He cannot follow our father to the throne if his head tops a pike before your gates. What good would this do Serabee, then, to sacrifice his men and expose the Fakir, if his puppet burns within the flames of Arravan's anger? If you returned to your home, my Lord, to find your family slaughtered and your palace walls breached by men of Lyoness, would it matter what my brother said to you? Could he convince you to give him a horse and let him ride for home?"

"That is not likely, no," Owen answered.

"Just so. This avenue of thought makes no sense, then. Even Joaquin would see his own death in such a plan," she agreed. "And for my father to devise such a thing? This would merely enrage you and incite all of Arravan into a frenzy that would demand vengeance for their slain. And let us not forget," she added, "you were not meant to be here. My father would want you dead above all others. Why deal with the lion on the battlefield when you might tangle with the cub instead? Better to attack you within the Green Hills and hope that both you and your sons would be killed."

Jessa studied her bracelets once more. Absently, she turned her wrist and slid them free. She spread the fingers of her right hand above them as they sat upon the table. The metal bangles began to turn, slow at first and then with a purpose. They made a strange, low sound upon the wood of the table as they spun, slight and scratching. It was a parlor trick, really, but it helped her think. Her power was such an integral part of her being that to be without its presence even in the smallest of things did little to help the deeper edges of her logic. *Why am I here?*

"There has been no war between our two lands for many years," Jessa continued. "My Radha told me once that the last war was very costly for my father, both in gold and influence. And still he did not win what he wanted."

"He did not," Owen acknowledged, his eyes drawn to the spin of the bracelets.

"And though Bharjah still retains absolute power, the Lords of Lyoness are not so eager to answer another call to arms, for their memory is very long and many sons of my country were lost. To have an army is one thing, but to go to war with an army that does not wish to fight? This does not seem like a good thing to me."

Owen's lips turned in subtle agreement.

"To push Arravan into invading Lyoness with such righteousness behind us?" Darry asked. "It would be a very foolish thing to provoke. It would take Bharjah farther away."

"It would take him farther from what he wants. The Lowlands would be behind us as we rode against him," Owen agreed as he followed her logic.

"Or this is about *me*," Jessa suggested boldly as the bracelets came to rest beneath her touch. "And how best a pawn such as I might be used to capture a king."

Owen's eyes widened.

"If I die upon Arravan soil, the Nightshade Lark and the only Princess to the House of Bharjah? Daughter to the only queen to have ever shown mercy toward the people of my land, murdered within the House of Durand after I had been offered up in a grand gesture meant to bring about peace?"

Darry set a hand upon the back of Jessa's chair. "A sacrifice."

"Bharjah would have his reason to ride to war," Owen declared.

"With all the might of his Lords behind him," the queen added.

"The last piece of jade in my father's tower…just as he claimed."

"They were sent to kill you then," Darry said.

"Perhaps, my love," Jessa answered as she turned to her. She saw the fire in Darry's gaze and the tightness of her body. She looked so fierce, in fact, that Jessa wanted only to hold her until she calmed and fell still beneath her kisses.

"But why my family as well? Why provoke me so?" Owen demanded. "Better to send an assassin than an army."

"My Lord." Jessa held tightly to Darry's gaze and saw Tannen Ahru upon a piebald stallion as she laughed in the sun. His question was a good one, and she was afraid she knew the answer. "There need not be a reason *why*. They were Fakir. If Serabee El-Khan finds his way back to Lyoness, then the Fakir will ride to war with my father. If war is what he intends, to assuage the grievous insult of my murder."

"But you are not dead," Owen answered quietly.

"And who is to know that?" she inquired. "Serabee may say whatever he likes if he even has the courage to face my father in light of his failure. And what bird of a Lyonese spy will fly to my father's wrist, bearing tidings he does not wish to hear?"

Owen let out an unexpected snort of amusement.

"Unless, of course," Jessa added almost casually, "I return to Lyoness with the truth."

"With Joaquin tied to your baggage?" Owen asked, his tone curious.

"However you would permit my return. Throw my brother into the deepest hole you might find, if that is your wish. But if my father rides to war upon the justification that I was murdered within the walls of your palace, then my return would expose him."

Owen sat back in his chair slowly and with ease as he marshaled his thoughts into order. That she was a master tactician he had no doubt, for her mind worked as Jacob's did. Her thoughts flowed with ease and grace, not unlike a strong dark wine poured into the finest of goblets.

He wondered, then, who had trained this princess. Who had been so keen and proficient as to cultivate such critical logic, as well as her affinity for the long view? A logic that was clearly on display, impressive in its knowledge of men and the dark games they were capable of. Games that might lay waste to entire countries with little regard for anything else.

But he would not let her ride to her death, taking his own daughter with her. "No," he declared.

"I quite agree," Darry said in support.

"I could try."

Owen knew he was being tested, and he knew as well that she was utterly serious in her suggestion. He waited for her to look away, waited for her to take it back. When the silence stretched on and she did neither, he felt his heart beat with a smooth swell of pride for her. "No."

"I cannot be the cause of a war." For the first time there was a tremor of emotion within her voice.

"You are the cause of nothing. If the plot that you propose is true, then you are merely caught within the tide, as are we all. And if you are right, then your father may ride to war even as we speak."

"This isn't your fault, Jess." Darry added. "If he used you as a pawn and moved you as such, that was not your doing. The consequences of his actions are not your responsibility."

"Though if Bharjah does not ride to war," Owen suggested, "if your father sits upon his throne and dozes in the afternoon sun, thinking of nothing more than his jade and how he might torture his children?" He watched as her eyes acknowledged the truth of his insult. "It does not matter. For I intend to ride to war against the Fakir," he announced in a deadly voice. "And against your father as well, should a single man loyal to his flag raise a sword against me."

Jessa's eyes reflected understanding. "But to reach the Fakir you must cross the border into Lyoness. And if you cross in force…"

Owen smiled, though he felt little amusement. "Then so be it. Your father's resistance will merely slow us down on our way to the Kistanbal Mountains."

"You will need a faster horse than the one you have," Darry replied, and Owen lifted his eyes to his daughter's. "Talon has a brother you may be interested in if you wish to keep up."

Owen smiled in earnest now. "This is good to know."

"Do not underestimate the Lords of Lyoness," Jessa interrupted their banter.

"I will ask them to hand over the men of the Fakir first and foremost, how does that sound?"

"I told you once," Jessa replied evenly, "that I hold the hearts of my people with great care. Nothing I have said since that moment negates that fact. *Nothing.* That you seek to destroy the Fakir? This pleases me more than you will ever know. And if the Lords of Lyoness and my father's army oppose you in this pursuit, then they deserve to fall before you."

"But?"

"But I would ask that you have a care for those caught unwittingly between you and your goal. The people of Lyoness have been at war since my bloodline first took the throne."

"I do not understand."

"That is because your people live in peace," she explained. "That is because you are a good king, by all accounts, and have seen to the well-being of your people. You have tried to make their lives better with your power and would see them prosper. This is not the sort of rule my people have known. Their circumstances are of capitulation and servitude to my family's will and cruel whims. Their war is of survival, and from what I have seen, they have found an unforgiving opponent."

"I will do what I can, but this will be war, Princess."

"That is all I ask—thank you, my Lord."

Jessa's eyes were intense as the fingers of her right hand rubbed against the bracelets still upon the table. The tension in her shoulders held a movement she had yet to make and it was a posture surprisingly familiar to Owen. A smile pulled at his lips. "I can see you thinking."

"I am thinking we must take care of what is most important at the moment."

"Which is?"

"Baiting the trap for my brother. And keeping in mind, of course, the sort of king the sons of the Jade Palace are used to dealing with."

Owen stared at her, the fingers of his right hand tapping softly upon the tabletop as he did so. After a bit of time he glanced at his daughter, and she did not turn from him. "And I am thinking," he said, unable to keep the deep spark of affection from his eyes, "that perhaps you are in over your head with such a woman, Darrius... just as I have always been."

Darry's left eyebrow went up slowly, a mirror image of her mother's infamous gesture.

Owen let out a bark of sudden laughter and slammed a fist upon the table, those around him startled as it shook from the blow. "I may be the only one that look doesn't work on," he growled and pushed to his feet. "Open the throne room and ready what's left of my guard, Gris. Send Colonel Briggs to bring the priests of Gamar, and find me a bird that will answer to Captain Biro in Baylon Town. I want the riders of the Thirteenth and those from the Green Hills to be diverted there. I want them to bring the Baylon Kingsmen home to Blackstone when they ride through those gates."

"It will slow them down. They won't reach us until midday tomorrow at that pace."

"That's exactly what I want." He strode to the doors that led to the Great Hall, and despite his limp, he moved with vigor. "And find me my bloody crown."

Jessa watched Owen leave the hall, and then looked up and found Darry's eyes. "Are you in over your head, *Akasha*?"

Darry's smile was slow and certain. "Absolutely."

Jessa considered her lover's answer. "I'm not sure how I should feel about that."

"How do you feel so far?"

"Rather lovely, for the most part."

"Aside from the general mayhem, betrayal, and blood loss, I'd have to agree with you."

Jessa could feel her smile reach deep in her eyes. Darry's

humor was completely unexpected and yet most welcome. "Has your daughter always been so splendidly cavalier, my Queen?" she asked, well aware that they were not yet alone.

Cecelia's chair scraped upon the floor as she pushed to her feet. She stepped about Owen's empty seat and moved for the doors with an amused expression and warmth in her eyes. "Yes, and I've just realized that it's no longer my problem."

Jessa let out a breath of laughter. "Thank you, my Lady."

A moment of silence passed between them before Darry took a small step and the backs of her fingers brushed against Jessa's cheek in a tender manner. "Cavalier or not," Darry whispered, "I am yours to command."

Jessa took Darry's hand in both of hers and turned it over, her touch delicate as she opened Darry's fingers and placed a sensuous kiss upon her palm.

CHAPTER TWELVE

Jessa followed Cccelia about the tower chamber and felt more at home than she ever had before. Not even her terraced rooms in the Jade Palace had offered such an overwhelming sense of belonging. Though she and Radha had made those forgotten rooms into an oasis of kindness within the brutal desert of Bharjah's presence, she had never felt truly safe. The word home had always been something of a conundrum for her, and though she had thought she understood its varied manifestations, she realized now she had known nothing at all. She had never felt this way, not even in the chambers she had come to love within Blackstone Keep.

Situated on the northern edge of the gardens upon the very edge of the maze, the tower structure was austere, though it complemented the aesthetics of the vast paradise.

"Years ago," Cecelia explained as they moved down the stairs that curved along the west wall, "this place was used to host the architects and gardeners hired by King Boris to help him build the maze, and even the great sorcerer Sebastian stayed here for a time. It's his name that stuck. But it's been abandoned for some time."

Upon the upper level, a bedroom of massive proportions had been arranged. There was a dressing room with deep closets, and a washroom with a tub that might rival a fountain. A feather bed big enough for several people stood beside the window facing the maze, fresh linens, pillows, and quilted covers upon it. There were water pulleys and contraptions the likes of which Jessa had never encountered before, and the mere thought of what she had yet to find made her laugh inwardly with unexpected joy.

Cecelia pointed to one of the windows by the tower's main door. "The maze has a will of its own, as you'll see. If the gardeners did not trim the ivy back, this entire place would be swallowed by the hedgerow and disappear completely."

The first level of the tower contained a workshop, the circular chamber filled with shelves, closets, and several workbenches. There were two separate fireplaces already prepared and a washroom, as well as a place for contemplation beside the hearth within the southern curve of the wall. Deep-cushioned chairs and a wide divan with pillows on it seemed to wait patiently to fulfill their purpose. There was a kitchen of sorts, with a working pump and stove, and the larder had been stocked with provisions.

"Your things can be brought here within the hour," Cecelia said as Jessa ran her hand along one of the workbenches, "as well as Darry's, from her loft in the barracks."

Jessa smiled at her. "It's very clean for an abandoned building."

"Yes, well, being the queen does have some advantages."

"Does it?" Jessa asked, and there was a slight tease in her tone.

Cecelia's eyes lit up. "Occasionally, yes."

"I do not know what Darry's plans are, my Lady. I will go where she goes," Jessa said, eyeing the shelves to her right. There were scrolls there, some piled three rolls high, and she felt a small thrill of excitement. It was early evening, and though she knew it to be true, it was hard to believe just that morning they had fought and won their battle against Serabee El-Khan and his warriors.

"Well, whatever your plans may be, they won't happen overnight. You will need a place to stay, and I have it on good authority that my daughter would rather trip over the edge of a cliff than spend another night beneath her father's roof."

"Did she say that?"

Cecelia made a face of mild displeasure. "I believe something with a bit more *carnage* was involved, but I understood her point."

"When your son returns, he will not like it," Jessa warned. "Will I be made to disappear into the night when he throws his tantrum? Will his men come knocking at the door, or will they sneak in and drag me from my lover's arms?"

Cecelia said nothing.

"Even though I was never meant to be his, or perhaps because of that, while I lie beneath my lover in the throes of our passion, should I be looking over her shoulder?"

Cecelia laughed unexpectedly, the sound filled with more than a touch of bitterness. "By the gods, girl, you have a wicked tongue when you want one."

Jessa's right hand lifted just a bit and the wood in the hearth by the chairs stirred with movement. The cut timber upon the brazier burst to life as it caught fire. "And I am not the meek and mild Aidan McKenna, either," Jessa declared, the name of Darry's former lover a bit uncomfortable upon her tongue.

Cecelia lifted her eyebrow in a slow arch and then walked around the chairs before the fire. She set a hand upon the round stones of the hearth and leaned over. Her right hand pulled the chain and the flue snapped open with a rusty sound. "It's quite possible he's noticed that fact, Jessa," Cecelia replied with an acerbic tone not unlike Radha's. "Although if he hasn't, you have my permission to let him know it before Darrius does."

"Perhaps I shall," Jessa agreed, no longer content to be thought of as the shy, foreign princess, especially where Malcolm was concerned. She did not want Darry to stab him full of holes, either, fairly certain that this was the queen's main source of concern.

"And what makes you think that Aidan was meek?" Cecelia inquired, her tone replaced by genuine curiosity. "Or mild, for that matter?"

Jessa leaned her hip against the workbench. "They were lovers, yes?"

"Yes."

"Then she must have been. No woman who has known my *Akasha*'s touch, or her eyes in the dark of night, would ever give her up. There is no price too high. It would always be paid."

"Just so," Cecelia acknowledged. "Though I would say she was more quiet than meek."

"It was not a slight."

Cecelia's eyes were warm. "I know that, actually. You're not wrong."

Jessa smiled, Cecelia clearly caught off guard. "I love this place, my Lady, I love everything about it, and I have never loved a place before."

Cecelia nodded. "I thought you might."

"I believe Darry will like it, as well, though she may complain at first."

"She used to play here as a girl."

"Here?"

"Yes, when I forbid her the maze."

"She did not listen to you."

"So it would appear. She is the panther from the maze, is she not?" Cecelia asked, though from her tone she had already made up her mind.

She had been more patient than Jessa had predicted. "Yes, you have met before."

"Aye, I knew it as soon as I saw her." The queen's eyes were dark but accepting of the knowledge. "They are *Cha-Diah*."

"It is an ancient majik," Jessa explained with care, not all that surprised that Cecelia knew the phrase. "Your daughter is aptly named, for the Gold Panther's blood runs within her veins. They are joined together."

"Her temper," Cecelia acknowledged.

"Yes, that is one part of it. When the anger comes upon her, it is just a facet of that power. She has no control over its presence, though she has learned to channel it. She is like a cornered animal when this happens, and anyone in her path that provokes her further is right to be afraid."

"Her fever, when her eyes changed."

"It was the majik stirring in her blood." Jessa moved from the workbench and gestured to one of the chairs beside the fire. "Sit down, my Lady."

Cecelia did so in a tired manner as Jessa sat in the opposite chair. "I will introduce you and you will see. Hinsa shares her eyes, only they are opposite."

Cecelia stared at her, her shoulders pulled in just a bit. "Her eyes were blue once, like her brother Wyatt. They had the same eyes. And I remember that damn cat, with green eyes, and by the gods, how I wanted to scream out. And there was Darry, just pulling at her. Blessed Gamar."

"Hinsa still likes to play."

"She was just a girl."

"I think it was very hard for her as a child, you are right," Jessa said. "I cannot imagine the strength it took to control her blood. When her majik is high, my Lady, she is indeed wild."

"Yes."

They were quiet for several minutes, and when Jessa whispered in Lyonese, Cecelia moved gently from her thoughts. The older woman looked utterly exhausted. "Yes, it's very peaceful here, Jessa." She looked about the workroom, more than comfortable within her plush chair. "I hadn't thought it would be, for some reason."

Jessa spoke once again in Lyonese, the words of her homeland more of a relief to her than she thought they would be. It was not easy to constantly move within the confines of a foreign language. Only in her dreams was her native tongue present, and it was a blessing to her.

"Yes, I'll have them bring your things, and Darry's."

Jessa smiled. "My Lady?"

Cecelia took a deep breath, blinked, and met Jessa's eyes. "Yes, child?"

"Thank you for your kindness."

"Thank you for saving my husband's life."

Jessa was truly startled by the statement.

Cecelia smiled. "He likes you…quite a lot, actually."

Jessa had no response, her cheeks hot. "He is my king, my Lady." She frowned. "That is, you must not thank me for such a thing."

Cecelia chuckled and the sound was filled with warmth. "I can thank you for whatever I damn well please, girl. I'm the queen, remember?"

CHAPTER THIRTEEN

Jessa got up from the bed and walked in her bare feet across the worn wooden floor. She wore one of Darry's shirts, but that was all, as the cool summer breeze drifted through the tower's bedroom chamber. Her black braids and curls fell about her shoulders and down her back, and the hem of the white shirt brushed her thighs.

Darry sat in one of the huge chairs before the banked hearth, her arms upon the rests with her hands hanging over the sides. Her feet were bare and her clothes were untucked and loose, her hair scattered gold against the lush red color of the chair cushions. She fought to keep her eyes open and Jessa knew she was utterly drained. They both were, but Darry obviously struggled against it with every fiber of her being. Darry's sword lay across her knees at the ready, though Jessa was uncertain if it would do her any good should the worst of her thoughts suddenly come true.

Their things had been brought to the tower as the queen had promised, and it had taken but another hour or so to arrange them into some semblance of order. Jessa had found Darry's Boys useful to have at her disposal, in any number of ways—there were trunks and chests of clothes, medicines, tapestries, and scrolls that needed to be settled. But those details could be dealt with at a later time.

Jessa stepped to the chair and Darry looked up.

Jessa lifted the sword from Darry's knees, held it out to the side, and let it drop. The weapon's tip sank into the floor, and the sword stood tall, swaying slightly.

"I need that," Darry argued, in no position to back up her words.

Jessa climbed upon the chair with a smooth step and straddled Darry's hips, her knees sinking into the cushion as she balanced above Darry's thighs. "No, you don't."

"Yes, I do."

Jessa took Darry's face in her hands and kissed her, Darry's lips supple and pliant in response to her advances. "I love you, Darry," she whispered.

Darry's touch burned with heat against the skin of Jessa's thighs, and Jessa sat with care. "I was so scared for you," Darry admitted.

"I know, my love." Jessa undid the buttons of Darry's tunic. "As I was, for you."

"Sebastian's Tower…"

"Yes," Jessa agreed and smiled. "I like it very much, *Akasha*." She opened Darry's shirt and slowly trailed her hands down her lover's chest as Darry caught her breath in reaction. Jessa tasted her neck and Darry's nipples became hard beneath her palms.

"You're so beautiful," Darry whispered.

"I know why you can't sleep." Jessa grasped Darry's nipples and twisted slightly, just enough to elicit the response she desired. Darry's hips moved upward and her head pushed back into the cushion as Jessa leaned forward. "I know why, *Akasha*."

"*Jess*."

"I know, baby." Her touch was like a breeze, slight and soothing as she removed Darry's shirt and exposed her upper body. She ran her hands upon the bruises and the marks of battle, and she could feel Darry's strength lying in wait, dormant beneath the soft fatigue. It roused Jessa's passion, and she felt her love in the pit of her stomach, where it flipped over and burned its way downward in a delicious quiver. She was hard and wet and this was all it took, just the feel of Darry's skin beneath her hands. Her flesh began to ache, heavy with want.

She moved her touch above the bandaged wound on Darry's left side and could feel the heat beneath the gauze and poultice.

Jessa could actually taste Darry's majik, her *Cha-Diah* energy potent and openly present upon her body. She understood that Darry was using Hinsa's strength to stay awake, and she knew why. If Darry were to sleep, as she had the night before, what terrible fate might await them when she awoke? She could see it in Darry's eyes and she could feel it in the way Darry watched her. All day she had felt it, though it was only when Darry refused to join her in bed that Jessa knew what must be done.

"Where is Hinsa?"

Darry's face was flushed with her desire, her heartbeat quick at the base of her throat. "Sleeping."

"You must let her wake up now." Jessa undid the buttons of Darry's trousers with a light touch, and her fingers slipped beneath the edge of Darry's undergarment. "She must hunt—do not deny her so, love."

"I will kill them all."

Jessa kissed her. "Hush, my sweet."

"If they come for you again, I will kill them."

"Yes, I know, love."

Darry sucked in her breath at the touch upon her sex.

"You will never lose me, *Akasha*. Such a thing is not possible." Her fingers massaged Darry's arousal, and Darry's hips lifted as the muscles of her buttocks and legs tightened. "We are safe here," Jessa promised, and her tongue tasted Darry's upper lip. "I have warded our lovely tower against all intruders." Her fingers were wet with Darry's spirit as they moved upon her flesh, and Darry took hold of Jessa's waist, her grip firm as Jessa arched closer. "You must come to bed with me now." She opened her mouth against Darry's, her lover's soft, exquisite cry captured and taken in. "Do you not want to lie with me?"

"Yes."

Jessa slipped a careful finger inside, and Darry's hips pushed against the touch. Jessa's flesh throbbed in response and her legs tightened upon Darry's hips as she slid a second finger inside. "Come for me, *Akasha*," she urged softly, her lips beside Darry's ear. She cupped Darry's sex and lifted her touch deeper inside, the heel of her palm hard against Darry's flesh.

Darry's muscles seized and she thrust upward as she spent,

crying out as her hands pulled upon Jessa's shirt. Jessa's mind flooded instantly with the sweet miracle of it all, though she managed to whisper her spell regardless.

Jessa kissed her and felt Darry's majik ebb and flow away, Darry forced to release the iron grip she held upon her *Cha-Diah* power. Her warrior's body eased and her muscles surrendered with a glorious shudder.

"Can you touch me, *Akasha*?" Jessa's voice was both pleased and anxious as she spoke against Darry's mouth, and their eyes met.

Tears slipped from green and blue eyes, and Jessa bit her lower lip as the fingers of Darry's right hand slid between her legs. She took hold of Darry's wrist and guided her touch, Darry's left arm about her waist. Her hips drove smoothly, slowly at first and then faster as her mouth sought the kiss she needed.

She felt her control slip away beneath the sweet pressure of her need, oddly uncertain of where she would end up. Darry's hand began to stroke with more strength, and Jessa cried out, arched, and spent her spirit.

Darry's eyes were alive, and Jessa could feel her lover's soul invade her own. She could feel Darry's wildness and she could feel her sweetness. She could feel Darry's strength and her quiet, the silence of that secret place Darry loved beyond all measure laid bare before her. She felt it all, and entangled in the warmth and overwhelmed by the essence of Darry's majik, she let it wash through her.

Her own power rose up in a blissful, harmonious rush, and the Great Loom spun beneath them, its threads unbound and soft as they brushed past. Jessa tried to hold the unfamiliar runes that burst within her chest, for she had no idea what the spell was, or even what it might do, but it was beyond her power to do so. She let the runes surge through her blood instead, to eventually rest as they might choose.

CHAPTER FOURTEEN

The throne room of Blackstone Keep was long and narrow, with staggered pews that lined both sides of the room. Three rows high and made of deeply polished redwood, they would accommodate guests and witnesses to any formal function. The walls were made of a stone that was the color of sand, though Jessa could see that it was not the sandstone so common in her own country.

The many banners of the House of Durand hung upon the walls, fastened with golden spikes. Made of the finest Damassus silk, they would ripple and snap gently within the flow of air that moved through the chamber. The scarlet-and-black banner of the Sunn Wars, when the Lyonese people had paid a great price in a losing effort to secure the Lowlands, hung upon the wall to the right of the dais and was prominent above all other battle standards. There were flags for each Durand king, and they lined the walls on both sides of the main aisle, from the dais to the massive blackwood doors at the opposite end of the chamber. Hanging last upon the wall was the banner of Malcolm Laurus Durand, who was meant to be king but was fated to die young instead.

The windows were narrow and made of stained glass, the midday sunlight red and gold as it sliced into the chamber and splashed onto the burnished oak of the floor. Sconces made of gold and black wrought iron hung from golden chains as they lined the aisle down the center of the chamber, their light rich and filled with warmth.

Two thrones stood upon the dais at the far end of the room, and the largest one was the Blackwood Throne, as renowned as Bharjah's though not nearly as infamous.

The wooden throne was as black as pitch and polished to such a high shine that when the sunlight graced its surface, it was wise to look away. The seat was wide and the arms were broad, though it was the back of the throne that was the most impressive.

Carved with stunning skill and patience, the backrest of the Durand throne fanned out in a magnificent representation of the tree that was its namesake. Thick branches reached well over eight feet into the air and were decorated with hundreds of carved leaves that hung from every branch. Each leaf, suspended from golden rings that allowed for movement, was stained in a tone that was slightly different from the rest. No two stems were the same and the veins upon each leaf were unique. The throne was an almost living thing, and each detail had been rendered with exquisite ability and pride.

Jessa had never seen its like; the Jade Throne was gaudy and almost miserable when compared to the craftsmanship on display before her. The branches that spread outward to the left were curved and full and offered their shade and protection to a smaller version of the Blackwood Throne. Polished in a lighter color, the queen's throne was nestled beneath the comfort and protection of the king's, no less beautiful for its smaller size. Though it lacked branches and leaves of its own, the intricate carvings that decorated its smooth surface were said to incorporate the deeds of each queen of the Durand name, and paid honor to their own bloodlines.

An odd grin pulled at Darry's mouth as they stood to the right of the main aisle, some ten feet from the first step of the dais. Her expression was one that Jessa had not seen before. "I tipped that damn thing over once."

Jessa let out a startled breath. "You did no such thing, Darrius."

"I did. I like to climb trees."

"It would be too heavy—I don't believe you."

Darry sighed in mock offense. "If you rock it back and forth and your brother is pushing from the bottom? It will tip over, trust me."

Jessa felt the humor rise within her chest and she shoved it back down. She eyed the king and queen where they spoke with the commander near the doors behind the dais, Grissom accompanied by the new captain of the Palace Guard. "You're quite mad, Darry, I've always known it."

Darry smiled, satisfied. "Look up."

Jessa debated with herself for a moment and then did as she was told. Her eyes narrowed upon the massive crack that ran through the mortar between the ceiling stones, the wound old and jagged as it reached across half the room.

"A huge, booming voice that caused my grandmother to cover her ears," Darry whispered. "So huge that the ceiling stones cracked and the mortar crumbled."

Jessa laughed as she remembered the story of the Moonblood orchids within the Queen's Garden. When she looked back down, it was to find a white tulip, its thick stem held with care by a bandaged hand. A flower not unlike the one Darry's grandmother had used as a substitute for her much desired orchids.

"It was the best I could do on short notice."

Jessa gave a sigh and grabbed the lapels of Darry's jacket with both hands. "If I had known you were here, waiting for me, I would have crawled from Lyoness if I had to. I would have come for you, Darry."

"Had I known you were coming, I would've sent you my horse. She's very fast."

Jessa smiled, pulled her lover close, and kissed her, careful as she wrapped her hand about the flower still between them. "Stop being so bloody charming now," Jessa whispered as she pulled back slightly. Darry's eyes were filled with life, and a pleasant shaft of desire knifed through Jessa's loins. She looked down at the soft petals and tried to regain her composure. "And do not do anything foolish, either."

"Like kiss my backwards lover in the throne room, for all to see?"

Jessa turned and stood up straight. With care, she slid the tulip into the pocket of her cloak. "Do not be thickheaded, Darrius, I am the one who kissed you."

Darry smoothed at her jacket. "As you like."

"Are you ready, Princess?" Owen asked as he walked about the throne. "They are here."

"Yes, my Lord," Jessa answered and pulled at her cloak. The hood came up and she stepped back from the sunlight that reached through the stained glass windows and splashed the center aisle.

The shadows welcomed her and she wove the runes for the Veil of Shadows. The unnatural breeze moved through the chamber and the banners rippled in response, the king a bit startled as the leaves above his head reacted. One of the lamps along the aisle swayed with a clank of its chain and its flame went out, and then another, the sudden distraction the center of attention.

❖

When Owen returned his attention to the Lyonese princess, Jessa was nowhere to be seen. "Bloody hell and hounds," he mumbled to himself and took his seat.

His daughter stood strong and tall, dressed in clean, crisp clothes. He thought she looked strange without her Kingsman blacks. Dark brown trousers and a green tunic that buttoned, the crossover collar undone and draped down handsomely beneath a matching brown jacket that was cropped at the waist. It was all tailored and made of the best homespun, the green of her shirt a perfect match in color to her right eye. Her hair was held in a loose tie behind her neck, and the wild curls seemed to ache for their freedom as they always did. At her waist she wore a dagger and the sword she had claimed in battle, the weapons held by a brown leather belt that matched her boots.

Owen let out a sigh of amusement as he situated his chair cushion in order to favor his wounded leg. The wound wasn't bad, as such things went, but it was an unpleasant reminder that he was not as young as he once was.

"What is it?" Cecelia asked as she sat beside him. "Are you all right?"

"I'm fine. She reminds me of my brother, for all that she looks nothing like him. He might've even thrown more gold away than she does."

"At what?"

Owen scratched at his clean-shaven cheek. "Her love of fine clothes. Mal was a hound for thread as much as she is, though he favored silks more."

"They seem to be alike in many ways," she said quietly. "Perhaps it is a place to start."

Owen cleared his throat and leaned back upon his throne. His eyes narrowed slightly as he stared down the distance, as if he could see into the Great Hall beyond.

There was a sharp rap and the doors opened.

❖

Prince Malcolm and his party entered the throne room and they walked with purpose, Princes Malcolm and Jacob followed by Joaquin and Malcolm's advisor, Marteen Salish. Their clothes were dusty from the road and they looked exhausted.

"Father!" Malcolm called and his voice echoed through the chamber.

Jessa moved like a ghost behind Darry and the others, determined to find a place close to Joaquin. She would need to see him in full, if she was to make a proper judgment of his words.

Jessa noted Darry's face as Malcolm walked past her, and she could feel the majik in the room change. The unique scent that was Darry's majik rose up, and Jessa knew her lover's temper rose with it. She could feel the rage, and more than that, she could sense that a very exclusive and uncertain danger was suddenly at hand. Darry's *Cha-Diah* majik was unstable.

Malcolm's company came to a stop at the foot of the dais, and

Prince Jacob turned back. He smiled at Darry and reached out to her, a bid for her to come forth and stand beside them. His eyes were filled with uncertainty, and Jessa knew he must feel decidedly uncomfortable for a man who was used to knowing more than everyone else.

Darry winked at him and nodded toward the dais.

"I would speak to Prince Trey-Jak Joaquin," Owen announced, and his voice held an icy tone that Jessa had not heard before. It sent a shiver of anxiety along her spine, and she pulled her cloak more tightly about her shoulders.

Jacob stepped to the side and Joaquin came forward. "My Lord, I am here," he said. "And I am very pleased to see that all of you are well."

"Yes," Owen said smoothly. "I appreciate your concern."

Malcolm approached the foot of the dais. "Father, what has happened here? There are bodies burning in the north field, and I have never seen Blackstone so fortified. Why are there men of the City Guard walking the walls?"

"Your message said very little, but that you were safe," Jacob added. "Some sort of attack had come in the night, but that was all. Captain Biro only—"

"Jacob," Malcolm turned on him. "Let me speak, please."

"Did I not say that I wished to speak with Prince Joaquin?" Owen asked.

"Yes, Father, but I would—"

"Then shut your mouth and let me speak with him."

Malcolm was startled by the reprimand. "Yes, Father, but I need to—"

"Captain Jefs!"

"Yes, Your Majesty?"

"Be so kind as to take the Crown Prince and his advisor, Lord Salish, into the Great Hall and have them wait for my summons. If they protest, you have my permission to give them a tour of the cells beneath the south wing. Perhaps the damp chill there will settle their nerves."

"Aye, my Lord, but those cells are full now."

Owen voiced his annoyance with a rumble as Joaquin glanced at Malcolm with startled eyes. "Is there room in the south tower?"

"Aye, Your Majesty."

"Then take them there."

Malcolm was stunned. "Father, what in the hell is—"

Captain Jefs barked the order and the doors behind the dais opened. A squad of the Palace Guard came through them, armed with halberds and pikes.

Marteen Salish stepped close and touched Malcolm's arm. "Mal, let us—"

"Don't *touch* me." Malcolm jerked his arm away.

"Let us go," Salish finished, the skin of his neck dark with a sudden blush.

"Prince Joaquin is my guest, Father, and I have a right to be here," Malcolm declared. "No matter what the circumstances are, he is under my protection."

"He is *my* guest, Malcolm, and he is here by my pleasure only," Owen corrected. "Take them both to the tower, Captain Jefs. I will send for them when I have need of them."

"Yes, Your Majesty." Captain Jefs bowed his head and turned immediately to Malcolm. "If you will come with me, my Lords?"

Malcolm seemed to calm, though his face was red with his anger. As he turned, he saw Jacob beside Darry. "Bring her as well," he ordered, his tone spiteful. "If I have no right to be here, she most certainly doesn't."

Darry met her brother's eyes.

"The Lady Darrius may stay," Owen declared from the throne.

"*Lady?*" Malcolm replied. "Do not dishonor the word."

Darry moved before even Jessa could have predicted.

Her left hand landed hard upon Joaquin's right shoulder and shoved him out of the way as she attacked. Malcolm stumbled back in surprise, put his arms out in a meager effort to protect himself, and then he fell, the sound of Darry's fist as it connected with his jaw surprisingly loud.

Malcolm hit the floor with a resounding thud, and Darry wasted no time, her right knee upon his stomach as she yanked him up by his tunic and hit him again. Jessa watched as Darry's strength rolled down from her shoulders with the blow, and Malcolm's head snapped back and banged against the floor.

"Darrius!" Cecelia called.

Darry hit him a third time and then dropped him, Malcolm now unconscious and splayed out beneath her. She looked over her shoulder. "Yes, Mother?"

Cecelia stood before her throne and looked down at her daughter. "Perhaps this is not the best time for you to settle your grievances."

Owen had not moved, though his sudden laughter floated through the room.

Darry watched her father and Jessa saw the confusion in her eyes, though it was only for a moment. Darry looked down at her brother, and then used his body to push herself to her feet. She straightened her jacket and pointed at Marteen Salish. "You're next, little toad."

Two of the Palace Guards took Malcolm by the arms, flipped him over, and then dragged him back down the aisle. His boots bounced along the floor, and his head swayed back and forth to the awkward gait.

"Take him to his chambers, Jefs," Owen ordered across the room. "See that he stays there until I send for him."

"Lord Salish?" Captain Jefs inquired.

Salish turned to him with a start, his cheeks a bright red.

Captain Jefs extended a hand toward the doors at the end of the aisle. "If you would be so kind as to accompany me?"

"Where is your man, Joaquin? Where is Lord Serabee El-Khan?" Owen asked.

Joaquin turned from the sight of Malcolm being dragged away, with Marteen Salish close behind. "I do not know, my Lord," Joaquin answered and glanced at Darry as she returned to her place beside Prince Jacob. "When your men arrived to say that Blackstone had been attacked, we came at once. Lord Serabee was not to be found."

Jessa watched her brother with careful eyes, saw his left hand going flat against his abdomen just above his sword hilt. He applied pressure and a grimace of discomfort came and went. The gesture was familiar to Jessa—Joaquin's anxiety gnawed at his stomach, it always had. Abdul-Azim, sixth in line for Bharjah's throne if age were to be taken into account, could only eat his food if it had been ground into a fine paste and mixed with goat's milk. Rashid-Warith, fourth in line, had much the same problem, though he tended to spend most of his time in the privy. *And so go the sad sons of Bharjah, one way or another*, Jessa thought, not without some cynical amusement.

"Is not El-Khan your man?" the king demanded as his wife took her seat once more.

The blackwood doors that led to the Great Hall closed with a boom, and Joaquin glanced over his shoulder with a start. "Yes, my Lord."

"And he follows your command?"

"Where is my sister?" Joaquin asked. "Where is the Princess Jessa-Sirrah?"

Jessa took a step back at the mention of her name, careful of the runes that floated through her mind. She deepened the Veil as she waited for Owen to capture the first piece upon the board.

"She is dead," Owen answered. "Killed by your man, the Lord Serabee El-Khan."

Joaquin's right temple gave a hard twitch. "He is not my man."

"But you just said he was," Owen countered. "Which is it?"

"And the Lady Radha?" Joaquin demanded.

"Dead."

"If this is so, then El-Khan is not my man."

"But otherwise he would be?"

Joaquin smiled and Jessa knew he sensed a trap. "That is not what I—"

"You must have very little authority, *Prince* Joaquin, if your man is yours but not yours. I had not thought that Bharjah would send me his dregs to bargain with."

Joaquin bristled and his shoulders went back slightly. "You had no intention of allowing my sister to sit upon your wife's throne," he accused. "*You* were playing your own game, my Lord. Everyone is playing a game."

"Perhaps you should ask him yourself if El-Khan is—or is not—your man."

Joaquin's face paled.

"He's been very talkative."

"You lie," Joaquin shot back. "Serabee is a man of great power and majik."

"Do you think the priests of Gamar are so weak in their majik that they cannot cage a mad dog such as El-Khan?" Owen's tone was curious as he watched the young prince swallow hard and glance over his shoulder yet again. "Beneath the fires of Gamar, your Fakir dog has said much to me about why he did what he did. He does not like the heat much."

Joaquin remained silent, though his left hand moved slowly to the hilt of his sword.

"Why he brought an army of Fakir warriors in the middle of the night to murder my family while we slept. Why forty-seven of my men lie dead in the north pasture, waiting for their families to come forth and claim them."

"I knew nothing of that."

"Of what?"

"Of an attack upon your family," Joaquin answered quickly. "I knew nothing."

"And your sister and her Lady? They were targets, as well. They had no chance."

Joaquin's expression darkened but he remained silent.

"What did you know of that, Joaquin?" Owen shifted his weight and leaned casually against the armrest of his throne. "Let us see if your words match those of your dog, yes?"

"I refuse to participate in this any longer," Joaquin announced. "As a prince of royal blood, I should not be forced to defend myself against the words of a murderer. It is a poor way to wield your power, Your Grace."

"Defend yourself against what?"

"Against the accusation that I was somehow complicit in the death of my sister."

Jessa watched her brother's face from but a few feet away, and the Vhaelin rose up within her blood. Her brother's anxiety at an unexpected situation had quickly turned to fear.

"I said nothing of the sort, Prince Joaquin," Owen responded and then laughed quietly. "Is that what you think Serabee told me beneath the lash? Beneath the brands of the fire?"

Joaquin's brow came down and a flush of blood rose along his throat. "But you just said…"

"That El-Khan has accused you of plotting your sister's murder?"

"Did he?" Joaquin demanded.

"That you sent him to murder your sister's Lady, as well?"

Joaquin's lips curled in a snarl. "If you speak of Radha, she was but an old witch. She meant nothing, a servant."

Jessa stood very still as her power trembled upon her fingertips. Her hatred rose up as she realized how very easily he had sent Serabee to slay what was hers. To destroy her blood and to take what he thought was nothing. Now that she understood her power and what its presence meant, Jessa knew she could kill him where he stood. She had but to reach out and touch his cheek.

"Don't do it," Darry said softly, and Jessa responded instantly. Darry's eyes met hers in a fierce manner, despite the Veil of Shadows.

"Do what?" Joaquin demanded of Darry.

"Speak so to the High King of Arravan," Darry replied as she shifted her focus.

Owen snapped his fingers in a quick rhythm. "Over here, boy."

"I did not plan any killing," Joaquin insisted.

Jessa knew he was lying. He was a master of the untrue, but she had always been able to tell.

"I think you are lying." Owen's tone was bored as his words mirrored her own thoughts, and Jessa was pleased. "You are lying, Prince Joaquin. And El-Khan has given me proof."

"There is no *proof*," Joaquin said.

"You sent him to kill your sister and her Lady."

Jessa knew she should feel something more than resignation, but at the moment, all she wanted was for him to confess, to put an end to the game he was destined to lose anyway. There had always been a scheme in play—for as long as she could remember, the pieces had always been moving. She was tired of it, and angry, as well.

"I did no such thing."

"I know you did," Owen stated. "Though perhaps you might convince me to spare your life, with a good explanation. Otherwise, your head will ride a pike before my gates." The king rose to his feet and looked down at him. "And you will not have even spoken in your own defense. Explain why you sent your Fakir dog and his men to slay my family. Explain now or you die."

Grissom stepped forward and drew his sword. "Guard!"

"It was not me!" Joaquin exclaimed as he took a step back. He flexed his fingers about the hilt of his sword but did not draw it. "I did not do that, my Lord. I am not a fool despite what you may think."

The door behind the dais opened once more, and three guards entered.

"I have learned a few things in my many years," Owen admitted, "from your father."

The dogs used to guard the city armory were held upon thick leather leashes, and their heavily muscled bodies strained and struggled against their bondage. The scent of Darry's *Cha-Diah* blood swelled in reaction to their presence, and the animals became so incensed that the guards struggled to hold them at bay.

"Yes!" Joaquin shouted above the din, his eyes terrified as the dogs snarled.

Owen waved his hand and the guards pulled at the leads and shouted the dogs down. The animals fought against them, a tangled mess of chaos as they disappeared through the same door they had come through. Their howls could still be heard as they were led away.

"You sent Serabee El-Khan to murder your sister and the Lady Radha."

Joaquin stared at the king, a fine sheen of sweat coating his head and running down the back of his neck. "Yes." His voice was oddly meek and defiant at the same time. "Yes, I sent him to kill her, though what does it matter?"

"And you ordered them to murder my fam—"

"I never did!" Joaquin almost shouted as he stepped forward and pointed at Owen. "I did not do that, my Lord, I swear it." His hand fell to his side. "I don't know why he did that. I don't understand it."

Jessa lowered the hood of her cloak and the Veil of Shadows fell away. She stood but a few feet behind her brother. "I believe him."

Joaquin spun about, and Jessa met his wide eyes in a calm manner.

"I believe he sent Serabee to kill me, and for whatever reason, that was his part in this. But I believe him to be ignorant of the assault upon Blackstone."

Joaquin stepped toward her and she let him, his face filled with a fury that she recognized all too well. *Seal your fate,* fikloche...

Darry moved with a shout, but the back of his hand struck Jessa hard across the face before she could get there.

Owen yelled as Joaquin began to draw his sword, and Darry grabbed his braid and pulled him off balance. He bent back at the waist and Darry was around him in a heartbeat. She brought her right elbow down and struck him in the throat as she twisted her wrist in his braid. Darry let him hit the floor, her dagger drawn and shoved beneath his chin as he coughed and clawed at her jacket.

"Don't do it, girl," Grissom commanded in a hard voice.

Jessa was thankful for the strong hands that had kept her from falling, and she looked into Jacob's green eyes.

"Hello, Princess." He looked out of his element but he offered a smile. "I'm very glad to see you're alive."

"Jacob." Jessa tasted blood as she spoke.

"Let him up, girl," Grissom ordered Darry as he crouched beside the fallen Lyonese prince. "Don't do it like this. Do it right, if that's what you want."

Darry pressed the point of her dagger into the skin of Joaquin's throat, and it popped through. She looked up as the scent of his blood filled her nostrils. "He tried to kill her."

Grissom made a disgruntled face and scratched at his beard. "He did, that's true." He looked down at Joaquin. "Should I let her kill you?"

"Don't…" Joaquin managed, his voice cracking.

Darry pushed away, stepped back, and flipped the dagger. The knife's tip buried itself in the floor between Joaquin's legs. "We shall solve our mystery, yes?"

The blade's edge had sliced through his trousers and was nestled dangerously close to his manhood.

"Darry," Jessa whispered, and her lover looked up. It took but a brief moment for Jessa to realize that she was too late to stop all that would come next. "What have you done?"

CHAPTER FIFTEEN

Marteen Salish stopped beside the high-backed chair and waited in silence.

Malcolm stared at the raised etching upon his goblet and noted how the firelight caught upon the sword held by King Bertram. His armor had faded over the many years, rubbed down by the countless times the cup had been lifted to the lips. Not by Malcolm alone, but certainly by his hand as of late. Bertram did not seem to mind.

He was well into his fourth hour of being banished from the throne room, and he was sick of it. He was not a child and he was not an afterthought. He was soon to be the High King of Arravan, and he would make this fact known in ways no one would expect. He should have been there, to control what happened next.

Although he understood he alone knew what needed to be done to secure the kingdom's future, he had been truly surprised by his father's actions. Obviously the violence of the Fakir attack had been extreme, but the High King did not have the luxury of reacting as his father was currently responding. The High King was required to stay above the fray. He was required to make the hard decisions for the good of his country.

Perhaps his father was too old for it all. His continuing to make the wrong decisions would clearly indicate age—and the supposed wisdom that came with it—was no longer his friend.

Darry should have been clapped in chains and locked in the jails beneath the Keep for what she had done. He was not willing to accept that she was free and left to influence those around her. It was not his father's smallest misstep by far, but it was the one that galled him the most, for the moment.

He tasted the warm spring vintage and set the cup upon the table beside him before he looked up.

"Serabee has escaped, according to Jefs."

Malcolm allowed a smile to slip across his lips. "And?"

"And Darrius has challenged Joaquin to the Blooded Duel."

Malcolm closed his eyes. "He ordered the death of the woman who is to be my bride, the woman who will bear my sons." The logs of the fire crumbled and the ashes popped.

"It seems as if being regent in Lyoness until your son comes of age was not enough to satisfy Joaquin's ambition," Salish suggested in a careful voice.

"It was enough," Malcolm said as his temper rose, "and he knew it. More than enough for the likes of him. Bharjah's dregs could not hope for more."

"Perhaps he knew you would never keep your end of the bargain."

Malcolm let out a breath of laughter. "Perhaps."

"I'm not sure that I understand what he hoped to gain by such an all-out attack on the Keep," Salish admitted.

"The Nightshade Lark, murdered upon Arravan soil? Don't be an ass!" Malcolm came to his feet and Salish stepped back. "Do you think this was Joaquin's idea? Do you think he is clever enough for a game so vast?"

"Did he act upon Bharjah's orders, then?"

Malcolm frowned. "This was Serabee, you fool. The Nightshade Lark murdered in her bed, in the heart of Blackstone Keep? Bharjah's Lords will line up behind him and froth at the mouth to cross the Taljah. Joaquin is irrelevant, he always has been. This was Serabee's doing."

"But Serabee failed and has fled, leaving Joaquin behind."

"Yes, to take the blame. A stag for the doe will do just as well."

"Joaquin?"

"My dear sister may be many vile things, but she handles a sword better than anyone I've ever seen, even Wyatt. Joaquin will not last five minutes. Bharjah will have the death of a prince to avenge, instead of a princess." Malcolm walked to the fire and looked within it. His jaw hurt and his head ached. His left cheekbone was so tender it hurt to speak, and his lower lip was swollen and tasted of blood. "By attacking the Keep in force with my father here, Bharjah meant to put me on the throne, while at the same time removing my future claim to *his*. Jessa's continued presence is a variable he can no longer control. It was wise to use her to some advantage. I would've done the same."

"But what of Joaquin?" Salish asked. "He has secrets he might share with your father that are better left unsaid. Or worse yet, lies that will prolong what is left of his life."

Malcolm lifted a finger to his lower lip and touched the cut. He pulled his finger back and stared at the blood. "Send a bird. Tell our emissary, if you will, that he must make his move at once. Remind him of what will happen if he fails."

"Of course. And what of Joaquin?"

"Midnight will be upon us in a few hours. Bring Jefs to me. Joaquin will tell all sorts of tales—you're right. I'll take care of it."

"Jefs will expect more. If you bring him in further, it will cost us."

"Then he shall have whatever he wants."

"As you wish, Mal."

"And one more thing," Malcolm added as he turned. The back of his left hand struck Salish high across the cheekbone. The sharp sound echoed throughout Malcolm's chamber as he stepped forward and seized his advisor by the throat. Salish stumbled backward as Malcolm tightened his grip. "If you ever touch me in public again, there will be a price beyond blood to be paid. Is that clear, my pet?"

Marteen Salish said nothing, nor did he acknowledge Malcolm's words.

"I do not play now."

Salish grabbed gently at Malcolm's wrist. "*Yes*."

Malcolm let him go. "More than your life hangs in the balance, after your misstep."

Salish bowed his head at once. "Yes."

"Send the bird. Tell him to return the favor when it's done."

"Yes, my Lord."

Malcolm stepped back to his chair and retrieved his wine. He took a generous swallow and felt the better for it. "And find me the Princess Jessa-Sirrah. After my father allows me to leave my room, I would pay my respects and offer her my protection. With Joaquin's actions, no doubt her fear will be great. If Bharjah may take advantage of good timing, then so must I."

"Yes, my Lord."

❖

"And when does this bloody duel take place?" Jessa demanded as she pushed her chair back and rose to her feet. She was more angry than she had been, for the longer such knowledge sat within her thoughts, the more fearful she became. "Tonight? Or at dawn, perhaps, for dramatic effect?"

"It's a *Blooded* Duel, actually," Darry corrected, though her eyes held a spark that Jessa did not approve of in the least.

"I know what a Blooded Duel is, Darrius," Jessa snapped. "I said what I meant, thank you. If I know my history, I believe that the first duel of such a nature between Bloods was held in the province of Ana Idriss, in the southland of my own country. Two Lords fought over the rather dubious honor of a woman who was in love with a third man altogether."

Darry smiled, genuinely surprised. "Really? What was her name?"

Jessa took several seconds as her gaze raked across the table. "What?"

"I am looking for something to break!"

Darry picked up her plate and scraped what was left of her late dinner onto the serving platter before she held it out to her lover. "This should do nicely."

Jessa grabbed the plate and slapped its edge upon the tabletop. The heavy porcelain broke apart with a clatter, and she threw what was left toward the hearth. The collision echoed against the stones as the remains of the plate shattered into a dozen pieces. "Do not mock me, Princess, or you shall regret it."

"I'm not mocking you."

"I have been mocked down the Dark Ridge Mountains and back again, Darrius," Jessa proclaimed, and her stomach felt a bit quesy. "Do not do that to me, as well. Not you."

Darry stood at once and met Jessa's gaze straight on. "I am not mocking you."

"You have more stitches in you than the rag doll that Radha made for me as a child, and not quite as much stuffing, unless I miss my guess. You are in no position to be fighting over a game of roundball, much less a duel to the death."

"I shall be fine," Darry responded in a gentle voice.

Jessa narrowed her eyes. "Joaquin may be a fool, but he can handle a sword."

"I'll be fine."

"That's it? That's all you have to say?"

"I'm sorry, Jessa, that he's your brother. I can say that, in all truth. He sent his men to kill you and Radha as you slept. This crime, for which he has claimed responsibility, is punishable by death. At least this way, he might go out fighting."

Jessa's eyes widened. "Against you?"

"Who better?"

"Someone who is not wounded from head to toe, for one thing. And are you saying this is why you challenged him? To let him die with some scrap of honor that he does not deserve?"

"No. But that doesn't make it any less true."

"He deserves to die like the *fikloche* dog that he is." Jessa's tone was cold and she hoped that Darry could hear it. "The dog that he has always been."

Darry's expression was thoughtful and Jessa waited as patiently as she could.

"I'm sorry, Jess, but I can't take it back."

"Are you saying you would if you could?"

"No."

"Then why say such a thing at all?" Jessa demanded, and then took an awkward step back. Her chair tipped over as she bumped into it and it slammed to the floor. She blinked at Darry and put a hand over her stomach, uncertain beneath a sudden wave of energy. "What…what are you doing?"

"I will kill the fucking dog, as you have named him, that has plagued you." Darry spoke in a low voice, her eyes decidedly bright as she stepped along the edge of the table. "And I shall do it for all the world to see."

Jessa took a clumsy step to the left as she sidestepped her fallen chair and let out a slow breath of air in reaction to the *Cha-Diah* majik that rushed her senses. "Darry…don't come any closer."

"Do you think it was easy for me to not kill him in that moment?" Darry turned about the curve of the table as she advanced. "To let him go free, even for a heartbeat, after he had struck you? What did you think would happen, my love?"

Jessa remembered her thoughts within the throne room. *Seal your fate…*

"What did you think would happen?" Darry asked again.

"That he would die for his actions," Jessa answered. Her blood moved apace as her body reacted to Darry's, the pulse of her desire instant and wonderfully intense. She could feel her nipples chafe against the fabric of her blouse. "That he had sealed his fate."

"Since the moment I picked up your fallen shawl, my first, *best* duty has been to protect you. And it doesn't matter that you can break a man's bones with a whisper, or steal hellfire from the mouth of your gods. It doesn't matter that I exhaust every last drop of my power making you spend your spirit, over and over, and over again."

Jessa bumped into the wall with a start and her right hand went out, her fingers splayed flat upon Darry's chest. The heat from her lover's body poured into her, and she let out a moan as Darry heeded the boundary, at least for the moment.

"It does not matter that I make you come until I pass out cold, as weak as the day I was born. It does not matter that you will lie awake, staring at the ceiling and wanting more. Your majik is more than mine, I know this."

Jessa licked her lips as her eyes found Darry's mouth. Slowly, she fisted her hand in Darry's shirt. "I could not take more," she admitted in a breath of words. Her breasts ached and her flesh throbbed with need.

"My duty shall always be to protect you, whether you need it or not. I cannot help this."

Jessa nodded as her body eased back against the wall. Her blood was decidedly hot and the stones were a cool relief, even through her clothes. "Darry, please…"

"Please what?"

Jessa's right knee came up slowly as her thighs pressed together. She caught her breath and bit her lower lip as the muscles between her legs clenched.

"Please what?"

"I don't know."

"Do not infringe my honor…not you, Jess."

Jessa looked up. "Not ever, *Akasha*."

Darry slowly pulled the blouse free from Jessa's skirt, the silk fabric like the soft breath of a dream as it moved against Jessa's skin. Strong fingers undid the buttons with care, and then Darry was against her, their bodies pressed close as Jessa was trapped against the wall.

Darry pushed her face in Jessa's hair and her lips claimed a kiss just below her left ear. "I love you."

Jessa took hold of Darry's trousers and pulled, her need answered with firm, slow thrusts. Darry's strong hands were upon her breasts then and Jessa's head tipped back as they were taken captive and toyed with.

Darry took a nipple into her mouth and Jessa cried out as Darry sucked upon the tender skin. Darry's teeth grazed and her hips pressed and Jessa's hands went in search as her head dropped forward. "*Akasha...*"

Jessa dragged her face along Darry's neck as they moved together, and she answered each movement with one of her own. She was moments from spending her spirit and it sent her mind into a swirl of anticipation and frustration both. "You should've...you should've done this that night—"

Darry's open mouth closed over hers and they kissed.

Jessa tasted life within their union, and Darry's tongue was insistent, as hot and sweet as summer honey. Jessa tried to pull closer, her breasts sore and heavy with the tease of fulfillment. She wrapped her arms about Darry's neck and her mouth opened wider. Darry's thrusts became more urgent and her hand slipped between their bodies, her fingers pushing beneath the waist of Jessa's skirt.

"That night in the stables..." Jessa managed, her lips inflamed and wet against Darry's.

Darry caught a breath. "I'm doing it now, my love." Darry's fingers slid through the soft hair between her lover's legs, and her own need reacted to the hard arousal and swollen folds that waited. Jessa pushed against the advance and the heavy ache between Darry's own legs deepened.

The abundance of Jessa's spirit upon her fingers fairly burned, and her breasts ached to be touched. She needed the feel of her lover's flesh against them. "Unbutton my shirt," she insisted, unwilling to wait.

Jessa took hold of Darry's tunic with quick hands and pulled her close. She cried out against Darry's mouth and bit her lip. There was a sting to it but Darry smiled, for in that moment, she knew that Jessa was helpless to stop. It was a thrill to know she could cause such abandon, and a deep quiver of pleasure shook through her loins. "I want my breasts on yours...when you come."

"Hurry then!" Jessa responded with a desperate breath and yanked Darry's tunic open. The buttons popped from their threads and clattered to the floor.

Darry leaned in and her blood soared as her most urgent desire was fulfilled. Jessa's body was always so hot against her skin, and the satisfaction she received from this particular connection could not be measured. There was a twinge of pain down her side as Jessa's arms wrapped around her neck, but it was there and gone as her blood rose in defense.

Jessa came hard upon the next stroke, her hands within Darry's hair as their foreheads pressed together. Jessa's touch when she spent was unique, and Darry felt the jolt of her lover's power move down her neck and bleed through the muscles of her back. The sensation was akin to sunlight and its warmth raced beneath her skin, the fevered tendrils of Jessa's majik searching out the panther. Darry cupped Jessa's sex and messaged her with a firm hand.

"You promised...you would tell me first, *Akasha*," Jessa said in a breathless voice and then kissed her.

Jessa's tongue was sweet, but there was a fullness beneath it that made Darry think of her favorite dark-tree spice. Her senses had become richer since Hinsa had left the maze, and she could almost feel the colors of her desire, reds and molten golds with swirls of black smoke chasing through both. She met Jessa's sable eyes as she slipped her hand free and took her by the hips.

Darry pressed her against the wall. "I didn't think," she answered and her voice was somewhat strained. Her sex throbbed with the most delicious pain, heavy and thick with longing. "I'm sorry."

The kiss Darry received in answer was open and aggressive, the pleasing awareness of Jessa's full breasts against her own pouring Darry's thoughts into a realm of singular purpose, in a distinctive arc of bliss. "I want...your mouth on me," Darry said as their lips clung together. Jessa's hands tightened within the curls of her hair. "I want your tongue."

Jessa's face was flushed and her dark hair was scattered. "*Yes.*"

They turned toward the bed, and before Darry could orient herself properly within the room, she was lying upon the huge feather mattress and sinking into the quilt. She felt Jessa's hands upon her body, and she closed her eyes as she tried to steady her breathing. The Vhaelin sunlight that was Jessa's passion flowed through the muscles of her legs, sensuous and pure like a river of the finest silk.

Her trousers and undergarments were pulled off, and Jessa, too, was naked as Jessa slid her body between Darry's legs. Jessa's stomach stroked Darry's sex and Darry's muscles clenched as her hips lifted in response.

Jessa's tongue was deliciously wet upon her skin, and Darry moaned at the feel of it. Her left hand opened within the thickness of Jessa's hair, and then closed tight at the base of her neck. Jessa's sunlight turned smoky as it came to life and pooled into a ball of heat within Darry's fist. She would hold it for as long as she could, but she had already learned that such a captive could not be held for long.

Jessa toyed with Darry's left nipple, circling with her tongue and flicking the tender skin until it was raised and hard, and then her lips closed upon the flesh, sucking it into her mouth. Darry arched beneath her and moaned.

The sunlight burst beyond the strength of Darry's legs as Jessa's hips thrust against her, and Darry cried out, the sound ripped from her throat. The Vhaelin light rushed within her loins and swirled in a never-ending spiral about her pleasure, stroking and then tightening. Expanding, pulsing and alive, as it filled her with its essence.

She spent amidst a rush of overwhelming sensations. Her legs tangled about Jessa's, her muscles clenched tight and then reaching out. The sleek, feminine strength of Jessa's shoulders as her back rolled and she moved with purpose. The heady taste as their mouths joined, and their tongues mating as she tried to breathe and cry out at the same time. Her panther's blood rising, pounding through her veins and then leaping free as Jessa's majik fell back beneath its rough, untamed power.

They moved as one as Darry tightened her embrace, and Jessa came with an aching cry that matched her own.

❖

Jessa nestled in the curve of Darry's right side, Darry's arm lax upon Jessa's thigh as Jessa ran her hand upon the smooth skin of her lover's stomach. Even in sleep, the muscles of Darry's abdomen were raised and pronounced in their strength. Her bruises were many, and Jessa's heart beat fast at the sight of them, her thoughts better suited to their current situation than they had been several hours ago. Darry's right shoulder was bruised and it bled down beneath the skin to her ribs and the outside of her breast, Jessa's touch but a whisper upon the wounded skin.

The burn upon Darry's jaw from a garrote, she had said, was almost gone, what was left of the minor wound but a scrape. Her forearms were littered with small bruises, both slight and deep, though each one had been a blow taken.

She lifted Darry's left hand and studied the palm.

The wound marking her separation from the Durand line was still pronounced, but it did not bleed, the precise cut closed with a seal of old blood and new skin that was both flexible and thick. The hand healed differently though, and with the power of Hinsa's blood, Jessa had no idea what Darry's body might do to recover its strength.

Your majik wastes very little time, Akasha.

She touched the edge of Darry's poultice and the resin used to hold the bandage in place lifted with little effort. Just below the dressing there were scratches upon the black-bruised skin, fresh marks she had made herself at some point during their lovemaking.

Jessa let out a hard breath at the dark mixture of yarrow root and fresh blood that stained her fingers.

Her hand became a fist and she closed her eyes as she remembered how she had tightened her embrace and writhed brazenly against her lover. She had lost track of how many times she had come, once Darry's blood had taken over and the Vhaelin had responded, and when Darry's touch had been so deep inside her, she had felt a glorious lack of restraint, one that she had become lost within, and joyfully so. They both had, for Jessa had let the panther have all that she wanted.

Radha's words were harsh within her head. *You must mind the strength and the nature of the animal that is within her and have a care when her power is high. The panther is a wild creature, always remember that. Do not ever forget that, Jessa, or you may both regret it...*

Tears slipped free as she opened her eyes.

"It is hard to see a weakness, *Akasha*, when it wears the clothes of so much strength," she whispered and shifted upon the ruined covers of their bed. Darry's lips were soft beneath her own and she kissed them with exquisite tenderness. "And though I shall do nothing that threatens your honor, my love, I am more than within my rights to enter the fray beside you."

❖

Darry stood before the tent and knew that she was expected to enter.

The night air was cool and crisp and the grass was thick about her legs. The smoke that rose from the center of the tent smelled of birch wood and sage, though there was something just beneath it that she could not name. It was the earth, perhaps, for its presence was ancient and indifferent.

She looked down and her feet were bare, her faded trousers much too worn and far too long without her boots. Her tunic was soft and almost threadbare, as if she had put it on years ago and forgotten to change it. She felt the material and she did not recognize the texture, or the color, for that matter. Perhaps it had been red once, though now she could not say.

The skin of the tent was heavy and clean, the light from within muted and somewhat eerie in the night. Shadows danced across the surface, but she sensed no movement from within, and so she glanced over her shoulder.

The moonlight was her only companion, and in the far distance there was but the horizon, the sky not quite as black or as thick as the earth beneath it.

She had never seen these stars in her life, or so many. The city of Lokey never seemed to sleep, and there was always the play of light from somewhere.

Nights upon the Zephyr could compare, and Darry felt peace at the memory of her time as a seaman upon her father's fastest ship. At times the sea was so still that she could name the constellations upon the water, an endless deep of blackness but for the deck she stood upon. She had sometimes lifted a hand to the sky, while on the crow's nest, on the midnight watch, though she caught no stars in her grasping hand. The turn of the distant clouds and the white fire of stars that burned hot and raced across the dome of the world had lulled her soul into a sort of peace, and she had welcomed it. It had been a peace she had never known before those moments, and the serenity had only haunted her since its loss.

She had named the loss loneliness, which she had never felt upon the *Zephyr*, and her memories of those nights at sea had followed her for years in her dreams. As she stood beneath a sky just as vast and filled with mystery as the skies above the Sellen Sea, she understood how very wrong she had been. She had been homesick for something she had no name for.

She walked to the tent and pushed the flap aside, the light from the fire so bright she felt as if she had stumbled into the sun.

"Give it a moment..."

The timbre of the quiet voice was rough, as if perhaps it had been broken once upon an age and never quite recovered.

Darry closed her eyes, let the tent flap fall shut behind her, and stood still within the warmth. It washed over her skin like a quilted blanket and her body gave a pleasing shudder. When she opened her eyes, the sun had settled into dusk and she was surprised at how small the fire actually was.

Darry followed the familiar sound of a blade pushed upon a whetstone, and her eyes found the source of the voice.

The woman was dressed in soft buckskin and sat cross-legged upon an open bedroll, the sword she held as bright as a star as its edge caught the firelight. Her dark blond hair was long and thick, falling onto her shoulders, braids and beads peppered through its loose curls. When she looked up, Darry noted at once the long scar that ran down the left side of her face.

Her feet were silent as she walked around the fire, the soft rugs upon the ground like clouds beneath her feet. She sat easily beside the stranger, and though she did not know why, she felt no embarrassment as she reached out. The woman closed her eyes as Darry's right hand touched her face, and Darry trailed her thumb along the scar. Darry was graced with a sweet smile in answer and a firm hand at the back of her neck that pulled her forward.

The woman placed a gentle kiss upon Darry's cheek. "Let me see your eyes."

Darry obeyed and met the woman's gaze.

Her left eye was bright amber in color, not unlike the inner flames of the fire beside them. Her right eye was a deep brown, lush and warm like the earth of the Lowlands after a warm summer rain. Intense heat within both took the breath from Darry's lungs.

"I never thought to have a child," the woman whispered, and her eyes filled with so much affection that Darry was instantly overwhelmed. *"But I see my Hashiki did not forget."*

Darry awoke with a start, her eyes wide as she tried to adjust to her surroundings. Her heart was pounding and she felt the smooth tracks of tears against her temples. "Jess?"

She stretched beneath the quilt, the fabric soft against her naked skin, the twinge of hard pain in her side there and gone, though an ache remained. She felt quiet within the afterglow of their passion and her heart was satisfied, even though Jessa was not lying in her arms. The bed was still warm, though, so she could not have gone far.

While she waited for Jessa to respond to her call, her eyes drifted and lost focus, her lids heavy and still full of sleep. Her exhaustion filled her to the edge like the wind within a sail, determined as it pushed her once more toward a sea of stars.

CHAPTER SIXTEEN

P rincess, are you here?"
    Jessa stepped from beneath the lowest curve of the spiral staircase, her gaze clear as she watched Jacob Durand close the door to his secret study beyond the Queen's Library. The single lamp upon the desk shone forth into the darkness and made his red hair glisten as he locked the door, the Prince of Arravan handsome beneath a fleeting crown of flames.

She had been waiting for almost an hour, and she had used the time wisely. She had played the pieces and she had moved them upon the board as Radha had taught her. She had looked into the future as far as her mind could reach, and then she had looked again from another angle. She had sat upon the bed with her eyes closed and played game after game after game.

The secret study still held a scrap of Darry's essence beneath the dry parchment of endless scrolls and the cold ache of stone, though it was not a thing that just anyone might notice. They had made love in this room for hours upon end, and Jessa still felt those moments deep within her flesh. It had been here that she had first felt the passionate touch of another, and she would always cherish the memory. To have finally tasted the addictive power of Darry's flesh, and to have been held within her arms after a lifetime of longing, was a remembrance with no rival.

She could still feel Darry inside her, every fiber of her body alight with the recent touch of her lover. When she smiled, her lips felt swollen and tender, and it was a very sweet sensation.

Prince Jacob walked to the desk and glanced at the scrolls that were open. Smooth round stones had been placed upon the curled corners of the aged vellum, and he did not disturb them. His green eyes were sharp as he looked deeper into the chamber. "Princess?"

Jessa pulled her hood back and let fall the Veil of Shadows.

Jacob's eyes widened and then he smiled. "'Tis a lovely spell, my Lady."

"No doubt a spell that might come in handy for the Prince of Spies." Jessa walked to the desk and stood upon the opposite side. "That is what they call you, yes?"

"Either that, or the Bookworm Prince."

Jessa frowned. "But that is not right. I know you're a very learned man, but that is not an insult to throw at someone—it's a privilege."

Jacob's eyes filled with warmth. "I am not the swordsman like Wyatt and Darry are, nor the Crown Prince as Malcolm is, nor the bold and wicked-tongued Emmalyn, admired by all. I am the middle son. The Lord of dusty rooms and moldy parchment. The Bookworm Prince."

Jessa scoffed at his words. "But that makes you the most dangerous one of all."

Jacob stepped about the desk and pulled the chair out for her. "Sit, Princess, please."

Jessa took the offered chair and waited for him to find his own.

"Your words are most kind, Princess," Jacob replied as he sat and faced her. "But I'm not sure if—"

"Call me Jessa, Prince Jacob. I am no longer a princess of Lyoness."

Jacob looked her in the eyes with a steady gaze. "Yes, my father has spoken of your oath and it negates nothing. You shall always be a princess. Just as I shall always be the Bookworm Prince, you shall be the Woman Within the Shadows and the Nightshade Lark."

"Then let us dispense with formalities and be comrades." Jessa held out her hand to him. She could not help but smile as she remembered her own first offer of friendship. "Darry taught me this."

Jacob chuckled and shook her hand. "Well met, Jessa."

"For certain."

Jacob leaned back in his chair. "Just two friends meeting in the dead of night…in a secret chamber hidden behind the stacks in the Queen's Library."

"Yes, well, I thought it might be best." Jessa sat back as well. "You have questions, yes?"

Jacob's expression changed slightly. "How so?"

"You are the Prince of Spies, Jacob, and yet I think you have never had the information you truly need. There is much guesswork that goes on, I have seen it. I am the only daughter of King Abdul-Majid de Bharjah of Lyoness, and though I am considered but a trinket among powerful men and the Lords of my people, I have been privy to information that has never left the Jade Palace. My Radha was not a nursemaid to me, nor a servant. She has been my teacher these many years, and she is a High Priestess of the Vhaelin."

Jacob's eyes showed genuine surprise and Jessa smiled, for he looked so much like Darry when he was startled. "But Serabee El-Khan is a Lord of the Fakir, and Bharjah worships them." He gave a wave of his hand as he sat forward. "To allow a High Priestess of the Vhaelin within the Jade Palace, under his very nose? That's not possible."

"My mother was a prophet of the Vhaelin, stolen by Bharjah from our people. Radha went with her for many reasons, I have recently learned, but most of all for the child she knew would come."

"You?" Jacob asked quietly.

"It would appear so."

"But surely Serabee knew."

"Who is to say?" Jessa shrugged. "But I do not think so. The Fakir are a proud race, and to know what Radha truly is and allow her freedoms he himself did not enjoy? It would have given him great pleasure to expose her before my father. He took her for a

Vhaelin witch, and a powerful one, but nothing more. They enjoyed the game, the taunting and the tease of it all, both Serabee and my Radha. She is prideful, and she is good with a lie when she likes."

"The frail nursemaid?" Jacob asked with a grin.

Jessa let her own smile blossom. "Yes."

"Your brothers..." Jacob's voice was eager. "Who will succeed your father?"

"I do not know."

"But surely there must be a name that stands above the others."

"I believe Sylban-Tenna to be the most dangerous of my siblings. But you are asking the wrong question, Jacob."

He stared at her.

Jessa's thoughts moved easily to a secondary path that might lead more quickly to her goal. "Who is your spy?"

Jacob's expression changed in a subtle manner, his green eyes careful in the flicker of the lamplight.

"He is most certainly a Lord, or you would be wasting your resources," Jessa reasoned. She hooked her right knee over her left and straightened her skirt in a casual manner. "He would have to be of your father's generation, with a son, perhaps, lost in the battle for the Lowlands. Or perhaps he lost all of his sons in a war that the Lords of my country did not fully support."

Jacob did not move, nor did he look away.

"Lord Almahdi de Ghalib lost all of his sons, three of those in battle during the retreat to the Taljah beneath the final onslaught of King Owen's army. His fourth and last son was named Jal-Kadir. Jal defied Bharjah and spoke out, saying that my father's army must leave Arravan or suffer a loss that Lyoness would never recover from. And so Bharjah brought him before all the Lords of his army before they could waver in their commitment, and he slit Jal's throat.

"Lord de Ghalib has great-granddaughters, young girls who have been promised by Bharjah to men who are old even now. Young girls who will be pawns, such as I was, when they flower with their first blood. They are the heirs of his fallen sons. Lord Almahdi de Ghalib sits upon my father's council. My father loves his praise, especially from an obedient man who has learned his lesson. And a broken man is a wonderful plaything to have. The fate of de Ghalib's family has been an effective cautionary tale."

There was silence between them and Jessa considered her logic yet again. "Lord de Ghalib and King Bharjah share the attentions of the same Master Healer."

Jacob's left eye gave the smallest of twitches.

"Officially, he attends only to my father. Unknown to many, he is related by marriage to the former daughter-in-law of Lord de Ghalib, the widow of Nasir, Almahdi's firstborn son who fell at the Taljah. He is the only man alive who would know if my father is ill, other than Bharjah, of course."

Jacob's smile, when it came, was both grudging and filled with warmth. "And so where does your tale end?"

"Well, I imagine it will end when my father's soldiers ride to the house of Lord de Ghalib to collect his granddaughter Fayha, who is promised to a worshipper of the Fakir, and they find that she is not there. Nor will they find any of the children born of Almahdi's line."

"And where shall they be?"

Jessa enjoyed his look of respect, his eyes bright in the lamplight. "Wherever you have decided to put them, Jacob, Prince of Spies."

Her reasoning was sound and she knew it. Radha's teachings had been most thorough, though it was not until recently that she understood just how methodical the old woman had been. She had given her majik, faith, languages, and secrets, and she had given her precious information about even the most mundane of subjects. It was all terribly valuable, even the smallest of details. *May the Vhaelin keep you safe, my mother, even though you vex them.*

"What question should I be asking, Jessa?" Jacob finally said.

"Who has the most to gain when my father dies?"

"If there is no clear line of succession, there will be a civil war," Jacob replied in a quiet voice. He leaned forward and rested his elbows upon his knees. "Even if Bharjah were to name an heir, once he is dead, all may claim their right to the Jade Throne. It's not like Arravan. If we rule out your lesser brothers, those with no sufficient following either in the military or among the people—"

"You are left with only five real contenders," Jessa concluded as she leaned an elbow onto her own knee. He thought fast and hard, and she liked the pace. She would see now how accurate his information actually was.

"Malik-Assad."

"Yes," Jessa confirmed. "He is the best warrior among my brothers, and those within the military love him."

"Qasim?"

"Right again. His wife has as much jade as my father does. He has garnered much power throughout the mountain regions, and with the Blooded families along the Dark Ridge."

"Rasul-Rafiq, he has the armies of the south."

Jessa nodded. "And many ships, as well."

Jacob sat up straight and Jessa did the same. "And Sylban-Tenna, of course. He worships the Fakir and he has proven himself in battle with the Horse Clans of the north. His victories along the Arramis River are legendary, even across the border. With the information I have, I see only four who might fight for the throne and win it. The others would have little hope of victory, for they have no real support. When the fighting begins, they would have no choice but to ally themselves with one of the four, or disappear into the night."

"They will be killed before this is possible."

Jacob did not look surprised, though neither did he look certain.

"They will be killed," Jessa repeated, "unless they have already fled Karballa."

"Not a kind fate."

"Nor should it come as a surprise if they have been paying attention. Are you certain you see no one else?"

"There is you, of course," he answered quietly. "But if you were the sacrificial pawn, as you suggested to my father, then your part has already been played in this game. Played by Bharjah himself, though to no avail."

"Do I not still have a right to the throne?"

"Well, your son would have a claim, but you have no son." Jacob smiled. "In Lyoness, no woman may rule from the Jade Throne, you know this."

"And what if I gave your brother a son? A son, who by my own blood would have the right to rule in Lyoness."

"Yes, if you had a son, he would have a right to the throne," Jacob agreed. "Bloody hell, he would have the whole of Arravan behind him. A civil war will spill across the border no matter how strong that border may be. Refugees and sickness will come. If their war finds the Killy Mountains, it would not be long before Sommes Pass becomes a liability and those who live there would have to be evacuated. They would be displaced and the Lowlands would be in jeopardy." His eyes raced with thought. "With a son of Arravan, a Durand by blood who had claim to the Jade Throne? It would take very little convincing to raise the flags of war."

"Was it King Owen who accepted my father's proposal?"

"No," he answered, and Jessa could almost see his thoughts come to a hard stop. "It was not that we have no respect for you, but such an idea would not be in the best interests of Arravan. Your son would have a claim to the Blackwood Throne, and to give your father such an incentive—it would invite a war. Even if your father is dying, the risk would be too great."

"Ask your question once more, my friend."

Jacob's green eyes darkened with the endgame and he leaned back in his chair. His gaze did not waver. "Who has the most to gain when your father dies?"

"Who is the fifth contender for the Jade Throne?"

Jacob said nothing, and though she waited, still he remained silent.

"I have been trying to figure out why I'm here, since before I arrived," Jessa explained in a somewhat tired voice. "The question was never *am* I a pawn, but *whose* pawn was I? Who might use me to their advantage? Who has the most to gain from my presence here? Bharjah knew an offer of this sort would not be welcomed by King Owen. From what I can see, your father does not enjoy the game and plays it only when he must. As you said, a child of Lyonese blood upon the Blackwood Throne would, at some point, invite a war."

"But if you were murdered within the walls of Blackstone, an emissary of peace"—Jacob followed her thread—"Bharjah would have one last chance at claiming the Lowlands, with more support than he had the first time."

"He would come for the throne."

"Most likely, yes," Jacob agreed. "He would have nothing to lose."

"And so goes the first game, for though I am not dead, a prince will do just as well."

Jacob rubbed absently at the stubble upon his chin. "Your brother will not fare well against my sister, Jessa. I'm sorry."

"Do not be sorry. I have no regrets as to his fate. He ordered Serabee to steal through the night and slit my throat, and my Radha's, as well."

"So either Bharjah rides to war to avenge the death of an heir," Jacob prompted.

"Or he dies at the hand of another before he names his successor," Jessa said. "Civil war will follow, and Lyoness shall be ripe for the picking."

"Your father has the wasting tumors, or so Almahdi de Ghalib has told me. But this is not a quick illness." Jacob confirmed her guesswork as to his spy with a sly look. "Bharjah will be failing in health for a year or two before he becomes too weak to rule."

"Then we shall know soon enough if there is a fifth contender for the Jade Throne."

"What you have suggested is a thing of terrible consequence." Jacob's expression was filled with grave conviction. "Though I'm not sure that it is treason yet, exactly, it comes very close, and it puts the crown in a precarious position that we might never recover from. There are Lords within Arravan who feel they have equal claim to the Blackwood Throne, and they have felt this for many generations. I can think of very few things that are worse than a game such as this, a plot that will jeopardize thousands of lives."

"I know you see the pieces, Jacob, just as I do," Jessa stated plainly. "Your brother, the Crown Prince, has his own game in play. If Bharjah falls, Malcolm has but to wait. Wait for my brothers to destroy each other…and for his son to be born."

"Yes, I see the pieces," he snapped, and for the first time there was a hard edge to his words. "I see them."

"Am I wrong?"

"I don't know," Jacob answered and though his tone was reluctant, Jessa knew he told the truth. "Gamar knows I don't want to believe it, but somehow it fits." He made a face and rubbed his eyes. "I have been trying to figure things out, as well, and Malcolm has refused to let me in. It has been months now, well over a year, in fact, since I've been privy to his thoughts. He has shoved me aside and taken only Marteen Salish into his confidence. There have been secret meetings and an unexplained trip last year to the Great Library at Hockley that took him away for almost a month." Jacob stared at the maps on the desk. "I sent several trusted men to report back on his actions, but Malcolm wasn't there and he never had been. I love him, and he is to be my King one day…"

When Jacob did not go on, Jessa's voice soothed him. "What is it, Jacob?"

"There are things he has done that I have questioned." Jacob shook his head. "I am not a meek man, as many have named me, but neither do I crave the power that Malcolm does. He always has." His expression was one of extreme sadness. "He has long been dreaming of Lyoness, Princess, and not just as a curiosity."

"If I am right," Jessa said softly, "you must know none of this is your fault."

"Melora Salish is Marteen's sister," Jacob said with care. "When she told Darry of our father's betrayal and his manipulations concerning Aidan McKenna's family, she did so with a very certain purpose. Malcolm used her as his weapon in order to elicit a reaction beyond my sister denouncing her title and status." He took a deep breath and let it out slowly. "And this is not the worst he has done."

"That is not your fault."

Jacob's features were pale. "If Malcolm seeks to provoke a civil war he will need an assassin, and if that is true, it will bloody well change everything. He will have crossed a line." He tipped his head back and spied the faint light of dawn as it fell through the skylight. "And my father speaks to him at first light. There is little time."

A shiver moved along Jessa's spine. "Does Malcolm know yet?"

"About you and Darry?"

"Yes," Jessa answered in a breath, uncertain of what Jacob's own reaction would be.

He reached his hand out and Jessa took it. "Not yet, my sister," he said with kindness. "Though I think we might have a more serious problem, if that's even possible."

"We have no proof."

Jacob nodded. "We have no proof."

CHAPTER SEVENTEEN

The Hall of Lords was built deep within Blackstone, beyond the throne room and the private meeting chambers that populated the heart of the Keep. Many of the walkways were open aired and fertile with greenery, the arches supported by black marble columns that caught the summer sun and devoured it. Red and gold Jubilee flowers bloomed in fine fashion, tangled through rich vines of ivy beside orange-flamed lilies that opened with the sun.

The walkways were laid with stones of smooth red granite, the deep scarlet tone a stark and beautiful contrast to the black. The red granite had been brought from the mines of Artanis, and Jessa knew that such a decoration was not a trivial expense. The rock was brought north little by little, for too many times through the centuries rough winds had taken their toll upon heavily laden ships. The ocean floor was paved along one such route with blood as well as stone, and those who sailed it knew it as the Red Corridor.

The Hall of Lords itself was perhaps the largest chamber Jessa had ever seen, for though the Great Hall was a rival to the terraced banquet rooms of the Jade Palace, they all seemed to pale when compared to the Hall of Lords.

From east to west the room was nearly half as long as the practice yards, the planks of the floor made of aged oak, the chamber open down the middle from the doors to the dais at the east end. The Blackwood Throne and its mate sat upon the dais, though Jessa had no idea how both had been moved, and it was inconceivable to her that there would be duplicates.

Upon each side of the long chamber, tiered rows of seats flowed upward to the walls, wide and smooth until they stopped beneath the overhang of the balconies. North and south the balconies fronted the hall, providing space for minor families and those spectators who were quick enough to find a place.

Dozens of flags decorated the balconies above the tiered rows, the banners of the Blooded Lords and important families of Arravan well represented. They were silken and bright and filled the vast hall with life as they caught the sun that poured through the skylights. Jessa found this honor to be one more difference between Lyoness and Arravan, the lesser Lords of a kingdom held in such high regard by their king. There were no banners but Bharjah's in the Jade Palace.

Jessa had not expected the noise, and if she were to guess, the Hall of Lords was filled to capacity. Lords and Ladies and countless bystanders leaned over the balconies in search of familiar faces among the crowded tiers, and their conversations filled the room with a buzz not unlike the locusts that would torment Lyoness in times of drought.

Jessa's shoulders jerked in surprise as Emmalyn's hand slipped carefully into her own.

"She'll be here after my father speaks," Emmalyn promised. "All will be well."

Jessa noted the bruises her friend wore, and the terrible black handprint that stained her throat looked extremely painful. Her dress was a lovely soft blue and her red hair was pulled back in an understated manner, though nothing could hide the consequences of the assault she had suffered. Jessa tightened her fingers about Emmalyn's and gave what she hoped was a confident smile. "This does not happen in Lyoness," she explained. "The people are not welcome within the Jade Palace."

Emmalyn looked about the room from their seats near the dais. "It does not happen so often here, either, not like this."

"I seem to be more of an attraction today than I was the night Darry danced the Mohn-Drom," Jessa commented dryly. A secret smile turned her lips at the memory of Darry's body moving to the music of the once forbidden dance. "I would not have thought that possible."

"Well, that being the case, perhaps you might sing for us later?" Emmalyn suggested, and Jessa turned to her as if she had been struck. She was greeted with a wry smile. "Sorry."

Jessa laughed at once with an equally dark humor. "Do not be sorry. I am glad your humor has returned."

Emmalyn took a deep breath and looked back to the crowd. "The Lewellyns are known for their sharp tongues, even in the worst of times. My mother's family is notorious for it, actually."

"And the Durands?"

"Stubborn. As stubborn as mules in the mud who wish to go the other way."

"Yes. Yes, I have seen this."

"I bet you have. There's Jacob," Emmalyn said and nodded her head toward the opposite balcony.

Jessa looked up at once and met Jacob's gaze across the vast chamber. He was dressed in a rust-colored jacket and white tunic. He lifted his hand slightly and gave a nod. She returned the gesture and let her eyes travel down the balcony. Nina stood not too far from Jacob beside Alisha and her parents, Alisha's brother tall behind them as he spoke to Nina. Nina touched her sling as she replied, a smile there and gone as she spoke.

Jessa did not see Malcolm, nor Marteen Salish for that matter, and she did not find comfort in their absence. If his game was indeed in play, he would not miss such an event. *Although you did not count on your father being the man he is*, she thought. *Nor did you consider me...or my heart.*

"I do not see Malcolm," Emmalyn commented as if she had read Jessa's mind.

"Neither do I," Jessa replied.

There was a resounding bang that echoed down the vast chamber and drew everyone's attention, and then another as the doors behind the dais opened. Those who were seated rose to their feet, and all within the chamber bowed their heads as the High King and Queen entered the Hall of Lords.

Owen and Cecelia stepped to the dais and Cecelia smoothed her skirts as she took her seat. Her dress was a beautiful cream color awash in bronze highlights, subtle yet filled with energy. Her collar covered the wound she had received during the siege, and her hair was braided and pulled behind her head, the rich gold of her crown nestled beautifully among the graying red strands.

Owen turned to the room and stepped to the edge of the dais as he took in the crowd.

He wore a uniform not unlike those of the Kingsmen, though it was shot through with the blue and silver of Arravan's colors, his family's crest embroidered upon the left side of his long jacket. The hem brushed the backs of his knees, and his black boots caught the light. He wore his sword upon his left hip and the ring of his station flared as he rested his left hand upon the hilt.

"Be seated," he ordered, and his voice was full and filled with command.

Amidst another wave of noise, all eyes remained upon the king as Jessa wondered how heavy his crown must feel. It was made of rich gold, and from what she could see, the stones set about its base were large and well cut, various bursts of colored light alive within the air around him. But the crown's actual weight was not Owen's burden at the moment, and Jessa said a prayer to the Vhaelin in his honor.

"Several days ago, Blackstone Keep was deliberately attacked by men of the Fakir." Owen's voice carried in a splendid fashion, though he did not seem to raise it, the acoustics of the room designed for just such an effect. "A religious cult born deep in the Kistanbal Mountains and the sworn enemy of our allies upon the Ibarris Plains, they have long been a dark scourge upon the land."

Jessa let out a startled breath as his words repeated within her head. For Owen to ally Arravan so closely to her own people before any other statement was made filled her heart with a relief so immense she could barely comprehend it. Emmalyn held more tightly to her hand and Jessa looked down as she took an extremely controlled breath and banished her emotions before they overwhelmed her.

"Lord Serabee El-Khan, First Councillor to King Abdul-Majid

de Bharjah of Lyoness, is the unquestioned leader of the Fakir. He is their Lord and their High Priest. He is the voice of their gods, and he long ago swore fealty to King Bharjah." Owen's gaze was made of the same steel he wore at his side, his brown eyes certain as they searched through the faces of the crowd. "And as you know, Lord Serabee El-Khan was a guest of Blackstone—indeed, of Arravan herself. He arrived with a prince of Lyoness, Trey-Jak Joaquin, Bharjah's very own son. They arrived here on a mission of peace, perhaps even one of love. They arrived with an offer of marriage between your own Crown Prince, Malcolm Edmund, and Bharjah's only daughter, the Princess Jessa-Sirrah de Cassey LaMarc." Owen stepped to the right and looked to the balconies. "I did not foresee such an offer, nor did I ever suspect that such a gesture would be presented to the House of Durand."

Owen turned again and for a moment he looked down, though not for long. "My hatred of Bharjah is no secret," he admitted, and Jessa could hear how very tired he was. "My own brother fell on the battlefield, my only brother, who was to be your king, not I. When he was gravely wounded and past defending himself, it is said that Bharjah finally entered the fray and dealt my brother a deathblow and so claimed personal victory over the greatest swordsman many of us have ever known. This was not honor. This was not the act of a king. It was not for my brother to die so on the field, a Prince of the Blood afforded no respect."

Owen walked slowly across the dais and lifted his eyes to meet Jessa's. "My hatred of Bharjah is no secret."

Jessa felt the heat in her cheeks but she accepted it boldly and kept her eyes upon him, despite the shame that raced through her veins.

"And so when the Nightshade Lark entered the gates of Blackstone, I was not the one who looked to the future. I was not the one who looked to heal old wounds and dream of new beginnings. It was my son, my brother's namesake, who did so."

Jessa looked across to Jacob.

"And though I commend Prince Malcolm's intentions, and I am proud of his hopes for peace, he acted as a young man who has never known war. He acted as a man who does not truly understand that Bharjah does not want peace. Bharjah wants the Blackwood Throne."

The chamber erupted in a roar, and Jessa's shoulders jerked in surprise as angry shouts rose from the crowd and a deep banging commenced. The tiers shook beneath the wave of voices as the people within the balconies pounded their hands upon the stone rails in unison.

Owen held up his hands, and as quickly as the riot of noise had begun, it ended.

"And so under the guise of bringing peace to our two countries, Bharjah set his plans in motion. He sent his First Councillor and he sent his son. He sent his Fakir warriors under the cover of a High Majik that even the priests of Gamar would struggle against. He sent them...and I let them in."

A ripple of noise moved through the crowd and then hushed.

"And so when my family was at its most vulnerable, when the House of Durand had let down its guard, if only slightly, Lord Serabee El-Khan carried out Bharjah's orders and attacked in the dead of night. And not only did they come for the blood of my children, they came for the blood of Bharjah's own daughter."

Jessa could feel the eyes of everyone in the chamber as Owen held up his hand.

"Prince Joaquin himself gave the order, he has confessed to such!" The voices turned quiet, though a low rumble of talk remained. "He has admitted to sending Serabee to murder his own sister and the Lady Radha who serves her."

Voices were raised and fell, and Owen let them as his eyes found Jessa's for a brief moment.

"What better reason for the Lords of Lyoness to ride to war than if his only daughter, his supposed emissary of peace, is slain within the walls of Blackstone itself?" Owen demanded and his voice was raised for the first time. "Which one of you would not ride to war if the Princess Emmalyn were slain in such a manner?"

The crowd surged and shouts could be heard amidst the general clamor as the Lords of Arravan stood and gave the call to arms.

Jessa watched the king as he stood, so calm beneath the outrage and certain of his path. She could not imagine Bharjah in such a situation, standing in such a manner, his shoulders back and eyes aflame with righteous anger. She saw the knuckles of his left hand turning white upon the pommel of his sword.

Owen held up a hand. "Peace!" he shouted. "Peace, my Lords."

It took several moments for the crowd to settle, and Jessa kept her eyes upon the king, every fiber of her being desperate to have Darry by her side.

"And so many good men are dead. Men of the Palace Guard and the Kingsmen, men of the City Guard sworn to defend our fair city of Lokey. Their families mourn, and their children shall come of age without their fathers. My own children, my own blood, wounded and battered, and the House of Durand besieged."

Owen turned to her again, and Jessa held his gaze. "And so I say to you now, I will not stand for such vile treachery, and it shall be answered with the strength of steel. And I say, as well, that even if only the Princess Jessa had fallen victim to Bharjah's betrayal? I would still ride to war."

There was utter silence throughout the hall.

"For if my oldest enemy has accomplished but one good thing in his wretched life, it is she."

"Is there to be a marriage?" a voice shouted from deep within the chamber, and Jessa looked away from the king, completely at a loss.

"There will be no marriage!" Owen called out and turned back to the crowd. He held a hand up for quiet and it was obeyed. "I cannot sanction such a union, nor does the princess want such a thing. To give Bharjah and his sons a blooded claim upon Arravan is something neither of us desire, and she has told me this from her own lips. She was not sent here of her own free will, and yet she has given us her loyalty. She fought beside us in the Siege of the Great Hall, and as a priestess of the Vhaelin she wielded her powers to help defeat our enemies and to chase El-Khan like a mad dog from our lands."

Owen cast her a glance and smiled. "And though she's but a slip of a girl, when your king was in the thick of it, out of practice and a few seasons too old for the melee"—Owen set a hand upon his stomach—"and perhaps, a victim of one too many peach pies..."

Jessa was startled to hear laughter and looked to the crowd.

"She saved my life more than once," Owen concluded and drew her eyes to his.

Jessa was surprised when Emmalyn kissed her cheek, her friend's eyes bright with affection as the pounding started once more and the tiers shook with it.

"Do we ride to war?" a voice yelled from the crowd.

"We must prepare for it," Owen answered, "as if we were. Troops will leave within the week for the Emmerin Gap, in order to reinforce General Nasha's command. And a contingent of the Kingsmen will reinforce the Lowland Rangers at Tomm's Town. The call has gone out."

"What of Prince Wyatt and the Seventh?"

"Birds have been sent. Prince Wyatt will bring the Seventh home, and he will welcome every man along the way who offers his sword for the coming fight. The Fourth will join him in Kastamon City. The House of Lewellyn will also gather its forces, and ride beneath the banner of the High Queen. The Council of Lords will meet three days hence, and all who are present may have their say. There is much to be considered and it will take time. It will take weeks, perhaps a month, to fully prepare. We have ships that must return before we march, if march is what we do, ships laden with vital supplies, for an army does not live upon righteousness alone."

"What of Solstice?" a woman's voice called out.

"Solstice celebrations will go on as planned. Bharjah does not have the power to stop the sun," he said with a smile, and there was laughter. "As much as he might like to."

"And what of Joaquin?" Lord Alistair Lewellyn asked as he rose to his feet. He was a tall man with a head of wild red hair and green eyes. His mustache was long past his lips and as red as fire. "Justice must be served."

Those within the chamber fell quiet, and Owen stepped from the dais and walked closer to the crowd. "Joaquin has been challenged to the Blooded Duel."

"When?" Alistair demanded. "My family's blood was spilled here, as well, my Lord."

As if on cue, the bells rang out from the barracks tower, deep and full in the distance. Owen let them finish and their music still hung within the air as he spoke. "In the Circle of Honor beyond the practice yards. When the bells for the second watch ring out, as they have done just now, on the morrow."

"There must be an official challenge!" Lord Alistair called, his face flushed.

Owen smiled just a bit and signaled down the hall with a wave of his hand.

Captain Sol called out the order and the arched doors were pulled inward as all eyes turned to watch.

Jessa stood as Darry entered the chamber as her men, Darry's Boys, fanned out behind her, walking in step. They were dressed in their old uniforms, their black trousers pressed and their black boots polished, though their cropped jackets had been altered slightly with blue trim upon the cuffs and collars. Perhaps it was the lack of insignia, or the green tunics they wore beneath instead of the stark white shirts of the Kingsmen, but it was a bold change made with minimal effort.

Darry's Boys came armed into the Hall of Lords, and her lover's stunning new sword—won from Serabee El-Khan himself—looked most fine and deadly as it hung from Darry's narrow hips. She walked with her left hand upon its hilt as they moved down the center of the hall, and as the crowd began to quiet, Jessa was fairly certain it was not the beauty of her lover's weapon that silenced them.

Hinsa walked beside Darry with an easy gait, and the giant panther moved as smoothly as Darry did, her eyes keen upon the High King as he stood alone in the center of the room.

Some ten feet from her father, Darry came to a stop, and Darry's Boys followed suit within the next heartbeat. Their heels clapped against the oak with a sharp bang that echoed throughout the chamber, and Owen pulled his shoulders back in response.

Hinsa did not stop, however, and a collective gasp moved through the crowd as the golden panther advanced upon the High King.

Darry let out a soft cluck of her tongue, and Hinsa answered her with a step to the side and a hiss that bared her fangs. She turned in a smooth circle and sat as her tail swished back and forth upon the floor.

"Lady Darrius." Owen bowed his head to her.

"Your Majesty." Darry nodded in return.

"You have business with the crown?"

"I challenge Prince Trey-Jak Joaquin. By the right of law, honor has been broken and the debt must be paid."

CHAPTER EIGHTEEN

Jessa spoke the spell beneath her breath that released the lock upon the last of the four trunks that had been Radha's. The mechanism turned with a slow grating sound, and then popped the latch as Jessa smiled. She undid the strap and lifted the lid.

It was the night before the duel, and after taking their dinner in Sebastian's Tower, she and Darry had carried the trunks up the narrow stairs, Jessa determined to find what she wanted no matter how long it might take.

They were both dressed in Darry's clothes, and Jessa loved the feel of the soft homespun trousers and tunic against her skin, the freedom afforded her by a man's dress oddly unexpected. The fire was high in the hearth against the cool evening breezes, and the lamps had been lit, bathing their expansive bedroom in golden light. The moon was not yet too high, but its pale light fell through the nearest window in an intrusion that was destined to fail as time continued its march into the night.

Jessa understood what the next day would bring, but the night would be theirs, and if she could, she would give Darry what knowledge she could find about the threads from the past that were entangled with their present.

"What are these?" Darry asked as she scooped an armload of scrolls from the first of the trunks to be opened. "Something that will turn an unsuspecting suitor into a desert snake of some kind?"

She sat on the floor and crossed her legs as she tried not to drop them. She caught the yellow ribbon that held the nearest scroll in her teeth and pulled.

Jessa laughed. "Do not open that."

"Why?" Darry asked. "Will something bad happen?"

"It might," Jessa answered. "Radha's method of arranging things has always mystified me. I believe that to be the main reason I never found what I was looking for—sheer trickery on her part, meant to annoy me, no doubt."

Darry grinned and the ribbon fell from her lips. "Were you a bad child, my sweet?"

Jessa's amusement filled her throat with more laughter. "Never."

"Well, you've certainly been naughty since," Darry said drily and held out the scrolls. "You pray to your gods with the same tongue you've used to make me cry out in reverence to a rival deity—it's no wonder she had to resort to deception."

Jessa stared at Darry, her hands in midair between them as Darry tried not to laugh. "Does the wicked Lewellyn tongue speak ill of the competition?" Jessa demanded as she grabbed the scrolls, and several spilled to the floor.

Darry chuckled, her eyes filled with a sudden sparkle as her dimple pressed deep. "I see you've been talking with Emmalyn. The Lewellyn women can be quite sarcastic, you're right. Even odious, I'm told."

"Odious?" Jessa asked.

"Unpleasant, I suppose, perhaps even nasty."

"Naughty?"

"No, that's something different."

"How so?"

"Naughty is rarely a transgression, but nasty often is."

"I rather like naughty," Jessa replied with sass and placed the yellow-ribbon-tied scrolls into their own pile. "But I don't think that makes me nasty."

Darry chuckled happily. "No, it makes you bloody well perfect, my love." She swiveled to her knees and dug deeper into the trunk.

She lifted out a heavy scroll that was tied with a strip of rawhide with a thick braid of black hair wrapped just beneath it. "What about this one?"

Jessa's eyes went wide. *"Hiyah,* love!" She scrambled to her knees but her hands stopped just short of the scroll. The parchment was thick and dark, and though Jessa had never known exactly what she was looking for, she knew at that moment she had found it.

She took in the scroll's texture, and the ties that held it shut. She could smell the singed edges, and she could sense the power of the words still hidden within. When she smiled at Darry, it was a smile that had been waiting for over a decade. "I have been searching for this one my whole life."

Darry inspected it with keen eyes. "What's in it?"

"The past," Jessa said softly, "and perhaps the future." She took hold of the scroll with no small amount of reverence, set it carefully on the floor between them, and then sat back upon her heels. "We must speak of things before we open it."

Darry shifted her position, crossed her legs, and set her elbows upon her knees as her curls fell forward about her shoulders. "Is something wrong?"

"Do you remember when you spoke of what you felt in Tristan's Grove? Of how you felt about you and me?"

"Of course," Darry answered. "And that feeling has only grown stronger."

Jessa used her hands to pull herself forward, and the knees of her borrowed trousers slid upon the floor. The scroll was pushed until it was trapped between them as Jessa came to a stop and touched Darry's face. "You said your love was beyond what you understood, and that it was old and bottomless. You said it was meant to be, perhaps even from the moment you had been born."

Darry took Jessa's hand from her face, kissed it, and then held it within her own. "Aye, this is true. I'm sorry I can't explain it better. It sounds sort of silly, actually."

Jessa smiled. "But you're not wrong."

"I know."

"How do you know?"

"Because it's the truth."

Jessa gave a soft laugh. "Yes. It is *Senesh Akoata*."

"The Great Loom of the world, you said."

"Yes, *Senesh Akoata* is the spirit woven upon the Great Loom." Jessa paused, organizing her thoughts. "Some spirits are new to the world, and a new color is added to the tapestry when they enter into their life, a new thread is born. But some spirits…some spirits have been woven within the Loom since the gods first fashioned it."

"Even when the body is gone from the world, the spirit still moves upon the Loom," Darry said. "I remember."

"Yes." Jessa gave Darry's fingers a squeeze and then lifted both her hands into the air. "This air around us, there is a pull, it creates a desire within us. You can feel it deep within your soul." Her hands moved in a graceful arc. "And there is energy everywhere. Inherent within the air, and in all living things"—she set her hands upon her knees—"but it is also present within each of us, and in the things we feel. This creates forces in the world that are too numerous to count. When you see something of great beauty, and it takes your breath away, this feeling you have inside"—Jessa touched her chest—"the sensation of happiness, the joyous reaction you have, this is a kind of majik in and of itself. All things have energy like this, though most especially love. Love can pull you through time itself, and time is not what people think it is.

"But those souls, those spirits that have the ability to absorb this energy into their own life force—those spirits walk a deeper path upon the Great Loom. Some threads become weak, or their colors fade as they lose sight of this power, and though their splash of color within the tapestry may be bright, it is short-lived. But those that are strong, who allow this majik into their blood, they live long upon the Loom, and though their bodies die, their spirits do not. They move on, and some never fade. They move in threads of power and love through the tapestry, always in search of a familiar touch. They look for a new place to bloom, if only in part."

Jessa smiled and took hold of Darry's collar. "There are gifts in life that need substance, yes?"

"If I could not have the feel of your mouth upon my breasts?

If I could not look up from my thoughts and see you standing in the sun, or see your hair shine in the light from the fire? To hear you laugh again?" Darry said.

Jessa gave Darry's collar a gentle pull. "Yes, my love."

"I would search every thread upon your Great Loom, until I found even the smallest piece of you."

Jessa smiled happily. "And I would blossom within the birth of a new thread and make it old with my presence, bringing all that I could into a new body and a new life. I would endure any loneliness or any danger for just one more taste of the majik that was my love for you."

Darry's eyes were bright.

"This is *Senesh Akoata*," Jessa proclaimed and brushed the backs of her fingers against Darry's cheek. "But always there is a harmony, a pattern, a cohesion of substance. One spirit may travel down the ages, floating along their family's bloodline as if it were a boat upon a river. Another may be drawn to the beauty of a very specific object or a place, always returning. Those things that may pull at a spirit, they are as many as the stars in the sky. Only the gods may know them all. And some things? They are just meant to always be, and the Loom will let them travel as they will."

"This is a strong precept of your faith, yes?"

Jessa nodded as her attention strayed to Darry's lips. "Yes."

"I have heard this story before."

Jessa's eyes snapped up. "Where? Where did you hear it?"

Darry's expression was somewhat bemused. "I don't know."

"Do your priests tell of this?"

"No."

"Is there a face with the memory?" Jessa asked with care. "Can you see the person who spoke to you, in your mind's eye?"

Darry's grin was almost sheepish. "No."

Jessa's heart was filled with love. "It's all right, *Akasha*."

"What's in the scroll, Jess?"

"You and I, we move within the realm of *Senesh Akoata*. This is what you felt within Tristan's Grove, and what you continue to feel now."

"I've loved you before, haven't I."

It was not a question and Jessa knew it. "Not as Darry, no. You are who you are now, and no one else. But there is that in your spirit which has traveled through the Loom, and I believe your thread is very, very long."

"I think I understand."

"It is the same with me," Jessa added. "I have loved you before, *Akasha*." She reached out and laid her hand upon Darry's chest. "I have loved your beautiful spirit always," she whispered. "And in my dreams, you have always been there." Jessa dropped her hand to the scroll and picked it up. "And this," she said, "may have a great deal to do with us."

"Then let us read it," Darry replied simply.

Jessa undid the rawhide tie and the braid of hair came free as well. Darry grabbed them both before they hit the floor. She brought them to her nose, her expression filled with surprise.

"What?" Jessa asked.

"Jasmine."

Jessa laughed softly, leaned close and claimed a soft kiss. "I love you."

Darry's eyes flared brightly. "Open it already."

Jessa took hold of the lower edge and unrolled the scroll, the heavy parchment revealed before them as it settled upon the floorboards. The scroll was thick with writing, several languages accounted for, and littered throughout with runes, filling the surface to the edges.

"Bloody hell," Jessa cursed.

"I can't read that," Darry said in a disgruntled tone.

Jessa laughed. "Neither can I."

"*What?*"

"Not all of it," Jessa amended. "My lovely Radha plays to win." She ran her fingers gently upon the uppermost text. "This I can read"—her touch skated down the parchment—"but this is High Vhaelin, and written by a Shaman. I will need several books to translate it properly."

"Do you have them?"

"In my rooms within the Jade Palace. But this, this here…"
Jessa felt the runes near the bottom of the scroll, mixed within a
script she did not recognize. "I have no idea what this is."

"That is most unfortunate," Darry commented, her tone
annoyed and amused at the same time, "and quite possibly, the very
definition of nasty."

Jessa laughed.

"What does the top part say?" Darry's touch was careful as she
ran a finger along a line of letters. "It's very pretty, actually."

"Let me see, my love," Jessa said softly and leaned over as
Darry pulled her hand away. "Unto the hide of the stag, here I
commit the history of the Vhaelin High Priestess, Neela Jhannina de
Hahvay, mother of all sacred peoples, and that of Tannen Ahru, War
Chief of the Red-Tail Clan and protector of all sacred peoples. All
knowledge in its proper time shall be revealed."

"Tannen Ahru?"

Jessa's eyes were quick to find her lover's as her heart gave a
hard beat within her chest. "You know this name?"

Darry was shocked by the question. "Do *you* know of Tannen
Ahru? I mean, you have to, don't you?"

"Yes, I know of Tannen Ahru. But how do you know of her?"
Jessa insisted.

"Are you asking me how I know about one of the greatest
swordswomen to ever live?" Darry sat back. "My mother used to
tell me stories, when I was small and I would grow angry at my
wooden sword while my brothers held only the finest of steel. She
said the day I could put a proper name to the brave deeds and the
daring adventures that were my bedtime stories was the day she
would give me a true sword."

"*Cecelia* told you of Tannen Ahru?"

"My mother is very well-read, and I had no idea the tales she
told me were of a woman until I read about the Craven Men at the
Singewood. I spent many hours in the library at Gamar's temple,
which I'm sure was my mother's true purpose." Darry's pleasure at
the memory was obvious, and then Jessa watched the joy in her eyes
change into something else altogether.

Jessa's left hand found her lover's face. *"Akasha."*

Darry tipped to the side and Jessa's hand was quick to find the back of Darry's neck in order to steady her. She slid closer and Darry stared into her eyes.

"All is well, *Akasha*." Jessa felt tears well up in reaction to the stricken look upon her lover's face. "You are Darry, and no one else. You are still the girl who lamented her wooden sword and tipped over the Blackwood Throne. You are Hinsa's *Cha-Diah* child and Bentley's dearest friend. This thread has always been a part of you, remember? There is nothing new that has suddenly been added."

"Lovers?" Darry asked softly.

"Neela Jhannina de Hahvay, hers is the thread that I walk, just as you walk Tannen Ahru's. And in their time, they were the greatest of lovers." Jessa smiled. "If we must live up to anything, let it be that, yes?" Jessa kissed her and her lips lingered for a tender moment.

"Your mother's name," Darry whispered as she began to regain her balance. "Jhannina."

"Yes, I didn't know she was named for Neela."

"A name for the poets."

Jessa kissed Darry once more as she remembered their night upon her small terrace in the Keep. To have finally spoken her mother's name aloud had been a great victory for her. "Are you all right?"

"Yes, I'm fine, truly."

Jessa looked hard into Darry's eyes and made the judgment for herself. "There's a bit more that I can read...should I read it?"

Darry considered the question and then gave a nod.

Jessa let her go and turned, then pulled the scroll closer with a quick tug. She flipped the lower half under and concentrated upon the Vhaelin script she could understand. "All knowledge in its proper time shall be revealed," Jessa read, "though a token is to be given at once, returned to its rightful owner."

"A token?" Darry asked quietly.

"First and foremost, my daughters," Jessa continued, "I return the Blue Vale sword of Tannen Ahru. Look no further, Darrius

Durand"—Jessa looked up slowly and searched across the room—"than your own sword belt."

Darry's eyes widened and she turned. Her sword belt hung upon the peg near the curved staircase and the twisted silver guard caught the firelight and flared brightly.

"Lost for fifteen generations, this blade is rightfully yours." Jessa looked up as Darry spun upon her hip, rose to her feet, and walked across the chamber. "Stolen in the Battle of Black Notch, at the foot of the Kistanbal Mountains, it is my greatest honor to gift you with its return."

Darry took hold of the scabbard and the belt slipped from the peg. She slid the fingers of her right hand about the grip, her touch slow and deliberate as she turned back into the room.

The sword felt good in her hand. It felt as if it belonged there, more than any other sword she had ever held. She had felt that within the Great Hall as she had moved through the Dance. The steel had sung its song and matched her every breath, and she knew even then that this sword would be hers until the end of her days. It was perfectly weighted and balanced like no other weapon she had ever seen. It contained the strength of a backbreaking wind, but it had moved with the ease of a soft summer breeze —the power and the simple grace made absolute within the steel as she had carved her way through the enemy.

"I knew it," Darry whispered and drew the sword.

The Blue Vale steel hissed from the scabbard and hit the air with a clean ping of sound, its bright edge instantly alight with reflected flames.

"The scroll says that it's called—"

"Zephyr Wind," Darry said. "She's called the Zephyr Wind."

"Yes," Jessa whispered.

Darry considered the weapon in her hand and then lowered it, her eyes traveling down its length as the firelight flashed in a bold manner upon the steel.

Her imagination had never been found lacking, and she had always taken pride in an open mind. That there were gods in the world that were not hers, she had accepted, and she had always respected them. Those that found comfort and strength beneath their grace were no different than she was, and she had always honored the freedom to choose.

But Gamar had blessed her at birth, and though she did not find her way to his temple as often as she should, the path to his door was her path. She had always known that, and she had been consoled by the certainty of his presence. She had prayed to him in need and she had honored him in wonder, and she had known peace in the fact that he would appreciate both.

It was said that Gamar honored a life well lived, and even in the dark times when she had lost her hope, she had tried to live well.

"*Akasha?*" Jessa asked softly.

"I don't understand all of this, not really," Darry admitted as she met Jessa's eyes across the room. Jessa wiped away a stray tear and smiled. "If you tell me that I once lived life as Tannen Ahru, I'm not sure I believe that."

Jessa pushed to her feet and took a tentative step. "Do you *feel* it?"

"I feel *you*," Darry answered, and it was the truth. All that she had ever wanted was but a few steps away, and that was a strange and delightful comfort. Strange, because she had lived without it for so long, and delightful, because she could not remember what that felt like at the moment. "And that is all I have ever believed."

"*Senesh Akoata* does not need your belief, my love."

"What about my faith?"

"Your faith is your own. The Great Loom of the world goes on whether we are here or not. It has no need to quibble with matters of individual faith."

"But do you, Jess?" Darry's quiet tone was laced with concern. If she could not believe in something so essential to Jessa's life, where would that take them?

"Not in the least." Jessa answered. "And besides, I have a much more pressing concern than discussing religious philosophy."

Darry let out a breath of laughter. "And what is that?"

"I need your arms around me."

Darry sheathed her sword and gave it a long look before she tossed it to the bed where it landed near their pillows upon the quilt. When she looked back, her eyes were dark and filled with feeling. "Come to me."

Jessa obeyed, her steps carefully measured as she crossed the room upon bare feet. She stopped only when she stood close, her eyes drawn to Darry's lips.

Darry closed the gap between them, and her hand slid upon Jessa's neck before it fisted within her braids. "This need you have, I share it," Darry whispered as Jessa rested against her. "And it has very little to do with your scrolls."

"No," Jessa agreed, moving against her lover. "No, there is only us, my love." Darry's hips were tight and hot to the touch as her hands moved beneath the waist of Darry's trousers. Darry's body was forever a temptation, always filled with sleek strength and sensual in its movements, even in the most casual act.

Darry spoke softly beside Jessa's ear. "I'm afraid there will be a price for this."

"I will pay it," Jessa promised. "Kiss me, please."

Darry eyes were bright as she pulled back, but she did not kiss her.

"I have loved you, *Akasha*, for as long as I can remember." The intensity of Darry's gaze thrilled Jessa beyond measure, for despite Darry's untamed expression she held control over Jessa's happiness in a very matter-of-fact and certain manner. "And I have missed you," Jessa added as heavy tears filled her eyes. They fell down her cheeks and she let them. "I have missed you for even longer."

Darry kissed her, her mouth open and yet gentle in her passion. Jessa returned the deed in kind and her knees went weak as Darry tightened her embrace.

"You are"—Jessa's lips pressed close as she spoke—"mine."

Darry looked into her eyes. "I've missed you, too."

"Do not do anything foolish tomorrow."

"I won't," Darry assured her.

"Do not leave me. You must swear it."

When Darry kissed her in answer, Jessa accepted her promise.

CHAPTER NINETEEN

L ike the Circle of Honor which lay before them, Jessa knew there were many arenas scattered throughout both Arravan and Lyoness where justice would be meted out. Nearly eighty feet in diameter, it was surrounded by four rows of tiered seats that stacked up and back, the ring completed by a simple platform at the north end for the king and queen and the royal party. The chairs set there were made of blackwood, and the carving was simple and clean. Though the cushions were made of silk, they might have been found in the home of any Blooded Lord.

The curved tiers were filled with important men and Lords of rank, the late-morning sun tinged with the first real heat of summer and bright upon the eyes. Jessa stood upon the dais between Emmalyn and Jacob and waited. Hinsa sat before them and swished her tail as she tipped to the left in a lazy manner, and Emmalyn stared down at her with curious eyes as the weight of the panther pushed against her legs.

"She likes to lean," Jessa explained, and she knew that her voice trembled. She had put on the sable-colored dress that matched her eyes, the dress she had worn for her first official tea with Prince Malcolm, and she felt hot and overdressed. Emmalyn wore a similar outfit, however, as did the queen, so she was certain that etiquette had been served. Her stomach rolled in a rather uncomfortable manner.

Joaquin stood upon the opposite end of the circle, looking freshly scrubbed and wearing his scarlet trousers tucked into his high boots. Commander Grissom Longshanks was nearby to attend to his needs, and Joaquin undid the top buttons of his white tunic with his left hand as he swung his sword before his feet. A small line of dust rose in its wake and he smiled.

The crowd stood in a single wave of movement as Darry entered the circle, followed closely by Bentley and Arkady Winnows. She wore black trousers tucked into her boots and a dark red tunic, the sleeves rolled above her elbows.

Owen and Cecelia stepped to the platform and moved to their seats, silent as Darry took her place but a dozen feet away. Bentley held out Darry's scabbard and she pulled Zephyr Wind free in a smooth move, the Blue Vale steel a lure for the sun as it flashed brightly into the assembled crowd.

Darry felt the weight of the sword in her hand and listened to the air around it as she turned the blade in the light, the song it sang a familiar one. She must've read the name in a scroll many years ago, she reasoned. It was the perfect name.

"Darry."

Darry looked to her left. Bentley looked in her eyes and then reached out and flicked his fingers against her chin.

Darry jerked her head back at the playful touch.

"Where's your head?" Bentley asked in a quiet voice, though she could not mistake the harshness of his tone.

Darry smiled. "Busy."

"Then bloody well fix it," he told her. "This is not the time for daydreaming about how lovely your Lady looks."

"Never you mind how my Lady looks." Darry frowned.

Bentley chuckled. "It's hot and sticky and I want my lunch. Don't make me kill that poor pig just to avenge your untimely death before I've eaten my first decent meal of the day."

"Perhaps you just wish to sit beside my cousin at lunch," Darry teased, and Bentley's eyes widened.

Arkady tilted his head and gestured toward their friend. "I think he's blushing."

"Of course he is," Darry replied and took a step away from

them as she gave her sword a wider arc. She felt the pull of her still-healing injuries and cursed beneath her breath.

"Leave your cousin out of this," Bentley responded. "She's not...I wouldn't ever..."

"Ever what?" Darry asked as she rolled her shoulders, her muscles loose and ready. She flashed him a smile. "Don't be cross, Lord Greeves."

The High King stepped to the front of the platform and all eyes turned to him, the silence within the circle and those gathered around it absolute. "Let the debt be paid," he said simply. "And let honor be restored."

Darry found Jessa's eyes for a long moment and let the touch of a smile come forth. Jessa wore the dress that she had once admired from afar, and for a brief second, she remembered the pain of knowing that Jessa had worn it for Malcolm as they had walked through the gardens. *But no longer is it so, and you are my love, sweet Jess, for now and for always.* Darry turned away and walked to the center of the circle.

Joaquin smiled as he came forward, his walk smooth and his shoulders back.

Darry sized him up with an expert eye. He had the range but not the legs.

"It's not the prick of the sword I would prefer"—Joaquin spoke softly as he flipped his braid back over his left shoulder—"but you might like the taste of this one, as well."

Darry stopped and took her stance, just beyond his reach.

"You know," Joaquin spoke only for her, his voice a tender breath of words, "you won't be the first woman I've killed."

Darry noted the hard turn of his right foot, his toes pointed inward slightly and his stress held on the outside of his foot. He brought his sword up and his weight was pushed forward as a result.

"Nothing clever to say, *cunta*?"

The bell from the watchtower chimed but once, and Darry struck high and to his right before it was done. Their swords rang out as Joaquin blocked her blade and moved awkwardly as he tried to correct his balance. Darry spun around him as her steel sparked along his own, and she struck before her circle was complete.

Joaquin sidestepped to the right, stood straight, and found Darry where she had stood but a moment before.

Darry tossed his long braid into the dirt between his boots. "Footwork."

Joaquin felt the back of his head and swung his sword between them. "Your brother was right," he offered, his tone sharp with anger. "You are the family amusement."

Darry let him attack and threw his aim off with a double blow of her blade as he lunged. The second impact surprised him, and he brought his back foot forward as he tried to follow her, her tempo clearly faster than he had anticipated.

Darry slid Zephyr Wind upon the false edge of his sword and gave her wrist a twist as she stepped back, forcing Joaquin to arch his back as he turned to meet her new position.

He felt his chin and his fingertips came away stained with blood.

"Footwork," Darry said softly.

Joaquin stepped forward and swung his sword from left to right as Darry leaned back smoothly. The blade passed her and she brought the back edge of her sword up as she moved the other way. The Blue Vale steel caught beneath the notch of his left ear and sliced through the cartilage.

A wave of noise moved through the assembled crowd as Joaquin stumbled beyond her reach. He pinned his ear against the side of his head and the blood ran between his fingers and down the back of his hand.

Darry kept pace with him and faced him as he wiped his hand upon his tunic. "Here," she said politely as she took up her first stance once more. "Try that move again."

Joaquin stepped forward and took his place, his face red and his eyes vivid with color. His weight was properly placed and his shoulders turned to match his style as Darry noted his focused expression.

She met his attack and gave ground in a measured manner as she deflected each strike of his blade. He was not a bad swordsmen, but he was not practiced, and he had perhaps never fought in earnest against an opponent that would do him harm if given the opportunity. *There are no personal guards to help you now, my good Prince.* His left shoulder lowered and his weight shifted hard onto his forward foot. She turned and circled his blade, her steel strung along Joaquin's until she could dip her weapon beneath his own and come back up. Zephyr Wind caught hold of the gold quillon of his wrapped guard, and Darry put her shoulder into it.

Joaquin's sword was flung from his hand and skittered across the hard-packed earth as Darry stepped a bit closer, placing the tip of her sword hard beneath the base of Joaquin's throat. Her arm was extended gracefully and with perfect form, the steel an extension of her body as she stood him straight and guided him backward.

"Footwork," Darry said again as she struck swiftly. The edge of her blade cut the notch beneath his right ear, the wound a perfect match to the one she'd already given him.

Joaquin jerked away from the pain, and Darry turned her back on him as she walked to his fallen sword and slipped the toe of her boot beneath the blade. His sword rose into the air with a kick, and she caught the grip as she turned back around.

Joaquin slid to an unruly stop, and Darry could smell his fear as she met his eyes, Joaquin's forward progress stalled by her smooth turn. Fear was a sharp, intense odor beneath his sweat, and Darry's blood surged and her majik rose.

"If I wound you for each time you have abused your sister," Darry said into the silence of the circle, "then we shall be here all day." Darry tossed him his weapon and he stepped back to catch it.

Joaquin narrowed his eyes at her, his hand fierce upon the grip of his sword. "What do you care about Malcolm's broodmare, *cunta*?" he said softly. "If it can't be my cock inside her again, it might as well be his."

Darry felt each word as he spoke it, and from the platform at the top of the Circle, Hinsa screamed her sudden rage. Darry's blood stuttered within her veins and then burst forth in a flood of instinct.

Joaquin thrust his weapon but Darry knocked it aside and then up as she ducked beneath it all and their bodies collided. His weight was greater than hers, but she lifted him nonetheless and his body flipped up and over her head.

Darry stumbled to the side as he hit the ground, the breath knocked from his lungs as the back of his head thumped against the hard-packed earth.

"Get up!" Darry shouted as all of her fury was released.

Many within the crowd surged to their feet as Joaquin rolled onto his side and pushed to his knees. He grabbed his fallen sword but before he could fully stand, he was forced to defend.

Darry pushed him back, her sword a blur of light as Joaquin tried in vain to protect himself. The sound of steel as it clashed filled the air, and Darry would not relent as Joaquin stumbled and the tip of her sword sliced open his right cheek.

The crowd reacted and individual voices became a single roar. The sound rolled in a swell through the heat, and several shouts rose above the hum as they sensed the end was near.

❖

Jessa let out a hard breath and moved without thought. *"Akasha."*

Owen reacted quickly and swept her back from the edge of the platform with a firm hand. "No, Jessa, you cannot."

Jessa took hold of his vest with both hands, and he pulled her close as Darry rushed Joaquin.

Jessa took a breath and remembered the first time Joaquin had struck her. She had been but eight years old, and the summer moon had been high, just two days before Solstice.

Joaquin's left sleeve was torn as the skin upon his shoulder was slashed.

Jessa remembered the first time he had grabbed and twisted her breast, the fierce pain it had caused suddenly fresh within her mind. He had been watching her as she slept, and she had awoken, terrified and defenseless until Radha had appeared but moments later. The old woman had incurred Joaquin's wrath, though he had stopped short of violence.

Joaquin's collarbone was next and then his right thigh in the downward arc of Darry's blade. His white shirt was splattered with blood.

Jessa remembered his voice within the throne room. *Yes, I sent him to kill her, though what does it matter?*

Darry's sword punctured his left biceps and Joaquin cried out in pain.

Jessa remembered the whispers and the tears when her maid Lahi-Jal had been found strangled. She had been raped, the cooks said, as Jessa had stood beneath the Veil of Shadows in the kitchens. It had been Joaquin, the woman said, *I saw him in the laundry with her that morning and then she was gone for sure, poor thing.* The talk had gone on and on—Joaquin had followed Lahi-Jal for weeks, and Joaquin had baited her with fresh grapes from the coast. *If that sweet little Lark isn't careful, she'll be next, just as pretty as her mother was...*

There was a sharp ping of sound as Joaquin's sword left his hand and seemed to jump upward, the blue sky bright behind it.

Zephyr Wind entered Joaquin's chest but a heartbeat later, and Darry stepped close as she pushed the strike home, earning a roar from the crowd as the killing blow was dealt and Darry's blade speared Joaquin's back.

Jessa watched as Darry stepped close and spoke to him, though they were too far away and the noise around them was too great for her to hear. Darry's left hand landed upon his face and she pushed him away as she drew her sword free.

Joaquin folded to the ground as the calls took on a definite rhythm. The soldiers who had gathered beyond the Circle called out Darry's name as Hinsa jumped from the platform and ran to her, unafraid of the cheers as she went to inspect their kill.

Owen bent his head close to Jessa's ear, and Jessa realized that she had turned her face to his chest. He smelled of soap and sandalwood, a clean, soothing scent. "It's over, my young Queen," he said in a gentle voice. It calmed her almost at once and she loosened her hands from his silk vest. "Your love has served justice upon the man who tried to kill you."

Jessa turned her head in time to see the gold coins fall from Darry's hand and land upon the chest of Prince Trey-Jak Joaquin, a Prince of the Blood no more.

CHAPTER TWENTY

Jessa stood behind the Healer as he tended Darry's wound, and Jessa held her tongue with no small amount of effort. Darry had ripped the stitches clean through, and when Jessa had finally reached her after the chaos of her victory, Darry's red shirt was plastered to her ribs and soaked with blood. To see the blood had been a physical shock to Jessa, and her legs had been less than confident as Bentley and Arkady escorted them from the yards amidst the crowd. Arkady's hand was familiar upon her elbow and his offered strength had been greatly welcomed. She had wanted to hold Darry in her arms but had refrained, uncertain with so many Lords of the realm and strangers around them.

The Healer applied a fresh poultice next and wrapped Darry's ribs with quick, expert hands as she sat upon the side of their bed. Jessa understood the wound would have to heal anew, and there was a greater chance of infection because of the reinjury. Neither of these things made Jessa happy, and her stomach cramped with anxiety as the Healer helped Darry into a clean tunic.

"Thank you, Master Devon," Darry said in a rough voice, her complexion pale and her usual fire completely absent from her demeanor.

He held out a wooden cup. "Drink it, Lady Darrius. I know your pain is great."

Darry's hand trembled as she took the cup and she looked up with a stubborn expression.

"Drink it," Jessa ordered, and she knew her voice was tight and somewhat harsh.

Darry obeyed, then handed the cup back to him.

"Get some sleep," he instructed and tidied his leather satchel. He stood up and gave Jessa a kind smile. "See that she sleeps, my Lady. In the morning, you should change the poultice. Do you have goldenseal?"

"Yes."

"Make a tea for her, two full measures to start with."

"Yes," Jessa answered again as the back of her right hand pressed against her forehead for an instant. "Thank you."

"You know what needs to be done, my Lady," he added. "All will be well...though you could use some rest, too, no doubt."

Jessa let out a startled laugh and met his eyes. "Yes."

"I'll let myself out." He touched her arm. "Send for me if you have need."

Jessa listened to his boots upon the stairs and took a step forward as she waited for Darry to look up. When Darry refused to meet her eyes, Jessa took another step. "*Akasha?*"

"I couldn't stop it," Darry whispered.

Jessa went instantly to her knees before her lover and raised Darry's face with gentle hands. "My love, my love..." She pushed at Darry's curls and saw the tears. "My heart, please don't cry, please," Jessa begged, and her own throat tightened. Darry's eyes were bleak and haunted, empty of their familiar brightness. "You must tell me what happened."

"I couldn't stop it," Darry repeated simply.

Jessa pushed upward and kissed her, her lips hungry for the flavor of Darry's mouth, though hungrier still for the taste of her presence. "What happened, *Akasha?*" she asked in a whisper so soft that not even her gods would hear.

Darry's eyes were heavy and Jessa could see that the passionflower syrup was already at work, Darry's pupils larger than they should be, her expression filled with helplessness. "Did he... did he rape you?"

Jessa's soul reeled in surprise at the words, her hands tender but firm as what was left of Darry's strength began to fade. "Joaquin?"

Huge tears welled up in Darry's eyes and then spilled over. "What good is all this *Senesh*...this *Senesh* threads, if I couldn't keep you safe?"

Jessa kissed her, her heart full with an ache so terrible that she could barely breathe. Her blood ran hot and she could feel the burn beneath her skin like never before. Runes and spells suddenly raced unimpeded, and it took all her control to rein them in. She stood slowly and Darry's head tipped back, Jessa's hands deep within her lover's wild, thick curls. Her lips brushed Darry's ear. "He never touched me," she said and her voice shook. She pulled back. "Did he say that he did?"

Darry's eyes were filled with pain. "I should've been there, Jess."

Jessa braced the back of Darry's neck as she began to tip to the side, and Jessa guided her onto the softness of the bed. "He never touched me, *Akasha*, do you hear?" Darry's eyes began to close. "Darry?"

When she received no answer, Jessa lifted Darry's legs up and over, grabbed the quilt, and covered her as best as she could. Darry's breathing was shallow but steady, and for a moment Jessa worried that Devon had given her too much.

Darry mumbled incoherently as her eyes fluttered closed and she slipped away.

"Hush." Jessa turned her head as soft voices floated upward from the lower level. Her fingernails dug into her palms as she stepped back from the bed, though she was unable to accommodate the bone-deep anger she felt merely by making a fist.

She turned with a swirl of her skirts and made her way to the stairs, her hand upon the stones as she descended. Her eyes took in the room, but there was only one person who waited.

"Devon says she'll be fine," Owen offered, though she did not accept his words. He took a deep breath as he considered her fierce expression. "Perhaps I should..."

Jessa held her tongue, afraid to unleash her thoughts.

"When Cecelia has such a look about her, something usually gets broken."

"Yes, and do you tell her to calm down?" Jessa asked, and her tone had bite.

"I usually give her something to break."

Jessa stared at him for what seemed like a lifetime, and then quite against her will, she laughed. There was an edge to the sound, but it felt right and she let it out. She covered her mouth and looked away, all of her emotions tangled together like the thick, dark vines of the Tarsem tree.

"And then if I'm lucky," Owen added, "she does not throw it at my head."

"Darry gave me a plate not two days ago." Jessa's voice was tired but decidedly amused. She wiped absently at her eyes, surprised at the turn of her emotions and annoyed at the resulting exhaustion. "A rather lovely one with a fine blue glaze."

"What did he say to her?"

Jessa held his gaze but did not reply.

"My daughter and I may not get along...and you needn't tell me that it's my fault. But I know her better than everyone thinks I do."

"It does not matter," Jessa answered, though she knew it was more relevant than most things. "He is dead now."

"It mattered to her."

Jessa leaned against the worktable and her body trembled with fatigue. It had become a familiar sensation as of late, to her displeasure. "I once told my Radha that my heart was of no use to anyone, and I believed it."

Owen held out his hand. "Please, Jessa, come and sit."

Jessa considered the offer and then accepted. She was not certain why he was here and not Cecelia, but he was, and it was an unexpected comfort to her. Owen took her elbow when she neared. He let her sit first upon the divan and then joined her, not too far away, and yet not so near that it would be improper.

"There was also a time, not long ago, when I thought I was free," Jessa mused aloud. "But that's not exactly true, either."

Owen gave a sigh in agreement. "Love is not always what people think it is."

"If he were not dead already, I would kill him for hurting her," Jessa proclaimed and knew it for the truth. "And if hurting her were not crime enough, I would kill him for using me to do it."

Owen glanced toward the stairs.

Jessa looked down at her hands. "I have eleven other brothers," she whispered. "And she will try and protect me from all of them."

"Of course she will."

"I can't allow her to do that." She looked up to meet his gaze.

Owen smiled in a rueful manner. "You really don't have a say in that."

"Of course I do."

Owen chuckled and then cleared his throat in politeness.

"You do not think I have a say in such things?" Jessa demanded as her anger rose to the surface once more.

Owen seemed to consider his response with care. "Part of my fear, concerning Darrius, has always been that she lives to the brim of her cup, as my mother used to say." His shoulders eased back against the divan. "When she rushed the Fakir in the Great Hall, I could not have been more horrified, yet I knew she would do it before *she* did, most likely. She has very little fear about such things." He glanced at her. "And this is not a comfortable feeling for a father to have. But what I always seem to forget is that her odds of walking out the other side always seem to support her decision to rush in."

"That is not enough," Jessa argued.

Owen chuckled. "Of course it isn't, but it's all I have at the moment."

Jessa smiled against her better judgment. "That doesn't do me a lot of good."

"No, you're right."

"What is it about men that makes them feel they may take from a woman that which she will not give?" Jessa asked. It was a question she had never been able to voice before, feeling certain for the first time that she would receive a truthful answer.

"Do you speak of a particular woman?"

"I speak of *all* women, I suppose, who possess something a man might covet. A woman who possesses gold or power, or the advantages of both. A woman who has skills to match a man's. Or one who is not considered beautiful by a man's standards but is his equal in every way. A woman who will not do as she is told. All of these women are the same. They are considered a liability and thus held to a standard they are not allowed to meet. They are a threat."

"Not all men feel that way."

"No, I know this. But I cannot help thinking, what was I?" Jessa replied simply. "Nothing but a piece of meat, to be bartered off to the highest bidder. It is no matter that it was a Prince of the Blood who laid down his coin, *your* coin, I might add. Or to be brought out, as I was, and paraded before Bharjah's allies like a prize they might win. To sing the songs of my people, only to have them made into a prank by my father, the words that my mother once sang with all reverence and faith. And all the while, my love was *here*, trying in vain to win something she had no chance of winning. Always left wanting as she followed your rules but was not allowed to succeed. Always trying in vain to understand why she was an outcast."

"I did not cast her out," Owen said, and his voice was somewhat curt.

"Perhaps—but did you have the right to deny her the girl she loved?"

Owen did not respond.

"And it is no matter that you did me a tremendous favor in that," Jessa added in a wry but slightly reluctant tone. "Had this Aidan girl had the chance to love my Darry free from fear, I would've had to wrestle the gods themselves, I'm sure, in order to win her away."

Owen smiled at that.

"Would you have done the same if Darry were your son and he had loved a pretty young boy? Would you have stolen your son's honor as easily as you did your daughter's?"

Owen grimaced. "Do you always talk so plainly?"

"Radha always says that to do otherwise is a waste of everyone's time."

Owen let out a grudging laugh. "I'm surrounded by a whole bloody pack of you."

"Answer the question, please."

Owen's brown eyes sparked, though he did not look displeased. "I don't know."

Jessa reached out and briefly touched his hand. "At least you answer honestly."

"We've never found much common ground, Darry and I."

Jessa allowed her surprise to show on her face. "But she follows in your footsteps," she disagreed with conviction. "There is common ground between you everywhere you look. It is just not the ground you expected, or were hoping for." She shook her head. "Your reasoning is not sound."

Once again, Owen was silent.

"When she's in pain," Jessa whispered, and the tears came so easily she had no chance to stop them. "I wish to lay waste to every *fikloche* thing in my path." She wiped at her nose with her sleeve and did not care.

Owen reached out. "It is the same with all lovers," he whispered as he brushed away a tear.

Jessa looked up at him. "And I should probably add that knowing I could do just that? It does not seem to help in the least."

Owen laughed softly and set his hand on the top of her head. "As to *that* one, my young Queen, you are most likely all on your own."

CHAPTER TWENTY-ONE

D arry stood at the end of the bed and watched Jessa sleep, her curls and braids scattered upon the pillow.

Jessa wore but a soft blue tunic that Darry had never seen before, and the faded color was quite lovely against the dark tone of Jessa's beautiful skin, its color almost unbearably soft against the texture of the fabric. Even in sleep Jessa looked exhausted, and Darry felt some guilt in that, for she knew she had been a major cause of Jessa's anxiety for the past few days. Her knack for finding trouble was not as amusing as it once had been, now that she had someone else to consider.

The sheet was tangled about Jessa's legs, and Darry gave a tender smile at the skin that was exposed.

The relief she felt at Jessa's words went to the very heart of her. The thought that Joaquin had abused Jessa in such a manner had thrown her utterly off balance, and it was a fear that she should have acknowledged sooner. There were many sons of Bharjah who, by their reputations alone, were considered quite vile, regardless of what the truth might actually be. That Jessa had come of age amongst them all, with very little authority that might have kept their desires and cruelty in check, was a hard fact.

While *Senesh Akoata* was a new concept to her, the fact that she had loved Jessa since before she had been born as Darrius Durand was not a revelation. It had always been Jessa, and though she had loved Aidan with the enthusiasm of youth, she had said what she meant the night that she and Jessa had first made love. Aidan had left because Jessa was coming, for Jessa was Darry's truth. She always had been and she always would be.

Tannen Ahru of the Red-Tail Clan? If you're in there somewhere, I hope you're not overly disappointed in where you've landed.

Darry touched the covers of the bed for a long moment and then crossed the room. She stopped at the stairs and considered her sword as it hung upon the peg.

The Circle of Honor had been a strange place and not what she had expected. It had been clean and oddly quiet and her mind had cleared the moment she had faced Joaquin. Every lesson she had ever learned and every skill she had absorbed into her style throughout the years had all melted into a wonderfully cohesive force. Pure and without restraint, she had felt her strength and knowledge become a single entity. The Dance was a weapon she had not needed, and she knew it the instant the watchtower bell had tolled. It had not been pleasant, the knowledge that she would kill him, but it felt like justice. And who better to mete out that punishment than Jessa's lover.

His words had tipped her balance, though, and a shiver moved up her spine as she recalled the flood of violence. The rush of her *Cha-Diah* blood and the instinct to kill her enemy had crushed everything in its path. It had been a fire that washed through her veins, and her senses had filled with the smell of his flesh. She could hear his heartbeat race and his heavy breathing had been a storm within her head. The rage had been absolutely pure.

She was surprised even now that she had been able to stop. That once Joaquin was dead, her temper had flowed from her soul like the last harsh wind of a spring storm upon the Sellen Sea. *Though that is not enough*, she thought and felt afraid. *If I have no control over my own blood, what shall our fate be, should I stand before such rage again?*

"Darry?" Bentley's voice called softly from below. "Are you ready?"

Darry turned away from Zephyr Wind and slowly took the stairs without her weapon, her boots quiet as she trailed her hand along the stones for balance.

❖

Darry walked through the dark corridor and did not mind the absence of light. Her eyes had adjusted quite well as she had walked through the maze, and even though she was less than fit, she had moved unseen through the solar doors. Though she did not employ her gift of stealth as Hinsa did, in the hunt for food, the skill had always provided an advantage when needed.

The entrance to the throne room was open, the right door pushed inward several feet as if to beckon her inside. She stopped at the threshold before she answered the invitation.

Her instincts were alive with the sense of danger and she did not question them. They were a part of her gift and her majik had never failed her. That its secret presence had set her apart had often been a burden, but no longer. When she had called Hinsa from the maze and their powers had finally been revealed, there had been a tremendous shift in her abilities. Her senses were deeper and more powerful, and though they were her own senses, they were now Hinsa's, as well.

Each smell was more pungent and startling, or more aromatic and sweet. Each taste was more volatile on her tongue, sharp and rich with spices she had once been oblivious to, or bitter beyond what she had known before, as with her karrem in the morning, the hot liquid much too overwhelming for her now.

Her physical power was more intense, and she could feel the urge to push things to their limits, to learn what more she might be capable of. Movements that seemed slow to her before were now sleek and fluid, and she was beyond them before her thoughts could catch up. She needed to establish a secure rhythm and a new pace. She needed to find her tipping point before someone else did.

Joaquin found it easily enough, she thought, *though without the consequences he was hoping for*. He had set off her fury, but he had been clueless as to what that would actually mean for him.

With her new strength she would need to learn new boundaries. She had not expected the uncontrolled and brutal rush of her emotions, and she recognized that this would be the most difficult problem to solve in her search for balance. Her restraints had shifted, and what she could once hide from others was perhaps vulnerable now to detection.

She could smell the rich earth of the Green Hills in the middle of the night, the fertile and heady loam of the earth and mud, as well as the tang of new foliage as it burst with life. The calls of the forest invaded her sleep, the movements in the undergrowth and the hum of the earth, the rubbing of a linnet's wings as it settled upon a branch far above.

But that she could no longer gauge the rush of her anger when it arrived in full force was something else altogether.

She could not stop life as it moved forward, so she would have to adjust more quickly if at all possible. She was not sure if she would have the time to do otherwise.

Darry turned her head and listened for a moment, then smiled within a breath when she heard what she needed. She pushed open the door and stepped over the threshold.

Her pupils expanded and then tightened in a heartbeat as she took in the room.

Malcolm sat upon the Blackwood Throne, his leg thrown over the left arm as he lounged upon their father's chair, but a single lamp lit above him.

Darry understood this would be the first real test of her control, and as she walked down the aisle she felt his eyes upon her.

"Well if it isn't the hero of the realm," Malcolm said in a quiet voice.

Darry made no comment as she approached, and after what seemed like a very long time, she came to a stop just beyond the edge of the dais.

"It's good to see you survived your altercation intact."

"Sorry about your little pet," Darry returned in a dry tone. She could actually smell the threat he represented, and she tried to arrange the knowledge within her thoughts. He was more of a predator as he sat at his leisure than he had ever been before.

Malcolm's right elbow did not leave the chair as he gave a dismissive wave of his hand. "Not to worry, dear sister."

"Why?" Darry asked. "Are there more where that one came from?"

Malcolm's eyes flashed and he smiled. "Are you going to play at politics now?"

"Are you in over your head and in need of my help?"

"Do not concern yourself with such complicated things. You are the stick that men such as I use to beat our enemies. You are above your station at the moment."

Darry noted that the tension within his body did not match the scene he had so carefully prepared.

"I see your lickspittle delivered my message. Thank you for coming."

"You need to leave me alone now, Mal," Darry said plainly. "I am no longer in your way, and I have no more concerns as to the affairs of the crown. I have relinquished my title and my command, as I'm sure you know."

Malcolm let out a breath of amusement. "Yes, thank you for that."

"So why am I here?"

"Do you enjoy fucking my wife?" Malcolm inquired and his tone had changed. It was slight, but Darry felt the sharpness of it like the taste of a misplaced needle. "Does her spirit taste hot and sweet upon your tongue when you make her spend?"

Darry resisted the urge to step forward before the impulse had fully formed within her muscles. "Your wife?"

"Does she moan and writhe beneath you?" Malcolm lowered his voice as if they were sharing secrets, and his smile was filled with condescension. "Does she cry out your name?"

"We can discuss that later." Darry struck quickly. "When did I miss the wedding?"

Malcolm ignored her and Darry felt his eyes rake over her from head to toe. He seemed to consider several comments, as if the confrontation he had plotted within his mind did not match the one he was actually a part of. "If only you had a cock to push inside her, your life would be complete."

His comment took Darry by surprise, though she was not sure why and her sharp tongue took the lead. "I know a rather naughty shop where I can purchase one, but I appreciate your concern," she returned in a wry voice. "For the love of Gamar, Mal, you sound like Melora."

Malcolm scoffed. "Why do you always assume you may have whatever you want? If something catches your fancy, no matter the consequences, you do as you please."

Darry waited, her eyes keen upon the flush of heat along his throat. She watched his blood pulse beneath the meager protection of his skin, and she wondered if he understood how fragile he was. *How fragile we both are*, she reminded herself.

Malcolm made a face of disgust as he pulled his leg back and sat straight upon the throne. "First you take an innocent, beautiful young girl and force her to engage in…well, I'm not sure what you made her do, but you soiled her without a second thought as to her fate."

Darry's eyes narrowed as they rose to his.

"And now the Princess Jessa, yet another innocent girl taken in by your false charm and diseased blood." Malcolm leaned forward, his eyes bright as if he had his victory already in hand. "And little did anyone know that your blood actually *is* diseased. You truly are a mongrel now, aren't you."

"You do not sound like a prince," Darry said softly. "You do not sound like a man who will be a king." She took a small step forward. "You sound like a jealous little boy, Mal, who's had his toys taken away."

"I have plans, Darrius," Malcolm responded. "Solid, exceptional plans for Arravan's future, and yet you care for nothing but your own pleasure as you discard the rules along your way."

"To marry Jessa and put your son upon the Jade Throne?" Darry asked with some degree of caution. The tension within his body had changed and not for the better. He felt his prey was in reach and the advantage was his. Beyond the confines of the maze, she felt Hinsa turn in the deepest forest of the Green Hills. She felt the spray of moisture as she exhaled, and the shiver that moved beneath her fur. "Was that your plan? Was your pet prince to be your regent until the boy came of age? Or should I say your puppet? And what of Jessa, Mal? She is not yours to take and do with what yo—"

"No?" His voice was raised. "But she is *yours* to take?"

"She is not anyone's to take, Mal. We've had this discussion before. Jessa is not a pawn in your game. She is a free woman, with all the rights and privileges that such a thing provides. And if that is not clear enough for you to comprehend, then understand that she is a Princess of the Blood and comes from a line that stretches back a thousand years before the first Durand was even born." Darry looked at him with a mixture of shock and rage, both of which she could feel within her chest. "I will not stand before you ever again and be belittled by you. This is beneath you." Darry spoke and felt her many years of frustration push against the door. "Move on. Make new plans. Find your own pleasure. Be a bloody prince, for the love of Gamar, and stop fucking with people's lives!"

Malcolm leaned back upon the throne and chuckled. "I don't know why I always engage with you," he responded. "I really don't. You never understand. No one really sees what the future can be here, least of all you."

Darry spied the movement within the darkness beyond her mother's throne, but she did not turn her head.

"You make me angry," Malcolm admitted and his tone was dark. "You are a backwards cunt and I am the Crown Prince of Arravan, poised to take the throne. And yet, here we are."

Darry waited, uncertain of what else she should do until he made his move.

"You're the hero of the realm who has dispatched our enemies in brilliant fashion, and me, I am left to pick up the pieces of Arravan's future." He leaned forward again. "Perhaps I'll make a new plan, if my old one doesn't work out. Perhaps I'll still get what I want. Perhaps Jessa will enjoy a change of pace. Do you think a cock for a tongue will please her?"

Darry realized that his words so far had served very little purpose but to provoke her. He disliked her, but so what? He disapproved, but who should care? He was jealous, but what did it matter in the end? Jealous of what and why, was perhaps the better question. She saw his moves played out into a endgame she had no intention of participating in. "I'm not going to hurt you, Mal, if that's what you're waiting for. I'm not going to beat you bloody again, so you may call the guards and have me thrown in a cell."

His eyes flashed and his jaw clenched.

"And I would not be so little-boy eager, if I were you, to pit your desires against a woman such as Jessa."

"A woman such as Bharjah's daughter?" Malcolm inquired. "She is still his dregs."

Darry laughed, unable to stop her reaction. "Have you not been paying attention?"

"Better than you have, apparently," Malcolm replied. "Have it your way, yet one more time, Darrius." He pushed to his feet.

Darry heard the crack and twang of the trigger and cord and reacted within the same instant, her instincts pure beneath the unmistakable sound. She was not at her best, though, and her muscles would not obey as they should have.

The crossbow bolt took her high in the left shoulder and she let out a hard breath as she was thrown back the other way. The pain burst throughout her chest and the impact as her right shoulder hit the floor sent a blast of light through her head that was its own agony.

Hinsa stumbled as she ran and her powerful shoulder hit the ground, the undergrowth and brush caught beneath her unruly slide and filling the distant night with noise. Birds lifted from their rest in a rush of wings and the call of a startled owl screeched out.

Darry caught one breath and then another as she craned her neck and looked to the open door in the distance.

Malcolm's boot pushed at her wounded shoulder, and Darry rolled onto her back with a cry of distress. The bolt shifted with her and she sucked in the pain as the broadhead of the arrow ripped through the skin of her back.

Hinsa's fierce scream echoed within Darry's head and drowned out her brother's words.

The smell of blood filled her nose, and she stared at his mouth as she tried to pull back from Hinsa's emotions.

Malcolm leaned down slightly, a curious expression on his face as he stood over her. "I said your temper is not what it once was," he repeated. "Is this better than a cell?"

"What…what have you done?" Darry asked and her voice was rough and unfamiliar to her own ears. The shock of it hit then, and she was swept along in its cold tide. She could feel the blood leave her body and settle beneath her back.

"I'm putting things back where they should be. It's not my fault if you wouldn't play along," Malcolm answered and his voice had softened. "So now you will disappear into the night, never to be heard from again. We shall all grieve, of course, and there will be tears. Mother's heart will be broken, but she'll bear it, just as she did when Jacey Rose left us."

Jacey Rose, Darry thought and she tried to focus. *The daughter whose place I took, in order to soothe a grief that would never go away. I brought you lilacs, Jacey, and cleaned the dust from the carvings on your tomb.*

"And I will console the Princess Jessa until she accepts her intended fate, you shouldn't worry." Malcolm crouched beside her. "And come Summer Solstice a year from now, we shall be married beneath the shadow of the gods, and she will know what it's like to have a real man in her bed. Not a pretender."

Darry licked her lips, the metallic flavor of blood upon her tongue. "I think…you're in…for a surprise."

Malcolm rose with a smile. "Then the joy shall be all mine, as she fights against me. Though either way, Darrius Lauranna Durand, I shall plant my heirs within her womb."

Darry blinked and felt her thoughts slip sideways as the familiar smells of the maze filled her nose. The ground was soft beneath her feet and she felt Hinsa's fear as the panther moved.

"Come and finish it, Marteen," Malcolm ordered quietly.

There was a loud clatter of noise and Malcolm turned with a start.

Bentley Greeves held a dagger at the base of Marteen Salish's throat as they walked clear of the shadows and moved about the dais. "Back away from her."

Malcolm moved to the side. "What you're doing is treason, Greeves. Let him go."

Bentley smiled and it was not an expression Malcolm had seen from him before. "Shall we speak of treason?" Bentley asked him. "Etienne!"

Malcolm looked over his shoulder and another man slipped from the shadows near the entrance of the throne room. He hurried down the aisle, the crossbow held before him and aimed squarely at Malcolm's chest as he approached. Malcolm took several steps toward the dais as he reassessed the situation. The man was another of Darry's bastard boys, Etienne Blue.

"Get her up," Bentley ordered.

Etienne set the loaded crossbow onto the stones and went to a knee beside Darry. "Hello, Captain. How's your evening going?" he asked as he inspected the wound. Darry lifted her right hand and Etienne leaned close as she whispered.

"You're both making a very bad mistake," Malcolm said and looked to Bentley. "And I promise—you shall all end your days in the same grave."

"Perhaps." Bentley flashed another smile beneath his mustache. He tipped the blade and Salish flinched within his arms as a thick line of blood ran down his throat and disappeared beneath the collar of his tunic. "But it won't be the first mistake we've made."

Etienne slipped a hand beneath Darry's neck. "That's true," he replied in a tense voice. The streak of blue within his hair caught the lamplight and flared silver. "The Solstice masque at Madame Salina's three years ago comes to mind."

Darry grunted in pain as Etienne sat her up in one smooth move.

Bentley shifted and tightened his hold upon Salish as they backed down the aisle several steps. Darry cried out as Etienne lifted her into his arms and stood up straight. "We'll leave the toad's body where you can find it easily," Bentley said.

"Mal?" Marteen Salish spoke and his voice was filled with an odd mixture of fear and disbelief. "Love, please!"

"Move a bit faster, my brother," Bentley ordered and Etienne quickened his pace toward the doors.

Malcolm's heartbeat was painful within his chest, as if a fist had reached in and closed about his lungs. He shoved at his panic as Bentley tipped his head to the side. "Love?"

Marteen Salish's eyes widened slowly but Malcolm looked away from him, intent upon Bentley's next move. "Do not mistake your place in all of this, Greeves. Do not presume more power than you have right now."

Bentley looked across the distance between them. "That explains quite a bit, actually."

"You're a dead man," Malcolm promised softly.

"Wouldn't you rather fuck me?" Bentley offered and Malcolm could feel the sudden flush within his face. The heat of his discomfort and shame rose up against every measure of his will and claimed a bold victory. "I'm told I can be quite a bit of fun."

Malcolm pulled the small blade from behind his belt and struck with speed, his lunge smooth and precise.

Bentley pulled his dagger back but he was too slow as the steel of Malcolm's knife sliced across the back of his hand. His dagger clattered to the stones and Salish stumbled and fell to his knees.

"Guards!" Malcolm shouted and his voice filled the throne room. "Guards!" He bent over and picked up Bentley's fallen dagger, regarding Marteen Salish who sat back upon his heels.

Malcolm considered his situation. The Greeves family held substantial power, but they were no match for the full might of the crown. "A price beyond blood," he said.

He grabbed Marteen Salish by the hair from behind and pulled Bentley's dagger across his throat.

Marteen's hair was soft within his hand, as soft as it always was, soft like the finest silk sheets. Soft like his lips about the shaft of Malcolm's manhood. As soft as his cries were, when he was taken from behind, the sounds of his pleasure at having a prince's favor muffled within the pillows.

Malcolm blinked and felt the the dagger's handle bite into his hand, and then Salish fell, the strands of his hair pulled beyond Malcolm's grip by the weight of his body.

He dropped at the base of the dais as Malcolm watched.

The blood was instant, and though Salish struggled briefly and tried to crawl away, it took very little time for the stillness of death to overcome him.

"Greeves?" Malcolm's voice shook as he turned about.

The throne room was empty before him, and Bentley Greeves was nowhere to be seen.

"If I were you…" Malcolm tossed Bentley's dagger to the stones as a strange surge of heat rose within his chest. He felt dizzy as he swallowed hard upon a tight throat and wiped his bloodstained hand upon his tunic. He stepped farther away from the body, unable to look.

"If I were you," he whispered. "I'd run."

CHAPTER TWENTY-TWO

*D*arry *struggled as her left hand found the small jut of stone,* but her fingers would not grab hold. As bits of shale crumbled and sprayed downward, Darry was forced to close her eyes and turn her face. Her left side ached as if she had run for many miles, but she was determined to reach the top. A flutter of fear moved within her chest, though, for no matter how hard she tried, she could not make her left hand work as it should.

She spit dust from her mouth and looked up along the sheer face of the rock. "Bloody hell and hounds."

There would be two good pulls before she reached a narrow shelf where she might rest, and she wasn't entirely sure she had the strength. She shifted her weight upon the toe of her right boot and glanced away from the rocks.

The landscape poured away from her in a vast roll of earth, the wheat-colored grass in constant movement as the wind moved south across the plain.

Darry could feel the sweat trickle down her back, and her legs trembled from exertion as she looked up once more. The dark gray rock seemed to rise straight into the sky, the brightness of the blue above almost too much to bear as Darry squinted her eyes.

She took a breath to calm her nerves and then she reached. Her fingers finally gripped and she pushed off with her right foot, but her strength did not last.

Darry grabbed with her right hand in a panic of movement as her left boot slipped free of the foothold and she bounced against the rock and lost her balance.

An iron grip seized her left wrist and held strong. "I've got you."

Darry looked up with wide eyes.

"Put your right hand to the left of where it was, and a bit higher...there's a notch."

Darry obeyed, found the notch, and held on tight. She established her feet once more and raised her eyes as her heart beat wildly in her chest.

The deep scar upon the left side of the woman's face crinkled in a curious manner as she smiled. "I know you're tired, but you can do it. I won't let go."

Darry struggled to catch her breath, but she did as she was told and pulled herself upward. Her feet found an outcrop of shale on the left and a divot within the rock on the right, and before she knew what was happening, she stumbled onto the shelf and into the strong arms of the scarred woman.

"*Essa-oh*, my friend," the woman said and smiled. "It is a hard climb, this rock."

Darry leaned against the wall of stone in weakness and tried to catch her breath. "Then why...am I climbing it?"

The woman laughed and looked happy. "That is a good question."

Darry leaned over at the waist and grabbed the fabric at the knees of her trousers. She gave a hard cough and wiped at her mouth with her sleeve.

"All of this land here," the woman said as she looked across the plains far beneath them, "this once belonged to my people. There is a heavily forested grove that grows past the horizon there," she explained and pointed into the west. "There is good clean water there, and the rabbits like the shade." She looked at Darry. "Do you like rabbit?"

Darry considered the question and stood up straight, though it took only a few seconds before she gave in and leaned against the rock once more. She pulled her left arm close and cradled it with her right. "With sauce, yes."

"Sauce?"

"Gravy."

"Yes"—the woman nodded—"I like that, too."

"Do you know why I'm climbing this rock?"

"I know why I am here."

"Yes, but why am I?"

"Because you must get to the top. The holy men of my people used to say it is better to reach the top and make your offering than to fall off and die. There would be no purpose in that."

Darry craned her neck. "I'd have to agree, but I don't think I can make that."

The woman tapped Darry's cheek with a light touch and Darry returned to her. "I think you should try. They say the gods sit up there and watch the sun set and smoke their pipes." Her mismatched amber and brown eyes widened and there was a flash of humor in them. "To sit and smoke a pipe with your god is better than a prayer, yes?"

Darry smiled and felt very tired. "Can we just sit here for a bit?"

"We can, but there is something at the top I need to show you, as well."

"What is it?"

The woman smiled. "You are like my *Akasha*, always wanting to know your surprises."

Darry blinked at her. "*Akasha?*"

"No," the woman replied in a firm voice. "I will not tell you what it means."

Darry nodded at the familiar answer and stared into the distance beneath the far horizon. "Where are your people, then?"

"They are all dead now," she said in a quiet voice that was colored with sadness. *"I am the last of my kind."*

❖

Jessa and Etienne sat Darry upright on the floor beside the banked hearth in Sebastian's Tower, the worktable beyond the sitting area covered by the contents of Jessa's medicine bag. Jessa braced herself against what she knew would follow and her stomach churned in an angry manner. "Cut it," she ordered in a tight voice and Arkady obeyed.

The horse clippers snapped through the shaft of the bolt but an inch from Darry's flesh.

Jessa felt the tip as it protruded from Darry's back, high upon her left shoulder. "Pull it, Etienne."

Etienne took a deep breath as he wrapped his hand about the broadhead. "Sorry, Captain," he whispered and then pulled.

The shaft slid from Darry's flesh and her blood followed after as Jessa packed the wound in the seconds that followed. She looked up as her hands kept to the task. "Put pressure on the front of the wound." Jessa waited until he had done so and then caught his eyes. "What did she say again?"

"We must follow Hinsa," Etienne answered. "But I don't know where Hinsa is."

"She will come. Where is Bentley?"

"He was right behind us, my Lady. What was she talking about?"

Jessa pulled Darry close and held her tight, her eyes upon the blood that slowly stained her hands. "Press harder, please," she said, and Etienne did as he was told.

Jessa looked up. "Arkady, the bells will ring soon, so we have very little time. Find everyone, no one gets left behind, do you hear?"

"Yes, my Lady," he answered. "That's easy enough. Grissom threw us from the barracks when we refused to sign up with the Kingsmen again. We moved our things to the stables."

Jessa considered his words. "Bring them, and bring the horses. Do not forget Vhaelin Star and Talon." She remembered their race to Tristan's Grove and how she had held Darry as she had wept. Until that day, Jessa had not known what it was to be truly needed. It had been the last moment of her old life, and the first of her new. "Bring your weapons, bring everything you can carry."

"Yes, my Lady," Arkady replied. "But bring it where?"

"Back here, to the tower. Go, do it now, and do it fast."

"We'll draw attention."

"Then ride, Arkady, and run them down if they try and stop you."

Arkady nodded. "Aye, my Lady."

"And no matter what you see, keep riding. Don't stop."

"Aye, my Lady."

"Go then, go!"

Arkady ran, leaving the tower door open behind him as he disappeared into the night.

"The bleeding is slowing down," Etienne said and gave her a crooked grin as he looked up. "I think I can take it now, if you wish to get dressed."

Jessa looked down and realized she wore but her blue tunic, which was now covered with blood, even as she was.

"I won't look, my Lady, I promise," Etienne added as he grabbed for more bandages with his free hand.

Darry's body was hot to the touch and Jessa lowered her face as she tightened her embrace. Darry's curls were damp with sweat and blood.

"Go on now, my Lady," Etienne replied in a gentle voice as he touched Jessa's hand. "Let go now." Darry tipped into his arms as Jessa released her, and Etienne laid her down with great care. "Darry ain't goin' nowhere." He looked up with a smile. "The path down that dark road is too rough for her in this condition, what with her dragging us all behind her."

Jessa reached out and her hand trembled against his cheek. "Do not let her die, please."

"No chance of that. She still owes me three silvers from our last game of Suns."

Jessa let out a breath of laughter as her tears finally fell. "Let Hinsa touch her if she arrives before I come down. Do not keep her from Darry, or she won't like it."

Etienne's eyebrows went up slightly as he pondered her words. "I wouldn't want that."

❖

Darry felt sick as she climbed beside the scarred woman, and her limbs trembled. Her left arm had gone numb and she knew if they did not reach the top soon, she would fall to her death. She wondered if she would hear the laughter of dead holy men as she fell.

"Here, love," the woman told her as she climbed ahead. "Right hand, just there."

Darry obeyed. "You could at least *sound* tired."

The woman chuckled and it was a rough, warm music that Darry found terribly familiar.

"Should I tell you of my people?"

"Yes," Darry said in a tight voice as she pulled herself up several feet and hugged the cold stone. It felt good against the side of her face, and she wondered if she had a fever. Her head felt tight and oddly too large for her neck. It was not a comfortable feeling.

"I am of the Fox People, descended from the constellation of the Dog Stars."

Shale slipped down the face of the cliff and Darry pulled her face away as it skittered past her. She found a better foothold and fought for it. "I don't know…"

"Here," the woman said and guided Darry's hand to the next notch.

"Those stars," Darry finished.

"People call it the Great Hunt, but it was never a hunt. It was a dance."

Darry let her weight settle upon her toes and tried to breathe as she took a brief respite. She thought about what the scarred woman had said and then laughed, out of breath and nearly out of hope. "You're right."

"The Dog Stars are the stars of the *Cha-Diah* people." The woman smiled down at Darry from above. *"They are your people now, as well, for you are Hashiki's descendant, and I am no longer the last of my kind."*

❖

Jessa stood at the entrance to the maze and watched as Darry's Boys rode toward her, bent low over their saddles as they thundered through a company of Kingsmen who dove out of their way. The watchtower bells still rang out and the barracks were lit from every window as men poured into the main courtyard. There were torches along the second and third levels of the Keep and men shouted in the distance.

She wore Radha's shawl about the waist of her homespun skirt, and she pulled one of the threads of fringe from the weave. It wrapped about her wrist as she raised her arm into the air and then it turned to smoke, thick and black as it expanded outward, a funnel of darkness that spun with ever increasing force. The light within its path was sucked into its rotation and disappeared completely as the tempest grew in size, the wind that swirled upon its edges fierce and filled with noise.

Jessa was pushed back a step and her hair whipped about her face as Hinsa stepped close and wrapped her sleek body about Jessa's legs. The panther's scream lifted into the night and was caught instantly by the cyclone, her pain and discontent magnified a thousandfold. The sound raked along Jessa's spine, and she wondered if Hinsa spoke for Darry, as well.

Men upon the balconies were thrown back and torches were extinguished. The Kingsmen in pursuit of Darry's Boys turned back or fell to the ground as the dirt from the courtyard was swept up and rolled over them in a massive, heavy wave.

The funnel cloud parted near its base and Darry's Boys rode through the opening as the two fingers of darkness separated up the middle and split apart. Now the tops of both clouds began to spread and the men upon the inner wall took cover as the stars above them were blotted out. One storm of darkness spun toward the barracks and the other swept into the Keep, shutters ripped from the balustrade and tossed into the night.

Jessa and Hinsa jumped aside as Darry's Boys crashed into the maze, the ground churned up and spit out behind them as they tore through the entrance and kept going. Arkady wheeled his mount to the side as the others rode past him.

"Where is Bentley?" she demanded above the roar as he vaulted from his saddle and ran to her.

"I don't know!"

"As soon as he gets here, I will close the maze around us."

"You can do that?"

"Only if he gets here," Jessa called out and pushed at his shoulder. "Go!"

Jessa turned back to the Keep and lifted her hands as she called forth the Hawk's Eye spell, her sight rising above the storm and swooping toward the walls of Blackstone. She saw Jacob Durand struggling past the solar doors as he fought his way to the rail around the stones of the patio, his right hand lifted to shield his face from the wind.

Jessa shifted the thread of fringe within the center of the storm, and the torches closest to the solar were blown out by the huge blast of wind that followed. Jessa's mind reached out as the funnel twisted and bent in the opposite direction. *Malcolm has crossed the line, Jacob. Believe in us, my friend, and look for the Lark that bears my song!*

The darkness spun along the stones and Jessa's vision followed in its wake, skating about the northern edge of the residence and then cutting to the left.

Bentley Greeves swung his legs over the rail halfway down the balustrade stairs and leaped to the ground.

Jessa cursed and tried to shift the thread, but it was too late as Bentley hit the ground hard and dove forward into a roll that turned quickly into several. He stumbled and limped as he found his feet but he was on the run regardless, caught within the torrent of wind.

Jessa spun about and let her spells overlap, each one on top of the other as she held the separate runes with confidence.

Leaves burst outward from the hedgerows as she spoke the words that would ward the maze against all who sought to enter. Greenery caught within the wind and filled the air with life. The frenzy would not last long, she knew, but it would last long enough.

As the maze groaned and branches broke and snapped and

grew anew, and the thick walls of foliage began to close around her, Bentley Greeves crashed through it all and sprawled at her feet.

❖

Darry pulled herself over the edge and crawled forward, her lower body dragged behind her as if her legs had no power of their own.

"It's all right, love," the scarred woman said softly as she knelt. She laid a hand upon Darry's shoulder. "We are at the top."

Darry's arms shook violently as she tried to push herself up, but she only succeded in part as she rolled onto her back and stared into the sky. The woman sat beside her and crossed her legs, her soft buckskins surprisingly tidy despite the mountain of shale and dust that had rained down on them.

"When our people walked this land, the gods would ride the wind and play their games. Balls of lightning would tumble from their fingertips and race through the air." She flicked her wrist and held her hand out. "They would knock each other from their gusty steeds as we would hide in the grass and watch."

"What is my surprise?" Darry asked as her eyes closed.

The woman laughed happily and set a gentle hand upon Darry's right arm. "Why did you climb this rock?"

Darry blinked into the brightness of the sky. "Because you told me to."

"Is that what happened?"

Darry thought about it. "Well, not exactly."

"You may sleep some, and then you may speak to your god if he is here."

"I'm afraid," Darry admitted as she began to drift.

The woman set her hand upon Darry's forehead and then stroked her hair in a gentle manner. "The gods are close, but you needn't fear. I won't leave you."

Darry tried to speak but could not.

"Yes," the scarred woman answered softly. *"I'll be here when you wake."*

❖

Jessa followed Hinsa as the panther moved quietly through the maze, a ball of witchlight connected to the great cat by a simple spell. It bobbed several feet above her head as she led the way, and the panther did not seem to mind.

Darry's Boys followed behind them both as they led the horses, laden with supplies and weapons and Radha's trunks, as well, all of it hauled along the twisted path by the soldiers and animals alike. Darry was carried gently in the massive arms of Jemin McNeely, their captain wrapped in the soft quilts from her own bed and seemingly oblivious to their journey. Tackle jingled as the hedgerows shifted around them in the odd light and flowers bloomed in their wake, and from time to time Jessa heard a startled curse as something moved within the greenery that could not be named.

The chaos of the courtyard could no longer be heard and their wild escape seemed oddly unreal as they traveled deeper into the maze. No one spoke of the fact that the maze was built within the gardens, and the gardens were contained within the walls of the palace.

After a dozen turns and a widening of the path that led them straight on for almost an hour, Blackstone Keep seemed gone altogether.

CHAPTER TWENTY-THREE

*D*arry opened her eyes and she was wrapped in the warmth of several sheepskins, her vision filled with the deep orange-and-gold colors of a small fire. Cedar filled the air with its rich aroma.

Stars filled the skies and Darry let out a startled breath at how close they were.

"She is awake." The scarred woman smiled as she poked a long stick into the fire. Ashes and sparks of flame rose into the night.

Darry pushed from the ground with her right hand as her left arm lay useless against her legs. She watched as the smoke and sparks from the fire danced above them. "There is no wind here."

"The wind can make it hard to talk and it steals your words. Who is to say where they will land? In the ears of your enemies if you have no luck. The gods do not like what they say to find the wrong purpose." The woman pulled her own sheepskin tighter about her shoulders. "You have a guest."

Darry looked to the left.

The man was tall and spindly as he sat before their fire, his legs crossed and pulled close beneath his body as he stared back at her. His torn pants did not reach his ankles and his feet were bare and dark. He could not have weighed much at all, and Darry wondered when he had last eaten a decent meal, his tunic as ragged as his frayed trousers as it hung from his bone-thin shoulders. His hair was dark and utterly chaotic about his head, and he wore a wild beard that had most likely never been combed. His eyes were dark within the firelight, but the whites around them were bright with life.

"I know you, don't I?" Darry asked, and though she did not know how, she knew it was true. She had seen him before.

"We met upon the stairs of Gamar's Temple, many years ago." Darry smiled as the memory blossomed within her mind.

She had stood beside Cecelia within the crowd that had gathered as the beggars of Gamar had danced and whirled before the main entrance to the temple. They had all been terribly poor and thin, but they had danced to the drums with all the righteousness and vigor of men who wanted for nothing. It had been a harsh winter, and Alirra Bay had frozen over, though the beggars had danced in their bare feet upon the cold stone. Darry had held to her mother's hand and watched.

The man leaned forward with a smile that showed his teeth. "I believe you need this back, little one," he suggested and held out a coin.

The fire caught the heavy silver and burst within the night like a ruptured star.

Darry stared at the coin. "That was for my birthing day."

"Yes," he answered. "You were very insistent that I take it, for you did not want me to be cold. You said if it was not enough for shoes, you could lend me yours."

Darry blinked at him and felt dizzy as his eyes seem to grow within his face. The stars from above were pulled within and Darry could see the constellations as they spun.

"And I told you I would keep it for you, until you had need of Gamar's favor."

"But you still need shoes," Darry whispered and licked her lips. She was very thirsty.

Gamar's beggar laughed happily and turned to the scarred woman. *"You are right. She is as sweet as berry-pear pie."*

❖

Jessa followed Hinsa into the clearing as the panther moved easily through the lush grass and bent clover. The witchlight hovered just beneath the high-up canopy of vines and branches, and Jessa's whispered words pulled more energy from the hedgerow walls around them. The intensity of the light increased and painted the greenery in a deep shade of gold as Jessa quickened her pace.

The soft earth gave way to a floor of uneven stones, and Jessa stopped in surprise as her boots sounded out upon the new surface. She called out in a soft voice and Hinsa waited for her. The stones were set in a dark mortar that had long since cracked and had begun to crumble, and a thin layer of moss had grown in its place, a bond that made the stones an integral part of the maze.

Jessa stepped a bit farther and went to a knee beside Hinsa, the panther's purr low in tone but loud in volume as it moved with a purpose into the air around them. The nearest horses shied away, and Jessa put a hand upon Hinsa's back at the hard jangle of bridles and tack and voices seeking to soothe the animals. The cat leaned against her, and her purr shifted into a higher pitch.

"Are you singing, Biscuit?" she asked in a whisper.

The wall before them began to move and the thorns folded over upon their thick vines as they turned and rolled. The plant life pulled back of its own accord and bunched up as it rose along a wall of stone. Jessa could feel the majik around them and it was unlike any spell she herself had worked. It was ancient and beyond her current knowledge and her blood raced with excitement despite her fears.

"It's her door," Bentley said as he entered the clearing. His voice was tired but filled with wonder nonetheless. "It's Hinsa's door."

Jessa pushed to her feet and looked over her shoulder.

"I was here before, when we were children," Bentley explained. "But it didn't look like this. It was much different."

Jessa approached the threshold as Hinsa continued her song.

There were two doors, actually, and though the wood was dark with moisture and heavy with age, Jessa could still see the wrought-iron hinges that only a man could make. She reached out as a harvest of ivy leaves floated down from the canopy above.

The metal handles were cool to the touch and with a deep breath, she pulled.

The hinges groaned as she backed up and a vine snapped

above her head, caught upon the edge of the wood. Darry's Boys approached one by one and stood upon the edge of the stone terrace, crowded together as Jessa let the doors swing wide.

Jessa raised her right hand and a dozen sparks of witchlight rolled from her fingertips into the darkness beyond the doors like a small army of fireflies.

The trees and undergrowth of the Menath Forest lit up in a ghostly manner, the sounds of the Green Hills alive around them. Hinsa brushed past Jessa's skirt and leaped through the gateway with a growl that turned into a satisfied scream.

Jessa spun and faced her companions. "We are at the Green Hills."

"Darry's land." Bentley smiled. "This is nearly a hundred leagues from Blackstone."

Hinsa growled from beyond the doors and watched them, impatient as she waited.

"We all go through the doors," Jessa ordered, her tone not without sympathy for their anxious, stunned expressions. "We follow Hinsa as Darry wanted. She will find us a place to camp. Darry's wounds must be seen to, and we must have a place to stay until she can travel more easily." And so went her hope, as it lifted to the pinnacle of her love and held on.

"I'm not tired, my Lady," Jemin replied in his deep voice. "The captain does not weigh much. But a feather, really, in my arms."

Jessa smiled at him with affection, surprised by his crisp and elegant accent. He had come from Artanis and she could hear it. "Thank you, Jemin."

"All right, in a line, my brothers," Bentley ordered as he tightened the silken nightshift that was wrapped about his wounded hand. "Jemin, you and Darry follow the Lady, and stay close. You too, Arkady." Bentley looked to the others. "Let's go, lads."

Jessa let Jemin cross over the threshold first, and then she followed, taking a single step that stretched a hundred leagues.

❖

The scarred woman looked down at Darry and smiled. "You should look around before you go," she suggested.

Darry was wonderfully warm and sinfully comfortable right where she was. "What about my surprise?"

"You will have to come back for it."

Darry blinked several times and then frowned. "I'm not climbing this rock again."

The scarred woman chuckled with delight. "That's what I said, too. But here I am again. I have made this climb at least thirty times now."

"Then I feel I should tell you that you've chosen a very unwise pursuit."

"Yes," the woman said with a glorious smile, her eyes alight with amusement. "*Essa*, but my *Akasha* must love you to the ends of the world and back again." She touched Darry's forehead. "Do not forget to rest," she whispered. "I always forgot, and it did me very little good."

Darry felt the rock shift beneath her, *and she closed her eyes as her stomach lurched.*

❖

Jessa stood within the depths of the Menath Forest and watched as the hedgerows and ivy devoured the doors. Vines of thorn and branches of yew cracked and split loudly as Hinsa's portal vanished and disappeared into the soft earth. The ground shook beneath her feet and she put her arms out for balance as she stumbled backward.

The fertile smell of earth and moss filled the air, and the undergrowth crawled across the ground, turning over rocks and sprouting new leaves. A fallen branch popped from the center outward, and Jessa took another step back as bark flew several feet into the air.

The air around her changed and the smell of singed wood was sharp within her nose.

And then she saw the runes, rising like smoke as they burst through the dirt and lifted into the air. As bright as witchlight they flared in the night as if the quill of a god had written them on the air, a work of great art that was only meant to last until the wind devoured them.

Despite her excitement, Jessa's mind took the runes in, wrapping around them as quickly as she could. The curves and the descending swirls. The edges that faded, and the edges that were as sharp as a blade. She had not seen this intricate language before, but as the runes were blown gently into the trees of the forest around them, she knew she would see it again.

As the normal rythmns of the Menath returned and the earth became still, nothing remained but a small hillock and the tangled roots of a fallen oak tree.

Jessa turned around slowly and the night was alive as the stars flashed above the treetops. There was only the scent of wild things and the sounds of their passage as Darry's Boys pushed on through the undergrowth.

"My Lady," Jemin whispered and looked up from his burden with a smile.

Jessa's heart lurched wildly at his expression, and she moved in a rush, a handful of quilt thick within her fist but a moment later. *"Akasha?"*

CHAPTER TWENTY-FOUR

The sweetness of the wine was almost too great, despite the aftertaste that left a touch of sour upon the tongue. The grapes had been harvested too soon for his liking, and though he was thirsty, he did not wish for more of the same.

Lord Almahdi de Ghalib waited for the servant to advance around the table.

The sun poured into the council chamber like an anvil of heat, and he felt each movement with an acute awareness. Beneath the layers of his white thawb, embroidered vest, and ceremonial robe, his tunic should feel softer. He knew it was soft. His first wife had made it for him thirty years ago. It could not be anything but soft, at this point.

She had been so very beautiful that at times his mind could not comprehend it. Asha-Aman she was called, named so for the music of the flowers that only bloom within the rain. Her long, straight hair had been as black as the Solstice moon and just as mysterious. He had not encountered the same scent since her death, nor had he known it before she had come into his life. She had brought it with her when her father had presented her before the elders of his family.

The smell of wildflowers and sweet peppers, the scent of her hair, had tamed the unbearable heat of one of the worst summers Lyoness had ever known. The aroma had been like the spice within the shama paste served with fresh, ripe tomatoes and milk bread. Or at least, this was how he remembered it. He could not eat sweet peppers any longer. The scent would overwhelm all other thoughts within his mind.

He would remember lying naked upon the tangled sheets of his bed, with Asha draped across his body as they both tried to breathe within the heavy heat. Most nights, the moon would sneak in through the terrace and steal what it could while they spent their passion regardless of all other concerns. She would draw pictures upon his skin, her finger dipped in the moisture of their sweat as they waited for even the slightest breeze upon the errant moonlight. She would sing quietly while he laughed and told her to stop.

He would drift within his memories while the flavors of his dinner lingered heavy upon his tongue, his eyes filled with thoughts of his lost love. So his second wife no longer served him sweet peppers.

He pushed the fringed ends of his kaffiyeh back over his left shoulder and considered whether he should have worn it at all. It was tradition in the province of Lahaba-Sha to wear the fringed blue headdress at all formal functions, but at the moment, it only served to make him more uncomfortable.

The servant moved at his left, and he put his hand over the mouth of his cup. "Not this. Bring me something sweet. Sweet like the honey wine from the north."

The servant bowed and moved away at once.

His youngest son had loved honey. All things he would eat with it, even fruit. Once upon an age, his cellars had been stocked with many bottles of the sweetest vintage known in Lyoness, a light, fruited wine that could make your heart race if you drank too much.

On the twentieth anniversary of his marriage to Asha-Aman, their last boy had taken his first sip. It had been a source of much laughter that day, for the boy had been determined to consume every drop he could find. *It will temper him as a man*, Asha had said with a smile. *He shall be sweet and beautiful, and great words shall tumble from his tongue. He shall entice the women to his side with even the worst of poems, from such honeyed lips.*

He looked up as the servant reappeared eyed and the cool pitcher beaded with moisture as his cup was filled.

He took up his wine and tasted it with a full swallow.

His eyes closed upon the flavor, for it was as he remembered. It was full and sweet and yet not so heavy upon the tongue that one could not indulge. It whispered of the papaya fruit as well as the fat, purple grapes of Hooba province. It was as familiar to him as a kiss from one of his children.

Taste it, Father. His son had smiled as he set a rare glass goblet upon the table. The boy-turned-man had been gone for many months upon a great and mysterious journey, for he had told no one of its true purpose. *I have bought the vineyard farm, just as my good brothers have suggested.* His vineyard had turned a heavy profit and made the honey-tongued young man into a noble of significant influence.

Almahdi sat back in his chair and took his goblet with him. His left hand pulled upon the rough thread of his vest as he shifted his shoulders.

"Lord de Ghalib?"

Lord Almahdi de Ghalib, First Warden and Lord of Lahaba-Sha Province looked across the table and narrowed his eyes so they might focus. He recognized the angular shape of the face and the pale green of the kaffiyeh. "Lord Shinza."

"Are you all right?"

"It is hot."

"Yes, but are you well?"

"I am well, Lord Shinza," Almahdi replied and tipped his head in acknowledgment of the concern. "It is hot."

"The rains have treated Lahaba-Sha well, I hope?"

Almahdi gave a sigh and lifted his cup. The bouquet of the wine filled his senses and, in his mind's eye, he watched his oldest son upon his first horse. Asha had sipped a sweet cup of a similar vintage as they had watched, and his left shoulder felt the ghostly weight of her presence as if she still leaned against him at her leisure. The mare had been gentle but with enough spirit so that Nasir might learn properly how to take command of his mount.

"Lord de Ghalib?"

"Yes," Almahdi answered and then savored another sip. "Forgive an old man, my friend. The rains have been good. Our wells are full and our cattle graze upon the fine summer grass."

Lord Shinza smiled and his teeth broke the mask of his dark skin, though Almahdi could not see the expression within his eyes. "Good. This pleases me. We should talk trade before you travel south."

"Yes," Almahdi agreed.

"Enough."

The quiet talk about the long table ceased at once and all eyes looked to King Abdul-Majid de Bharjah. The servants set their trays upon the opposite end of the table and bowed as they backed away. Well practiced in their retreat, they moved as quickly as possible until they disappeared into the shadows.

Dressed in a pale gold robe, Bharjah sat within his deep chair and cast his gaze along the men about his table as the rings upon his right hand clicked against the stony gray Tarsem wood. It was not the Jade Throne, but it was a replica in shape, if not size. The pikes that rose from the crest of the backpiece were infamous, for Bharjah's search for the perfect gems of jade had long ago turned ruthless.

"I have received news from Arravan," Bharjah informed them, "about my daughter, the Princess Jessa-Sirrah."

Queen Jhannina's daughter, Almahdi acknowledged, and the beauty of Jhannina's long-ago face filled his vision.

He had seen Queen Jhannina but a few times during her short reign, and always he had felt her kindness. He had even spoken with her once, at the fete to celebrate Sylban-Tenna's victory over the Obi River tribes, though briefly, before Bharjah seized her away. She had taken his hand and blessed his fallen sons by name.

Jhannina's daughter was even lovelier, and her obvious innocence as to her father's darkness only made her more compelling. He had heard her sing once, though he could not recall where or why she had done so. She was aptly named for her skill.

Almahdi looked slowly and with care about the table, and he

could feel how the energy had shifted at the mention of the late queen's only child.

"My daughter is the heart of my kingdom and well loved by all, is she not?" Bharjah asked simply.

"Yes, my Lord King!"

Almahdi could not tell whose voices had spoken up, for there were many about the table from all the provinces of Lyoness. They spoke the truth, however, for the Nightshade Lark was well loved. She was the living symbol of her mother, and though she would never rule from the Jade Throne, she gave them hope. Somehow, in some unexplainable fashion, her presence had given them back their dreams for the future.

"As you all know, she was sent to Arravan in hopes of a marriage between their Crown Prince and the Jade Throne," Bharjah announced. "A mission of peace, and one of—"

"Your daughter deserves so much better," Almahdi interrupted and Bharjah was silenced by the intrusion, "than a *snake* such as he is."

No one moved and not a further word was spoken. The punishment was great for such an offense and Almahdi knew that it was forbidden. The heat seemed to increase within the room and several Lords shifted in their chairs as the silence became uncomfortable. Almahdi did not know who moved, but a seat groaned as someone's weight shifted.

"Almahdi, my old friend," Bharjah called down the table. "You have something to say?"

Almahdi sat forward and savored another swallow of his wine before he set his cup upon the table. "Arravan is a green country, my Lord King."

"What is that old fool still doing here?" Sylban-Tenna asked upon his father's right as he leaned back in his chair. "He drinks more wine than Rasul-Rafiq."

Bharjah laughed and a response was given within seconds, those gathered obliged to join him. Even Lord Shinza laughed and Almahdi did not fault him for it.

Almahdi let out a breath of his own amusement and turned in

his chair as he looked down the length of the table. "The Nightshade Lark is most beautiful," he said, and his voice was tinged with a peculiar humor. Almahdi reached into one of the pockets of his robe. "It is odd that you mention her, for I brought these gifts." He coughed to clear his throat as he set the jade next to his cup. "They were to be in honor of her return home."

Bharjah leaned forward in his chair.

"Almahdi," Lord Shinza said in a shocked voice. "Where did you find such stones?"

"Blessed be Hamranesh!" Lord Ibish-Dega stood and leaned over the table in order to have a better view. "They are the size of acorn apples!"

"Bring them here, Lord Almahdi," Bharjah said firmly. "Bring them to me now."

Almahdi took up the jade and leaned heavily against the table as he rose to his feet, the huge stones held awkwardly in his right hand. He shoved his seat back with his left leg and sidestepped free of his neighbor's chair. His feet shuffled and his left shoulder hung down slightly, though neither of these suggestions of old age and long-ago war wounds was entirely the truth.

Bharjah sat forward upon the edge of his chair as Almahdi approached, his eyes fierce upon the stones. "Put them on the table."

Almahdi set the stones before his king and stood closer than he ever had before to the man responsible for the death of his children.

"*Essa ahbwalla!*" Bharjah hissed as he held a stone within each hand. "Where did you find these?"

"I have another, my Lord King."

Bharjah laughed with joy as he held the gems to the sun and they flared with brilliance. His face was flushed with excitement. "Then you are more foolish than your useless sons ever were. Give it over."

Sylban-Tenna's eyes were filled with envy as he stared at the finely cut jade.

Almahdi leaned over as he reached within his embroidered vest. The thread was crooked and the seams were rough. Asha-Aman would not have been pleased by the lack of artistry.

"And tell me where you found them," Bharjah commanded as he turned the jewels within the light. A sudden frown creased his brow. "Why are they not more heavy?"

Almahdi could smell the sickly odor of Bharjah's sweat, and he smiled as his hand came free of the vest he had never liked. "Nasir. Amjad. Haddad and Jal-Kadir. These were the names of my sons," Almahdi whispered close to Bharjah's ear.

One of the jewels slipped from Bharjah's fingers and hit the edge of the table before it fell to the smooth marble floor and shattered into a thousand pieces of glass.

Almahdi stood up straight and looked down upon his king, his laughter quiet but filled with life.

"*Shivasa!*" Sylban shouted and shoved up from his chair. "Guards!"

Bharjah stared into the distance as the blood poured from his opened throat and spilled down the front of his golden robe.

Almahdi de Ghalib, First Warden and Lord of Lahaba-Sha Province lifted his arms out, the curved, bloody dagger that had belonged to his wife still held within his right hand. "Asha-Aman!" he called out and his voice echoed with strength to the high ceiling.

The many doors to the chamber were thrown open and the Palace Guards rushed in as Sylban-Tenna drew his sword and grabbed his father by the shoulder. He yanked Bharjah from his chair, let him fall to the floor, and then stepped over him as Almahdi watched.

Sylban looked down at his father and watched as the blood pooled beneath his body, its flow unimpeded as it spread across the floor. He turned back to the Lords of Lyoness as the Palace Guards filled the room behind him and surrounded the table, as well. Several Lords were on their feet, but most were still seated as they stared in shock.

Sylban-Tenna let his gaze travel down one side of the table and up the other. "You will swear fealty to me, or die," he declared and turned smoothly.

Almahdi stared beyond the searching, dark eyes of Bharjah's firstborn son. As Sylban shoved his sword into Almahdi's chest beneath his left arm, Almahdi spoke his last words. "Asha, your sons have been avenged."

CHAPTER TWENTY-FIVE

Jessa walked through the bedroom chamber and tossed Darry's jacket onto the bed as she passed by. Several unfinished dresses were laid out, and Jessa was determined they should be completed by the night of the autumn moon. The fabrics were not the finest silks, but she had dyed them with the help of the maid, who was also an accomplished seamstress. The colors were rich bronze and rust, and the fabric had taken them well.

The house was larger than they needed, but she found she liked the space, the rooms filled with windows and terrace doors that were still open although the heat of summer had left. The fresh air was crisp and filled with the tang of changing maples and thick pines, and she did not tire of the mixture of scents.

The manor was set upon the edge of the Yellendale Forest, north of Ballentrae and south of the Lanark River. The forest came close upon the house and the stables, but it was a comfortable union and it served them well with Hinsa's presence.

The manor and estate lands had belonged to Emmalyn's first husband, Evan, and when they had arrived, they had been expected. The seneschal had been there to greet them, and he had liked Darry from the moment they shook hands. He gave over a leather satchel before they had entered the house, and within it were the deeds and papers that gave Darry ownership of the properties.

The house had been in the midst of major repairs, and before they had even settled in, Darry's Boys had taken up the tasks alongside the household staff. The stables had been repaired, and the fences, as well, and barracks had gone up within a month's time, a home made of sturdy oak and maple that none of the men had expected. Lucien Martins had designed the two-story building, and each man was beyond pleased to have the privacy of his own room.

Jessa heard the sound of weapons and she moved through the sitting room and onto the second-floor veranda, her soft boots quiet upon the painted oak planks. She leaned against the rail and searched the courtyard below.

Darry stood beside Bentley as she slipped the leather straps of a round oak shield onto her left arm, and Jessa's eyes widened at the sight of it.

Darry tested the weight. "It's a good fit."

"The wider straps should deflect the weight differently, when someone tries to lop your head off," Bentley explained and stepped closer. He tipped the shield forward and looked to the straps. "Lucas says they will, anyway."

Darry's grin was filled with mischief. "And we believe Lucas, because…?"

Bentley giggled. "Because he's the bastard son of a blacksmith."

"Perhaps he should stand in front of me and hold it while I test out his theory."

"Don't be cruel, darling." Bentley smiled. "Apparently he wishes to learn a trade."

Darry stepped back and held the shield in front of her, her arm firm. "Hit it."

"I'm not going to hit you."

"No, I want to see."

"Hit it with what, my head?"

Darry smiled and nodded toward the nearest fence post. "That rock over there, give it a good toss at my head."

"What in the name of Gamar do you think you are doing?" Jessa called out as soon as the words had crossed Darry's lips. Her heart had given a not-so-pleasant thud at the thought of rocks being heaved at her lover's head.

Darry turned with a brilliant smile and looked up. "That was just for you, my love, to see if you were paying attention."

"My wits are about me, Darrius, you needn't fear," Jessa responded with amusement, for she could not be angry when faced with such a captivating expression. Darry had yet to reclaim her full strength, but her wounds had healed faster than Jessa expected. Darry had lost weight and she looked lean, her muscles finely cut and her stride quicker than it had been, if that was possible. It had been nearly three months since their escape from Blackstone, but Darry had yet to regain the full use of her left arm. "Take that damn thing off."

Darry's eyebrow lifted and Jessa thought instantly of Cecelia as Darry's smile slid easily into a rogue's grin of disobedience. "But we're having fun, Jess. Bentley's lovesick heart wishes to play in the sun for once."

Bentley swung hard with his right hand and Darry ducked beneath his fist with a laugh as he stumbled past her.

"Remove it from your arm, or I shall not dance with you at the party," Jessa promised. "I shall dance with Bentley all night."

Bentley stood up straight and turned around with a handsome smile. "And I didn't even need a rock."

"You will dance with me no matter what I do, my sweet Lark, and you shall love every minute of it." Darry's eyes darkened. "Do not threaten me with such."

Jessa's stomach flipped at the brazen tone in Darry's voice, and she felt a wonderful rush of love cascade throughout her chest. Jessa happily took the offered bait and tasted the richness of it. "Bentley, my good friend, please tell Arkady that I shall dance the Mohn-Drom with him when the stars reach their peak of the autumn moon."

Darry pulled the shield from her arm and swung it.

Bentley caught it against his stomach with what must have been an uncomfortable loss of breath at the impact. "Bloody hell, woman…"

Darry's eyes were dark. "You have something else to say, Lord Greeves?"

Jessa turned at the polite but unexpected cough behind her, pulled from their play by the intrusion. Arkady wore an enigmatic grin as he stood beyond the veranda doors, an expression that Jessa had come to know and appreciate.

"Is that a promise?" he asked.

Jessa smiled. "She would kill us both and you know it."

"Probably just me, my Lady."

She glanced at the rolled parchment tied with a gold ribbon in his hand, the seal that held it made of green wax.

"Lucas brought this from Ballentrae," he explained. "He was not followed, nor was he questioned by anyone. He is still but a hunter from the north and of little interest to anyone. Orlando was his shadow and he saw nothing amiss. Neither of them witnessed the man who delivered it. Prince Jacob's spies are the best we've seen."

Jessa's heartbeat quickened with fear as she held out her hand. "Or not seen."

Arkady stepped forward. "Aye, that too, my Lady." His heels gave a hard click as she took possession of the message.

"Stop doing that, please," Jessa said. It was an order that she had given him a hundred times and he had yet to obey.

"No, my Lady," he said with a smile and turned about.

Jessa waited for him to leave and then returned to the bedroom as she broke Jacob's official seal. They stayed far from Ballentrae and the household staff were under strict orders not to speak of the changes that had taken place on the estate. Jessa entertained little fear that they would be found. She knew it would end at some point, but for now, they were safe.

Jessa stopped beside the desk and unrolled the parchment.

Darry stood in the doorway. "Jacob's colors."

Jessa did not look up. "Yes," she whispered.

Darry entered the room.

"The Lord Bentley Greeves is wanted for questioning in the suspicious death of Lord Marteen Salish. He has not been charged with murder, but there is a bounty for his return to Lokey, and there is a bounty for Etienne Blue." Jessa lifted her eyes as Darry stepped close. "A thousand gold coins offered by Melora Salish, for *each* of them…and the seal of the Crown Prince is upon the writ."

"But not my father's?" Darry asked with interest.

"It does not say, but by the inclusion of such information, it may be safe to say that your father travels a different course in this. Jacob would not waste his words."

"What else, my love?" Darry's voice was but a breath as she reached out and pulled with care at a dark braid of hair. The backs of her fingers brushed with warmth against Jessa's cheek.

"My father has been assassinated by Lord Almahdi de Ghalib, and Sylban-Tenna has taken the Jade Throne," Jessa said with an odd hitch in her voice as she looked up. "There is civil war in Lyoness. My brothers fight for the throne."

Darry took the parchment from Jessa's hands and glanced at it before she dropped it to the desk. "There is no surprise in this, Jess." Darry pulled her to the side and gathered her close. "Your reasoning was sound the moment I heard it. We knew this was coming."

Jessa took hold of Darry's tunic collar with both hands. "Malcolm's game is deep in play, Darry." Her thoughts began to assimilate the new information. "Lord Almahdi has avenged his children—though I did not predict that."

"Aye, and my father's war will be stalled at the Lyonese border," Darry added, "if indeed they march. There is no word of battle from Ballentrae, and nothing travels faster than word of war. My father's couriers are second to none, and his rookery will have doubled in size since last we were there. Arravan has yet to encroach upon Lyoness. Bharjah's death has changed things."

"And so what do we do, *Akasha*?" Jessa asked as she realized that Jacob's greatest spy was no more. Her thoughts faltered down a new avenue and it threw her into confusion. "I don't know what to do now."

"You will dance the Mohn-Drom with no one but me," Darry answered in a whisper.

Jessa was startled into a smile. "Is that what is next?"

"Aye," Darry responded. "Say it, my pretty Lark, and you shall be rewarded."

"And I will dance the Mohn-Drom with no one but you."

Darry smiled and her dimple pressed in her cheek.

Jessa laughed, her heartbeat quick at the desire she saw in Darry's eyes. "Thank you," she said. "'Tis a lovely prize."

"Our world is here now, Jess. We will rest until our own game begins." Darry brushed her lips upon Jessa's. "Until then, we live for *us*…we live for *now*."

The words moved deep within Jessa's heart and she pulled Darry closer. "And what else do you want right now, *Akasha*? You seem to have a lot of free time upon your hands. Perhaps I should give you a task to complete."

Darry's smile was filled with delight. "Will you give me a quest? How splendid of you, my Princess."

"I said a task, not a quest."

"Make it both," Darry said with whispered fire as her lips brushed beneath Jessa's left ear, "and I shall let the panther take you as I know you like."

Jessa bit hard upon her lower lip as Darry's mouth burned against her throat. Her reaction was instant and she felt her need pulse throughout her body. Her majik reacted as well, and everything faded beneath its hunger for more. "Just…you should…"

"Just what?"

Jessa caught her breath at the placement of Darry's hand as their bodies came together.

"What is my task, sweet Jess? Command me and it shall be done."

"Close the bloody door, *Akasha*," Jessa said within a smile and kissed her.

The taste of Darry's tongue upon her own was like the honeyed wine from the far north of Lyoness, the distant memory of its flavor brought to life by the sweetness of love.

About the Author

Shea Godfrey is an artist and writer working and living in the Midwest. While her formal education is in journalism and photography, she has spent most of her career thus far in 3D animation and design. You may contact Shea at: sheagodfreymail@gmail.com.

Books Available From Bold Strokes Books

Let the Lover Be by Sheree Greer. Kiana Lewis, a functional alcoholic on the verge of destruction, finally faces the demons of her past while finding love and earning redemption in New Orleans. (978-1-62639-077-5)

Blindsided by Karis Walsh. Blindsided by love, guide dog trainer Lenae McIntyre and media personality Cara Bradley learn to trust what they see with their hearts. (978-1-62639-078-2)

About Face by VK Powell. Forensic artist Macy Sheridan and Detective Leigh Monroe work on a case that has troubled them both for years, but they're hampered by the past and their unlikely yet undeniable attraction. (978-1-62639-079-9)

Blackstone by Shea Godfrey. For Darry and Jessa, their chance at a life of freedom is stolen by the arrival of war and an ancient prophecy that just might destroy their love. (978-1-62639-080-5)

Out of This World by Maggie Morton. Iris decided to cross an ocean to get over her ex. But instead, she ends up traveling much farther, all the way to another world. Once she's there, only a mysterious, sexy, and magical woman can help her return home. (978-1-62639-083-6)

Kiss The Girl by Melissa Brayden. Sleeping with the enemy has never been so complicated. Brooklyn Campbell and Jessica Lennox face off in love and advertising in fast-paced New York City. (978-1-62639-071-3)

Taking Fire: A First Responders Novel by Radclyffe. Hunted by extremists and under siege by nature's most virulent weapons, Navy medic Max de Milles and Red Cross worker Rachel Winslow join forces to survive and discover something far more lasting. (978-1-62639-072-0)

First Tango in Paris by Shelley Thrasher. When French law student Eva Laroche meets American call girl Brigitte Green in 1970s Paris, they have no idea how their pasts and futures will intersect. (978-1-62639-073-7)

The War Within by Yolanda Wallace. Army nurse Meredith Moser went to Vietnam in 1967 looking to help those in need; she didn't expect to meet the love of her life along the way. (978-1-62639-074-4)

Desire at Dawn by Fiona Zedde. For Kylie, love had always come armed with sharp teeth and claws. But with the human, Olivia, she bares her vampire heart for the very first time, sharing passion, lust, and a tenderness she'd never dared dreamed of before. (978-1-62639-064-5)

Visions by Larkin Rose. Sometimes the mysteries of love reveal themselves when you least expect it. Other times they hide behind a black satin mask. Can Paige unveil her masked stranger this time? (978-1-62639-065-2)

All In by Nell Stark. Internet poker champion Annie Navarro loses everything when the Feds shut down online gambling, and she turns to experienced casino host Vesper Blake for advice—but can Nova convince Vesper to take a gamble on romance? (978-1-62639-066-9)

Vermilion Justice by Sheri Lewis Wohl. What's a vampire to do when Dracula is no longer just a character in a novel? (978-1-62639-067-6)

Switchblade by Carsen Taite. Lines were meant to be crossed. Third in the Luca Bennett Bounty Hunter Series. (978-1-62639-058-4)

Nightingale by Andrea Bramhall. Culture, faith, and duty conspire to tear two young lovers apart, yet fate seems to have different plans for them both. (978-1-62639-059-1)

No Boundaries by Donna K. Ford. A chance meeting and a nightmare from the past threaten more than Andi Massey's solitude as she and Gwen Palmer struggle to understand the complexity of love without boundaries. (978-1-62639-060-7)

Timeless by Rachel Spangler. When Stevie Geller returns to her hometown, will she do things differently the second time around or will she be in such a hurry to leave her past that she misses out on a better future? (978-1-62639-050-8)

Second to None by L.T. Marie. Can a physical therapist and a custom motorcycle designer conquer their pasts and build a future with one another? (978-1-62639-051-5)

Seneca Falls by Jesse Thoma. Together, two women discover love truly can conquer all evil. (978-1-62639-052-2)

A Kingdom Lost by Barbara Ann Wright. Without knowing each other's fates, Princess Katya and her consort Starbride seek to reclaim their kingdom from the magic-wielding madman who seized the throne and is murdering their people. (978-1-62639-053-9)

Season of the Wolf by Robin Summers. Two women running from their pasts are thrust together by an unimaginable evil. Can they overcome the horrors that haunt them in time to save each other? (978-1-62639-043-0)

The Heat of Angels by Lisa Girolami. Fires burn in more than one place in Los Angeles. (978-1-62639-042-3)

Desperate Measures by P. J. Trebelhorn. Homicide detective Kay Griffith and contractor Brenda Jansen meet amidst turmoil neither of them is aware of until murder suspect Tommy Rayne makes his move to exact revenge on Kay. (978-1-62639-044-7)

The Magic Hunt by L.L. Raand. With her Pack being hunted by human extremists and beset by enemies masquerading as friends, can Sylvan protect them and her mate, or will she succumb to the feral rage that threatens to turn her rogue, destroying them all? A Midnight Hunters novel. (978-1-62639-045-4)

Wingspan by Karis Walsh. Wildlife biologist Bailey Chase is content to live at the wild bird sanctuary she has created on Washington's Olympic Peninsula until she is lured beyond the safety of isolation by architect Kendall Pearson. (978-1-60282-983-1)

Night Bound by Winter Pennington. Kass struggles to keep her head, her heart, and her relationships in order. She's still having a difficult time accepting being an Alpha female—but her wolf is certain of what she wants and she's intent on securing her power. (978-1-60282-984-8)

Windigo Thrall by Cate Culpepper. Six women trapped in a mountain cabin by a blizzard, stalked by an ancient cannibal demon bent on stealing their sanity—and their lives. (978-1-60282-950-3)

The Blush Factor by Gun Brooke. Ice-cold business tycoon Eleanor Ashcroft only cares about the three Ps—Power, Profit, and Prosperity—until young Addison Garr makes her doubt both that and the state of her frostbitten heart. (978-1-60282-985-5)

Smoke and Fire by Julie Cannon. Oil and water, passion and desire, a combustible combination. Can two women fight the fire that draws them together and threatens to keep them apart? (978-1-60282-977-0)

Slash and Burn by Valerie Bronwen. The murder of a roundly despised author at an LGBT writers' conference in New Orleans turns Winter Lovelace's relaxing weekend hobnobbing with her peers into a nightmare of suspense—especially when her ex turns up. (978-1-60282-986-2)

The Quickening: A Sisters of Spirits novel by Yvonne Heidt. Ghosts, visions, and demons are all in a day's work for Tiffany. But when Kat asks for help on a serial killer case, life takes on another dimension altogether. (978-1-60282-975-6)

Love and Devotion by Jove Belle. KC Hall trips her way through life, stumbling into an affair with a married bombshell twice her age. Thankfully, her best friend, Emma Reynolds, is there to show her the true meaning of Love and Devotion. (978-1-60282-965-7)

Rush by Carsen Taite. Murder, secrets, and romance combine to create the ultimate rush. (978-1-60282-966-4)

The Shoal of Time by J.M. Redmann. It sounded too easy. Micky Knight is reluctant to take the case because the easy ones often turn into the hard ones, and the hard ones turn into the dangerous ones. In this one, easy turns hard without warning. (978-1-60282-967-1)

In Between by Jane Hoppen. At the age of 14, Sophie Schmidt discovers that she was born an intersexual baby and sets off on a journey to find her place in a world that denies her true existence. (978-1-60282-968-8)

Under Her Spell by Maggie Morton. The magic of love brought Terra and Athene together, but now a magical quest stands between them— a quest for Athene's hand in marriage. Will their passion keep them together, or will stronger magic tear them apart? (978-1-60282-973-2)